1/25

Happy Xmas – Jan
to the kindest
neighbours I have
known –

Love
Elsie
X

A VICAR'S DAUGHTER

A VICAR'S DAUGHTER

Elsie G Compton

Book Guild Publishing
Sussex, England

First published in Great Britain in 2007 by
The Book Guild Ltd
Pavilion View
19 New Road
Brighton
BN1 1UF

Typesetting in Baskerville by
IML Typographers, Merseyside

Printed in Great Britain by
CPI Antony Rowe

A catalogue record for this book is available from
The British Library.

ISBN 978 1 84624 144 4

For Susie

*Thanks to my husband Brian for
his help and support*

Prologue

It was late spring, too cold to sit outside, but Mary Freeman braved the chill breeze and sat on the patio in her old but comfortable wicker chair. Her vacant pale blue eyes looked out on what was once a colourful well-tended garden.

The last year had taken its toll. The shrubs that should have been cut back in the autumn were now beginning to bud amid dead thin branches that took on a sinister look ready to hamper the life of any new growth. The weeds had already begun to choke the progress of flowers that had always provided Mary with a source of comfort and antici-pation in the past. Her muddled thinking strayed to her dead husband, but the hatred she felt for him blocked any thought of compassion from her mind. Thinking of her daughter made her blood run as cold as the spring breeze that flapped around her check cotton skirt as it periodically rose in the air and exposed her bare white legs. Mary clasped her hands tightly together as the awful memories of her husband and daughter played havoc with her mind.

Feeling for her long blonde hair she remembered how her daughter had hacked it off in a vicious attack. All that was left were a few blonde strands showing through the lifeless, thinning, grey hair.

She lifted her thin frame from the chair with the characteristic movements of a lady in her late seventies although she was only forty-six. The decision to move was not because she felt the chill of the evening air. She wanted to go round to the front of the house to make sure the unwelcome visitor had not returned.

Chapter One

Mary Freeman was born in 1942, the only daughter of the Reverend Peters, in a village called Denton in Hertfordshire. Her mother died just two weeks before Mary's fourth birthday and her father had fulfilled the roles of mother, father and vicar to his parish admirably. A live-in house-keeper, Mrs Davidson, had moved into the Vicarage a few weeks after Mary's mother died and had become affectionately known as Davy.

The Rev. Peters taught Mary the rights and wrongs of the world in a very loving and caring way. There was no real religious pressure put on her save the normal Christian parenthood. The Reverend Peters's belief was that to appreciate the good and the generous automatically prevented evil being done by any of his congregation and that included his daughter.

Mary had a very happy childhood. She made friends easily at school and both Mrs Davidson and her father encouraged her to bring her friends home to play in the woodland that almost encircled the Vicarage.

At the age of 19 Mary had won a scholarship to the University of London. The excitement of going to London to study was somewhat marred by the concern she had about leaving her father. She loved him more than anybody in the world and held him in such great esteem that there were times, as she was growing up, that she had believed he probably was God.

The week before leaving for London, Mary was walking through their beloved woodlands with her best friend Anne Stacey. They had been close friends since the age of seven. Unlike Mary's stable upbringing, Anne had an uncaring father and a very sick mother.

'You have been like a sister to me,' Anne said. 'I'm going to miss you terribly. You are truly my best friend.'

Mary touched Anne's arm,

'I'm not that far away, and I'll always be there for you.' The two girls vowed that nothing would ever mar their friendship.

The first four months away from home went very slowly. Although Mary was beginning to make new friends she was very homesick. She longed to see her dear Davy bustling around the kitchen in the mornings. She missed walking through the woodland at the back of the Vicarage. Quite often her school chums would gather there and indulge in teenage chatter. Most of all she missed Anne.

At the end of the fourth month she began getting excited about coming home for Christmas. Her father sent her the money for train tickets and told her he would meet her at the station. Such was her excitement that she found it almost impossible to concentrate on anything but her journey home.

As the train pulled into the station she caught sight of her father and her best friend, eagerly scanning the train for a glimpse of her. The hugs and kisses went on and on until the Rev. Peters took them both by the arm and marched them off to his old Morris Minor.

The following day was a Sunday and, of course, one of her father's busiest days. Mary dutifully went down to breakfast at 6 a.m., although her father had been adamant that there was no need for her to rise early.

It was a welcome sight seeing Davy bustling over the stove. Her father was bent over papers, strewn all over the breakfast table. He was going over his sermon and, as usual, had left everything until the last minute.

'Will you be attending church today my dear?' the Rev. Peters asked as she seated herself at the table. 'Yes, of course,' Mary replied. 'But not your early morning mass. I'll be there for the eleven o'clock service.'

Her father looked up and smiled. ' I know what your game is young lady. You want to compete with Mrs Lawson's Sunday hats.'

Mary threw her head back and laughed. 'Father, you can be quite wicked at times you know. Poor Mrs Lawson goes to a lot of trouble trying to impress you with her hats.'

They both laughed and the Rev. Peters noticed how grown up his daughter had become. He admired her long blonde hair with just a slight natural curl, her large blue eyes and slim but curvaceous figure; above all, her smile with such beautiful white even teeth that could light up a room instantly. So like her mother, he thought.

Once her father had gone, and Davy had finished telling her what a lucky girl she was to be getting an education that most girls could only dream of, Mary went up to her room.

After tidying the room and unpacking the things that she still had left in her case, she settled down to write an essay. It was about nine o'clock when Davy called her downstairs to answer the phone. It was Anne.

'Hello Mary,' she said cheerily. 'Do you want to meet at the coffee shop for breakfast? I'm dying to hear all about London.'

Mary explained that she had already had her breakfast and Mrs Davidson was preparing a big Sunday lunch. 'I've got an essay to write so why don't we leave it until tomorrow when we will have much more time.'

'Okay.' Annie replied sounding a little disappointed.

Back in her bedroom, her concentration having been broken, Mary wished she had taken up Annie's invitation. Unable to settle she decided to go for a walk in the woodland before going to church.

3

She could never have known that she would regret that decision for the rest of her life.

It was two weeks before Christmas and, although a little cold, it was a bright day. The dried leaves crunched under Mary's feet as she walked quite briskly through the trees. A warm glow of happiness engulfed her as she recalled the fun and laughter she had experienced growing up here in this almost fairytale atmosphere.

She wondered whether Anne still came here. She might not have the time now that she was working as well as looking after her sick mother.

Sitting down on the same old log that had been there ever since she could remember she recalled how they had used it as a make-believe canoe. Five of them, all sitting astride with branches from the trees as make-believe paddles. They had used it as a table for picnics and many other things. Her most cherished memories were of Anne and herself just sitting there talking about all manner of things.

'What is it really like?' Anne had asked one day. 'You know, your father being a vicar.'

'It's no different from your father being a postman,' she had replied. 'They're just Dads.' But today, gazing up at the sky through the trees, she knew she had been wrong. Mary's father was a good, kind man who would always be there for her. Anne's father had left and run off with a woman not much older than his daughter.

Anne had never forgiven or spoken to him again, even though he did not live far away. Mary remembered the hours she had sat on this very log consoling her.

Her thoughts were interrupted by the sound of footsteps crunching on the crisp, dry leaves. She looked round and saw the figure of a man approaching. At the same time she spotted a white van parked in a clearing about 50 yards away. As he got nearer, Mary thought that she recognised him. She began to feel very uneasy once she realised who it was ... John Stacey, her best friend's father.

'Aren't you the vicar's daughter?' he said, slurring his words as he plonked himself down on the old tree trunk next to Mary.

'Yes, I am. And you're Anne's father,' she replied, her voice trembling a little. Although it was only 10.30 in the morning there was a definite smell of alcohol about him. He was clean and, in fact, looked quite attractive in his beige corduroy trousers and dark brown sweater. The dark brown hair, identical to Anne's, was swept back tidily. In fact, he almost looked too young to be her father.

'I heard you were back from ... Where is it? ... Some fancy college in London,' he said.

'Yes, that's right,' replied Anne. 'I'm home for the Christmas holidays.' Without looking at him she went on, 'I don't wish to be rude, Mr Stacey. but I really must be getting back. I promised my father that I would be at church this morning.'

'Sure. Sure,' he said, getting up. Looking down at Mary he asked sorrowfully, 'Have you seen my daughter since you've been home?' Mary looked at the ground so as to avoid his alcohol-smelling breath. He bent down low over her and said quietly, 'Because she won't see me, I've written her a letter. I wondered whether you'd give it to her.'

Mary stood up and started to walk away. He called after her. 'Will you take it for me? I only want to try and help Anne, what with her mother being ill and all that.'

Mary stopped. Turning around she said, ' I'll take your letter, but I don't think you'll get a reply. I doubt she will even read it.'

'Maybe not, but it's worth a try,' he muttered.

'Have you got the letter with you?' Mary asked. 'Only I really must be getting back.'

'It's on the dashboard in the van,' he replied, excitement beginning to show in his eyes.

Mary gave a long sigh, 'Come on, let's get it. Perhaps you can give me a lift home or I really will be late for church.'

John Stacey opened the passenger door. Mary jumped in and saw a buff-coloured envelope on the dashboard. As she picked it up he jumped into the driving seat and locked both doors.

Mary noticed the envelope was not addressed to anyone. She looked inside, only to find it empty.

'Where's the letter?' she asked, her impatience beginning to show. At that moment his arm slid across her shoulders while the other hand gripped her thigh like a vice. What happened next would be stored away in Mary's mind forever.

She felt her arm being pushed up her back. The pain was so acute that she thought her arm would break. Then came a slap across her cheek followed by his excitable voice saying, 'This can be enjoyable or painful. It's up to you.'

Her head still spinning from the slap, Mary was dragged into the back of the van where she was pushed on to a stained, grimy old mattress. Mary lost her virginity to her best friend's drunken father.

He tore her skirt and pants down from her waist, then his knee forced her legs apart. The pain ripped through her body as he entered her. A strong arm was under her chin, forcing her head back so far she thought her neck would break. Between his heaving and grunting he muttered, 'Terrific. A virgin. I thought so.' It was then that Mary slipped into unconsciousness.

Mary regained consciousness slowly. She was cold. The pain between her legs and the warm moisture running down the inside of her thighs reminded her with a cruel jolt what had happened. She closed her eyes in the hope that when she opened them again she would find it had all have been a bad dream.

She knew she was no longer in the van because she could feel leaves around her. Opening her eyes again, she saw the sunlight penetrating the trees. Mary began to cry and the sobs shook her body so much that she began to vomit. Realising she was choking, she turned onto her side. Still shaking from head to toe, she sat up. Looking around, she found she had been dumped in a copse. From the waist down she was naked apart from one shoe. Her blouse, although torn, covered some part of her bruised breasts. Mary caught sight of her other shoe, skirt and duffle coat not too far away, as if they had been placed there in readiness for her. Crawling on all fours she picked them up but could find no trace of her panties or tights. As the realisation as to what had happened to her set in, she once again, vomited violently.

Like a fugitive, she hid in the grounds of the Vicarage. She had no idea how long she waited for Davy to leave the kitchen. Eventually she did, and went round to the side of the house to feed the birds. This gave Mary the opportunity to sneak in and run straight up the stairs to the bathroom. Within minutes, she lay soaking in a near scalding bath.

She tried to wash away all traces of her ordeal. On the outside she managed to achieve that, apart from an enormous bruise on her cheek. However, nothing could rid her mind of the smell of that man and the humiliation he had put her through. Putting her hands together, she whimpered, 'Oh why, God? Why?'

That evening, Mary told her father her first lie ever. 'I'm so sorry to have missed church,' she said across the dinner table. 'I was running, so happy to be back in the woodlands again, when I went smack bang into a tree. It made me feel quite bad, I can tell you. I thought I was going to pass out so I came home and had a nice hot bath.'

The Rev. Peters looked at the bruise on her cheek. 'Dear, dear Mary, are you sure you're alright? Perhaps you should pop in and see Doctor Wright in the morning. A knock like that can have repercussions, you know.'

'Please don't fuss so.' The reply was sharper than she

intended. Her father was quite taken aback by Mary's abruptness. 'My dear,' he said, ' I don't mean to fuss. I'm just concerned for you. You look so pale and shaken up.'

'I'm so sorry, Father. Perhaps you're right. I do feel a little shaky.' She pushed her uneaten dinner to one side, stood up and excused herself just in time to conceal the tears that were welling up in her eyes.

Once up in her bedroom, Mary broke down and cried herself to sleep. Sleep rescued her from the torment for no more than a couple of hours. Then she was awake, reliving the nightmare over and over again.

The following morning Mrs Davidson woke Mary with a steaming hot mug of tea. After placing the mug on the table beside the bed, she carefully pulled back the covers so as to examine Mary's cheek.

'Oh, my dear!' she exclaimed. 'Your father's right. To the doctor with you.' Mary opened her eyes and, forcing a smile said, 'No, really, Davy. I'm feeling so much better and Anne is coming over this morning.'

'Well, I'm glad to hear you're feeling better. It's a lovely morning and a walk down to the surgery will do us both good. Now, drink that tea and up you get.' Mary, recognising the tone of command in Mrs Davidson's voice, reluctantly agreed to go. Before leaving the room, Mrs Davidson looked down at Mary and whispered in a more conciliatory tone, 'Your father has enough to worry about, what with Christmas coming up. We don't want to add to his worries now, do we?'

Mary felt the huge knot in her stomach as she thought of her father. There was no possible way she could confide in him. Over the years they had been able to discuss most things, but in order to save him any embarrassment, sex had never been on the agenda. This had not given Mary a problem as Anne had always been there, and they had laughed and teased each other about sex and the changes in their bodies as they grew up. But this was different. How could you ever tell your best friend that her father had raped you. Realising she could tell no one, a feeling of isolation swept over her. Never before had she kept secrets from Anne. They had always been confidantes. Feeling lonely and violated, she made her way downstairs to phone and postpone her friend's visit.

Doctor Wright gave her his usual cordial welcome. 'Mary, how nice to see you. I missed you in church yesterday. I spoke to your father and he said you were going to be there.' Mary sat down in the chair beside the doctor's desk and explained how she had stumbled into a tree.

After cleaning her face with a swab and writing out a prescription for painkillers Doctor Wright leant back in his chair. 'Your father's very proud of you, young lady. To my knowledge, you're the first person in Denton to acquire a place at London University. He's very proud of you indeed.'

Your father's very proud of you! Your father's very proud of you! The words echoed around in Mary's head.

'Mary, is anything troubling you?' Doctor Wright asked tenderly.

'No, Doctor,' replied Mary fighting to hold back the tears. 'I'm sorry. I was miles away. Yes, my father is very proud of me and I'll do my best to make sure it stays that way.'

After thanking Doctor Wright for his time Mary met Mrs Davidson in the waiting room. They were about to leave when the door burst open and a very out-of-breath Anne Stacey came charging in.

She stopped in her tracks when she saw Mary. 'Hello, Mary,' she gasped. 'What on earth have you done to your face?' Without giving Mary a chance to answer Anne went on, 'I've had to run all the way here. I thought I was going to be late for my appointment. The doctor's got some new medication, which he thinks might make Mum a little more comfortable. She's still in a lot of pain you know.' The receptionist calling Anne's name interrupted them. Anne said, 'Must go. I'll call round this afternoon and you can tell me what happened.'

On the way home, Mrs Davidson told Mary that Anne's mother was getting worse and that the pains were now very bad. Soon she would have to be moved to a hospital.

'Does Anne know?' asked Mary.

'No she doesn't, and you mustn't tell her.' Mrs Davidson put her arm across Mary's shoulders and went on, 'Anne's mother doesn't want her to know until the time comes. She's worried that Anne will want to give up her job to spend more time at home with her.'

They walked the rest of the way in silence. As they came to the turning where Anne lived, Mrs Davidson shook her head and said quietly, 'That poor woman has never been the same since that toe-rag of a husband left her. And, as if that wasn't enough, he has to flaunt himself around the village with that Jezebel.' Mrs Davidson took her arm from Mary's shoulders and continued, 'They do say that Anne won't have anything to do with him. Won't even speak to him. Can't say I blame her.'

To Mrs Davidson's surprise, Mary quickly changed the subject. 'How many are we to expect at the Vicarage for Christmas lunch this year?' she asked. Mrs Davidson took this to mean that she did not want to discuss her best friend's business, and smiled at Mary's loyalty.

'At the moment there are six of us. But you know your father. I'm quite sure there will be a few waifs and strays that he will have forgotten to tell me about until Christmas morning.'

Christmas Eve arrived at the Vicarage and, with it, the usual preparations for Midnight Mass. Mrs Davidson bustled about the kitchen making sure that the mince pies were ready to go in the oven. The Rev. Peters was getting agitated because Mary seemed to be showing little interest in anything.

'Mrs Davidson, I forgot to tell you. There'll be three more for Christmas lunch tomorrow. I've had so much on my mind that I forgot to tell you.' The Rev. Peter's voice trailed away as he left the kitchen at breakneck speed.

After exchanging smiles with one another Mary said, 'You know my father too well, Davy. I don't know what he'd do without you.'

Mrs Davidson smiled. 'Well, when I moved in here to take care of you and your father I never thought I would still be here today. If I don't know the pair of you by now, then I never will.' She rubbed her hands down her front before removing her pinafore. 'Your father has been very good to me, as he is to everyone. Now come along, let's go into the dining room and start laying the table for tomorrow's lunch. You can tell me what's on your mind and why you're looking so gloomy.'

Mary, somewhat startled by her remark, made her way into the dining room. 'I can't imagine why you think there's anything on my mind other than all the work I've got to do before I go back to London.' Mrs Davidson looked at Mary wistfully but said nothing.

'Who do you think the extra guests are?' asked Mary, trying very hard to make herself sound cheerful.

'I have no idea,' replied Mrs Davidson. 'Although I wouldn't mind betting one of them is his friend from London, David Freeman. I know your father was most upset when he heard that he was going to be on his own at Christmas.'

Mary remembered David Freeman. Although she did not know him that well, she knew her father had a lot of time for him. She almost found herself saying, 'Isn't that the man who was studying for the clergy but gave up his ambitions for a relationship with a woman that didn't work out?' but stopped just in time. She was not sure her father would have confided in Mrs Davidson, so just said, 'Oh, that will be nice!'

11

Mary's memories of David Freeman were vague. He had visited the Vicarage on several occasions, but on opening the door Christmas morning she failed to recognise him. He was a tall, thin man, very upright with gaunt features and light brown thinning hair. He made little attempt to join in the conversation at lunchtime, and Mary found herself longing for the lunch to end in order to escape to the privacy of her room.

For the remainder of the Christmas holiday Mary spent as much time as she could with Anne. During this time she became more and more convinced that what had happened to her must remain a secret inside her head forever. Not being able to be honest with her best friend left her with a feeling of guilt that caused her to become more and more withdrawn.

It was at the end of February when Mary's worst fears were confirmed. She had been sick in the mornings for five consecutive days and she had been unable to attend several lectures due to her biliousness and the University of London was now a very lonely place for her.

How she longed to be able to sit down and talk to someone about her problems. Instead, she kept herself to herself and spent most evenings alone trying to make some sense of her depressing thoughts. One option that sent shivers down her spine was to have an abortion. But how could she, a vicar's daughter, murder a child? Another was to go into hiding. But how would she survive with no money? More than anything, she longed to talk to Anne. In her muddled mind she knew this was not an option. How could she tell her best friend that she was the daughter of a rapist, especially as the poor girl now knew of her mother's terminal cancer?

It was during this time that Mary began to withdraw and hide behind the dark shadows that crept into her mind.

Fellow students around Mary began to notice something was wrong. They began to talk about the vacant expression that barely left her face.

Mrs Jarvis, one of her tutors, asked her to stay behind after class. She asked if the pressures of university were getting her down. Mary just shook her head. After failing to get her to talk about what was bothering her, Mrs Jarvis suggested Mary go for some counselling. With a vague nod, Mary left the room – Mrs Jarvis not knowing whether she had made any progress at all.

Chapter Two

At the age of 36, David Freeman had recovered from what could only be described as a bizarre relationship with Rosalind Farrow. It had been suggested to him that the clergy was not a career that could encompass a relationship with a woman with Rosalind's reputation. Subsequently he had given up his career but, unfortunately, it was not too long before Rosalind decided to move on, no longer able to cope with his bizarre sexual needs.

It took him about a year before he decided that his next career move should be counselling. He now worked for an organisation partly funded by the church but reliant on charities to make ends meet. Two rooms above a shoe shop in Oxford Street served as his headquarters. He worked with a fellow counsellor by the name of Jane Bromfield. Most of their clientele were drug addicts, alcoholics and the homeless.

He led a depressing life, getting no satisfaction from work that he knew he was so bad at. Quite often he would lose his temper with poor, hopeless teenagers and Jane Bromfield would have to come to the rescue. She was very concerned at David's bad temper but, until she could find someone else prepared to work for nothing, there was little she could do about it.

David Freeman was financially very comfortable, with a substantial private income for the rest of his life. The family had been in the carpet trade and his grandfather had set up a trust fund for him. His parents could never understand why he had chosen the clergy as opposed to the family business and, therefore, had had little contact with him over the years. They had been delighted when they heard he had given up the clergy for a woman, but not so delighted once they had met the brassy blonde. Once again, their hopes of him ever returning to the family business were dashed when he announced that, although he could never return to the clergy, he would do the next best thing and work to help the poor and needy.

He lived in a small but comfortable mews cottage just off the Edgware road. This was very convenient for him. Delicatessen shops were open late at night and all other amenities were within easy walking distance. Apart from a cleaner that came in twice a week, he lived alone. He had always enjoyed his own company but, of late, was beginning to feel that something was lacking in his life.

Trudging up the stairs towards what he called his consulting rooms, the threadbare and dirty carpeting did nothing to lift his spirits. Walking through the poorly furnished waiting room, he could see through the half glass partition that Jane had already got someone with her 'Another useless dropout,' he thought to himself

An hour had gone by and he was about to make himself a second cup of coffee when Jane appeared at the door. David looked up and sighed, 'No customers yet. It looks as if I'm going to have a quiet day.'

Jane smiled. 'I had a very early bird. A pregnant girl and, would you believe it, a vicar's daughter who's been raped. I didn't have a chance to give her any real help as she had to be back for a lecture at eleven o'clock. But she agreed to come back this afternoon although I don't know whether she will. She was so nervous she just couldn't wait to get away.' The sound of the telephone ringing in her office sent Jane scurrying away.

Ten minutes later she was back looking flustered. 'David, that was my mother on the phone. My father's been taken to hospital. A heart attack, I think. My mother was all over the place. I have to go. Can you manage on your own?' Without waiting for an answer, she turned to leave and called over her shoulder, 'Don't forget that pregnant girl is coming back at four. Her notes are on my desk. Be gentle with her. She is a vicar's daughter, remember.'

At three o'clock, after having listened to two drug addicts and one alcoholic telling him how unfairly life had treated them, he made his way to Jane's office to get the file for the four o'clock appointment. 'Vicar's daughter,' he muttered under his breath. 'This could be interesting.'

As he looked down at the buff-coloured file, his face took on a look of disbelief. He quickly sat down on Jane's chair as the name Mary Peters danced before his eyes.

Like a man possessed, he began reading the notes. Mary had told Jane everything apart from who the father was. Momentarily he questioned himself as to whether it would be appropriate for him to deal with this case. Jane had strict rules about counselling friends and family.

Forgetting the ethics a faint smirk took hold at the corner of his thin lips. The Rev. Peters, he thought to himself. The man who had always seemed so perfect. The man who had lectured him about his foolish ways with the only woman who had ever given him sexual satisfaction. The Rev. Peters, the man who had always befriended him in what David thought a very patronizing way. He recalled their telephone conversation before Christmas: 'Oh David, you poor unfortunate soul. Nobody should be alone at Christmas. Come down and have lunch with us at the Vicarage.' Just like that poor unfortunate soul, he joined them for lunch. How he wished he'd not gone.

The sound of footsteps on the stairs brought him back to reality. He looked at his watch. It was only 3.30. Too early for

Mary. 'Damn!' he thought to himself. He did not want to be tied up with anyone else when Mary arrived, so sat quietly in Jane's office hoping whoever it was would go away.

He looked up as the door opened. There she stood with her long blonde hair, blue eyes, not as bright as he remembered them, and a face that looked a little pale.

Mary's legs turned to jelly. Holding on to the door for support she stammered, 'David. What on earth are you doing here?'

Moving from behind the desk he went and put his arm around her shoulders. Guiding her towards a chair he whispered, 'Don't be alarmed my dear. I work here. I've read your file and Jane has told me all about your problem. Now come and sit down.'

The room began to spin. Mary tried to compose herself but it was all too much. All she could think of was that David Freeman, a friend of her father, knew her secret. The room span faster and Mary passed into oblivion.

David swiftly went to get a glass of water. With his arm around her, he tried to force the glass between her lips. He was holding her close. Her long blonde hair brushed against his cheek. It had been a long time since he had held a woman in his arms and he found the nearness of her beginning to arouse him.

She regained consciousness, muttering, 'My father must never know.'

After placing the glass on the desk, David held both her hands in his and said, 'Mary. You mustn't be frightened. Everything that is talked about here is strictly confidential.'

She began to cry uncontrollably and David held her in his arms until her sobbing had subsided.

'You know, David, that this would break my father's heart,' she said, blowing her nose.

'I know, I know, but you need have no fear of him ever finding out from me. Is that understood?'

'Thank you,' she whispered. 'I suppose I'd better go, and come back another time if Jane isn't here.'

Placing an arm around her shoulders he said, 'Absolutely not. In fact what I think we should do is get out of this place and get ourselves a nice cup of tea where we can talk without interruption.' For the first time in weeks, Mary felt comforted.

They had tea in a café only a few minutes' walk away. There was no talk of an abortion. David knew this was something Mary would never consider. He seemed in agreement with the idea that Mary should go into hiding and, after the baby was born, arrange for an adoption. He even suggested at one point that she stay at his house. However, neither could come up with a satisfactory reason to explain her disappearance.

They walked back to his consulting rooms. There he checked for any messages and locked up properly. As she waited for him at the bottom of the stairs, it started to rain. The evening air was bitterly cold and so Mary accepted David's invitation of a lift back to the university without hesitation.

They had not gone far when David announced that a good hot meal would do her good. After some protesting, she agreed to go to his house where he said he would make her a pasta dish.

To her amazement she found that, for the first time in weeks, she actually felt hungry and finished every morsel on her plate including most of the green salad. David had insisted that she have a glass of red wine. She noticed that he drank the remainder of the bottle.

Giving a huge sigh of contentment, she leaned back in her chair and said, 'David, you are a dark horse. I had no idea that you were such a good cook.'

Offering to clear the table and wash the dishes, she leant across to pick up his plate. Once again he found himself feeling aroused as he caught a glimpse of the white flesh at the top of her breast. He quickly pulled his sweater down over a situation that may have frightened her had she seen it.

Watching her move around the kitchen made him feel good. He had a sudden urge to keep her there forever. Somehow he had to work out a plan that would enable him to do just that.

After dropping Mary back at the university he downed three large whiskies before going to bed. His brain was working overtime and he could not sleep. Finally he got out of bed and went into the living room and picked up the paper. He skimmed through the pages without paying too much attention. His eyes suddenly lit up. There it was. The perfect solution. He was looking at a sketch of a bridal gown designed for some American film actress.

'I'll offer to marry her!' he said out loud. Startling himself and realising he was a little drunk, he went back to bed and fell asleep.

Arrangements had been made for him to meet Mary the following evening. He was to pick her up outside the main gates at seven o'clock. The day seemed to drag by, even though he was kept busy having to see every client himself.

Towards the end of the afternoon Jane rang to say that her father was not critical and that she would be coming into the office the following day. 'By the way, David. How did you get on with the vicar's girl?' she asked.

Her question irritated him but he remained calm and replied, 'Oh, that's all taken care of. I persuaded her to go home and confess all to her father. She called this morning to say everything had worked out fine.'

'Is she going to continue with her studies?' Jane enquired.

'Yes, but not in London.'

David cringed as Jane continued, 'Oh, well done, David!' As he put the telephone down he muttered, 'Why do people have to be so bloody patronizing?'

Mary was already standing outside the gates, a faraway look

on her face, when he drove up. Her collar was turned up and the belt to her camel coat was tied tightly around the waist.

They had dinner together at a little Italian restaurant. Once again he persuaded her to have a glass of wine. He finished the remainder of the bottle.

While they were sipping their coffee, he put his proposal to her. Mary was so shocked that her hand began to tremble. She missed her mouth, letting the coffee spill down her front and all over the tablecloth.

After she returned from the Ladies where she had done her best to remove the stains from her dark green sweater, she looked at David in utter bewilderment. 'Why?' she asked, 'Why would you want to marry someone you hardly know?'

David leant across the table, took both her hands in his, and said, 'I owe so much to your father, Mary. He was always there for me, and this would be my way of paying him back. More importantly, I believe God sent you and expects me to help you.' He let go of her hands and a strange silence descended upon them. Mary found this extremely unnerving.

Picking up his napkin to wipe the corners of his mouth David said, 'I'm a very lonely man, Mary. I happen to think we could get on very well and it would solve your problem at the same time. We could tell your father we have been seeing each other. We could even say it was love at first sight and we want to get married straight away.'

Mary found something in the way he was looking at her a little disturbing. She was relieved when, after he had paid the bill, he suggested that he put her in a taxi back to the university as he had a lot of paperwork to do before the morning.

Back in her room, Mary began to panic. She did not want to marry David. She knew it was wrong but she could not think of any alternative. Maybe this was God's way of helping her. As she began thinking of her father, the black shadows she had experienced lately engulfed her and she sat peacefully staring into space.

The following evening, sitting in David's living room and having consumed two glasses of red wine, Mary related the nightmare of her best friend's father raping her.

'So now you can see why I could never let anyone find out the truth,' she said hanging her head. 'I can't bear to think of what it would do to poor Anne. She has a swine for a father and a mother whose life expectancy is no more than a couple of months.' She began to cry and David took her into his arms.

'Try not to cry, my dear,' he said, in a very compassionate way. 'If you agree to our plan we can leave in a day or two and tell your father we wish to marry.'

The Rev. Peters took the news reasonably well, although it was very apparent he was disappointed. His uneasiness was demonstrated by his tone of voice when he said, 'I trust you will continue with your studies at university. A lot of married women take degree courses, you know.'

David answered for her. Taking her hand in his he explained, 'We don't want to have separate careers. We have talked at length about this and Mary will be a great help to me in my work.' In Mary's muddled mind she could not remember ever having talked about it and responded with a faint smile.

The Rev. Peters was not a stupid man, and that night, once Mary and David had gone to their separate rooms, he sat alone by the dwindling fire holding his head in his hands. Like any father he was not convinced by their reasons for a hasty marriage.

He felt great sorrow at the thought of his little girl who was maybe with child but unable to talk to him about it. If he himself were to broach the subject she would be so hurt if it was untrue. He lowered his head and prayed to God for guidance.

Three weeks later the Rev. Peters presided over the wedding of his daughter to David Freeman. It was not a big affair, but most of Mary's friends were there. Anne Stacey was her bridesmaid. Both Mary and her father had tried to persuade David to invite his family, but he was adamant that he did not wish any of them to attend.

Mrs Davidson had shown her disapproval from the beginning and barely managed a smile throughout the whole day. When she hugged Mary and wished her well there was no warmth, just a look of sadness upon her face.

Anne hugged her repeatedly throughout the day and wished her well. 'Oh Mary, who would have thought?' she kept saying excitedly.

The day passed for Mary like a dream.

As people were saying their goodbyes, something brought Mary back to reality. She saw David and Anne standing together having what appeared to be a very intense conversation.

Somewhere in her head a voice was screaming at her. 'He's telling her, he's telling her!' Instead of getting hysterical, Mary found sanctuary in the dark shadows that she hid behind more and more now.

They drove back to London in silence save for a few polite remarks about the weather.

Chapter Three

The March winds made it difficult for Anne Stacey to keep her red woollen scarf in place. Having tired of repeatedly throwing it over her shoulder she tied it in a knot. 'Not very attractive,' she thought, as she made her way through the hospital grounds towards Marlborough ward.

It was now four weeks since Mary's wedding and she had not heard a word from her. Making up her mind to go home via the Vicarage, she went through the swing doors and climbed the stairs.

As she made her way down the long corridor towards the ward, her heart sank. She recognised her father walking towards her. Her face betrayed the anger she felt. Of all times for him to come snooping around. How she hoped he had not upset her mother. It was too late for her to turn back and hide, so she walked purposefully on with the intention of ignoring him.

As their paths met he caught her arm. She could see he had been crying. 'Let go of me,' she hissed. He now held both her arms and whispered, 'Anne. Don't go in there. It's too late. She's gone.'

His words echoed around in her head. She began to stammer. 'G-g-gone? Gone where?' At this point a nurse approached and, putting an arm around both their shoulders, ushered them into a small room off the corridor.

Anne watched her father's hands shake as he tried to drink a cup of tea. The hatred she felt for him showed no signs of diminishing even though she could clearly see that he was upset.

'Why are you here?' she asked, her voice trembling.

He lifted his head to look at her and said, ' I'll always be here for you, Anne. I've wanted to tell you this so many times.'

'I don't need you. It was my poor dear mother that needed you,' she said, dabbing her eyes with an already well-sodden tissue.

'Please, Anne. Let me come back to the house with you. There are things that have to be taken care of.' He tried to catch her eye but she continued to look away.

Even though Anne knew it had been only a matter of time, the loss of her mother lay heavily on her heart. She had no idea how or where to start arrangements for the funeral. In her sadness, she reluctantly nodded her head in agreement.

As they walked along the corridor he whispered, 'You know, Anne, my greatest wish is that one day you'll be able to forgive me.'

Anne stopped abruptly, and, looking him full in the face said, 'Never!'

The following day, after trudging around with her father organising death certificates, cars and, worst of all, choosing the coffin, Anne told him she was going to the Vicarage to discuss the service with the Rev. Peters.

The panic in his eyes was unmistakable. Anne put this down to his embarrassment at having to get too close to anyone connected with the Church. Pulling on her coat she said, 'Don't worry. You don't have to come with me. I doubt very much whether the vicar would want to see you anyway.'

That afternoon Anne sat at the kitchen table with Mrs Davidson waiting for the Rev. Peters to return.

Mrs Davidson saw a very sad, lonely girl. Her long brown hair had not been washed, and lacked the lustre that had always made it one of Anne's finest features. Her face looked pale and her large brown eyes looked sore from crying.

Moving her chair closer to Anne, Mrs Davidson said, 'My dear, don't ever feel lonely. I want you to know that I will always be here for you and will help in any way I can.'

Anne forced a smile. Wiping her eyes she said, 'Oh, how I wish Mary was here.'

'I know, I know,' said the old lady patting Anne's cheek. 'She'll be here for the funeral. Reverend Peters is going to call her again tonight.'

The banging of the back door and the Rev. Peters calling out, 'Davy, has young Anne arrived yet?' interrupted them. They looked at each other and smiled.

Some two hours later Anne was about to leave after choosing hymns and scripture readings when the Rev. Peters put his hand on her shoulder and asked, 'Is everything alright between you and your father now?'

Anne began to cry quietly. 'No, it's not. He wants to move back into the house and take care of me. He claims all he wants is for me to forgive him, but I can't. I really can't. I blame him for my poor mother's sickness, loneliness and death.'

The Rev. Peters led her back to her chair. Looking down at her he said, 'Anne, you are going through a very traumatic time. When Mary gets here you can talk it over with her.'

She nodded and replied, 'I've tried to call her so many times. I don't understand why there is never anyone there.'

The Rev Peters smiled. 'They are both very busy people, Anne. Counselling unfortunate souls is not a nine to five job.'

'No, I realise that,' said Anne.

He walked her to the door and, holding both her hands in his, said, 'You know, Anne, I think your mother would have wanted you to forgive your father, and I know for certain that God would.'

As she made her way home Anne knew she did not really care what God wanted. If all they say is true, she thought, it was God who was responsible for her poor mother's suffering.

She felt comforted by the fact that her best friend would soon be here. The long discussions she had had with Mary regarding her father had always made her feel better. A vicar's daughter she may be, but Mary had never thrust God down her throat.

Later that evening Mrs Davidson entered the study in time to catch the last few words of the Rev. Peter's conversation before he put down the phone. 'Well, give her my love, David, and tell her we all wish her well.

'Something wrong?' asked Mrs Davidson.

The Rev. Peters stood looking down at his desk. He shook his head before answering.

'Yes. It's poor Mary. She has a very bad attack of gastric flu and cannot come to the funeral.' With a worried expression on his face he continued, 'There's no point in Anne phoning. David says she can't get out of bed and he doesn't want her disturbed.' Picking up papers from his desk he muttered, 'I suppose he's right. It's not like Mary to take to her bed. She must be really poorly.'

'It's unlike like Mary not to make contact for the last four weeks either. I don't know! Young people,' Mrs Davidson tutted as she left the study.

Chapter Four

Mary had been unable to speak to anyone since arriving at David's house. She had been quite relieved when he told her that he felt it important that they respect each other's privacy and, in order to do so, should have their own separate rooms.

What she was not prepared for was that all the telephone extensions had been removed. The only telephone was in David's room, which he locked every day before he went off to work. In addition to this, he made sure the front door was locked from the outside to stop her from going out. She questioned him about this and he explained that it was for her own good as she was not used to living in London and it could be very dangerous out there. The situation was beginning to alarm her, but David put her mind at rest saying there was plenty of time to explore London when he was with her.

Her relief at finding that he had prepared the guest room for her was soon shattered. On the third night, he came to her room. Kneeling down by the side of the bed he explained that, as a married woman, she would have to perform certain acts. He made her kneel at the side of the bed with him and pray for blessing on what he described as two of God's people coming together.

That night Mary became the victim of David Freeman's depraved sexual demands. Not being able to bear the pain any longer she begged him to stop. He never heard her. His face was transformed into that of a madman.

Now, some four weeks later, she was able to conjure up the black shadows and hide behind them while he abused her body.

This morning she sat at the breakfast table toying with a bowl of cereal while he read the newspaper. Her eyes travelled up to the clock on the kitchen wall. It was 9.30. Another 15 minutes and he would be gone. He always left for work at 9.45 on the dot.

Folding his newspaper and placing it in front of him, he pushed his chair back and came and stood behind her. Mary shivered as he placed his hands on her shoulders. 'You're really not eating as well as I would like you to, my dear. Don't forget that little baby inside you gets hungry too.'

Mary was quite unable to think of a baby growing inside her. Instead it felt like a cancer that she could not wait to get rid of. Every time she inadvertently placed her hands on her stomach, she felt dirty and unclean at the thought of something evil growing inside her.

He patted her cheek, smiled and said, 'We'll write to your father tonight and tell him he's going to be a grandfather.'

She heard the keys turning in both locks of the front door as he left. David had dispensed with the services of his cleaner and she had quite willingly agreed to keep the house clean and look after her new husband. But her mind seemed so mixed up of late that she couldn't remember whether it had been his suggestion or hers.

Mary looked around the very modern kitchen. Plain white units surrounded three of the walls and on the other was a large picture of Christ. Along the gleaming worktops the most up-to-date kitchen appliances were on display. A smoked glass circular table and four black leather padded chairs stood on stainless steel legs in the corner.

Next to the kitchen was a large dining room that housed an antique oak dining table. On the backs of the six dining chairs were ugly ornate carvings. The room was devoid of other furniture and the emulsioned walls were bare.

The room had an eerie feeling, and Mary would have much preferred to eat at the little table in the kitchen. On her arrival she had suggested this, but David was adamant that dinner had to be eaten there.

Upstairs were four bedrooms. David had the largest room. Mary occupied the guest room and the smallbox room remained empty. The fourth room, although small, was used as a lounge. It was furnished with a dark brown chesterfield and a high-backed leather chair. A small mahogany coffee table stood in front of the chesterfield. Once again, not a single picture hung on the plain magnolia walls. A white venetian blind hung at the window, the same as every other room in the house.

Mary continued to look vacantly around the kitchen. No matter how hard she tried, she could not hold on to the picture of a Victorian kitchen with a plump lady bustling around that flashed in and out of her mind. With a totally blank look on her face she began to clear the breakfast table. David liked everything spotless when he came home for lunch at exactly 12.30.

He always brought something in for lunch but insisted on cooking dinner when he came home in the evening. The evening! Her muddled brain tried to remember what David had said about this evening. It suddenly came to her. They were going to write to her father.

Smiling, she said out loud, 'My father's a vicar, you know.' The sound of her own voice startled her.

Yes. They were going to write to her father and tell him about this diseased object that was growing inside her. Mary began to tremble, but became quite calm once the black shadows had engulfed her. She did not hear the telephone ringing behind his locked bedroom door, as it did most days.

Chapter Five

Anne Stacey took a long deep breath as she walked up the hill to the Vicarage. The evenings were getting lighter, and it was a particularly nice spring evening. As she inhaled the scent of the early blossom she knew she was beginning to fight her way out of the gloom and despondency that had taken control of her life since her mother's death.

Reluctantly she had agreed to her father moving back to the house. His attempts at taking care of her consisted in him making the odd cup of tea, and even this had faded into oblivion after the first three weeks. This really gave Anne no problem at all as she had been used to taking care of the house and preparing meals during her mother's long and tragic illness.

It was a small comfort to know that she was not alone in the house at night, even though it was only after the local pub had closed that he would return home.

However, there was something that made Anne a little uncomfortable. That was the way she sometimes caught him looking at her.

The only thing she had been unable to come to terms with was Mary's silence. It was nearly three months now, and not a word. She had phoned continuously, and no one ever answered.

Having prepared a ham salad for her father, she was now on her way to see Mrs Davidson who had invited her for supper.

Glad of the fact that the Rev. Peters would be out calling on his parishioners, she had eagerly accepted. It was far easier to talk when the vicar was not around.

She wandered through the grounds of the Vicarage and up to the big oak front door, engulfed in nostalgia. They had been such happy days when she and Mary had played here as small children, then as teenagers pretending to be film stars. Anne smiled to herself. Mary never liked that game much, and said that she would never leave the Vicarage. Now, Anne said to herself, here she is living in London and here am I, having supper at the Vicarage.

The front door opened before Anne was halfway up the drive. There was Davy, arms outstretched, ready for a hug. Anne's spirits were lifted immediately. What a welcoming sight.

After a wonderful meal of homemade steak and kidney pie, fresh vegetables and Mrs Davidson's speciality, crispy roast potatoes, Anne had difficulty finishing even a small portion of apple and blackberry pie.

The two women sat talking for a long time about Mary, the girl who had played such an important role in both their lives.

'For all intents and purposes she has disappeared into thin air,' said Mrs Davidson raising her hands in the air and letting them fall to the table again.

Anne left with a feeling of reassurance that dear old Davy was as uneasy as she was about Mary's lack of contact.

It was dark when she made her way home from the Vicarage and she was surprised at how long they had been nattering. Looking at her watch she was irritated by the fact that it was almost eleven. Her father may be home now, though she secretly hoped not. She felt a lot more comfortable if she was in bed when he came home.

On turning the corner into School Road that led to her small terraced house, she saw that the curtains were closed but the light was still on. A strange feeling took hold in the pit of her stomach as she realised her father was home but had not gone to bed yet. She had begun to feel uncomfortable at the way he looked at her when he was under the influence of alcohol.

'Well, there you are,' he called out as he heard her key in the lock. She was confronted by the sight of her father stretched out on the settee with his head propped up by a cushion, drinking a can of beer.

Anne's anger was apparent as she snarled, 'If you must sit with your feet up, will you take your filthy shoes off?'

Swinging his feet down onto the floor he replied in a slurred voice, 'Oh dear! Who's upset my little princess?' Anne hated him calling her that. She just glared at him with a face that portrayed her contempt. Try as she might, she could not rekindle any affection for her father at all.

John Stacey watched his daughter walk through the living room into the kitchen. Her white jeans fitted her slim figure like a glove and her short black T-shirt emphasised her firm bust and 22-inch waist.

'I don't suppose you want a cup of cocoa!' she called from the kitchen.

'No, I don't,' he laughingly called back. 'But bring yours in here and come and talk to your old dad.'

Anne entered the room with both hands wrapped around a steaming cup of cocoa. 'Sorry. I'm taking this up to bed with me. I've got to get up early for work tomorrow. Someone in this house has to pay the bills.'

He watched her walk across the room and, as she was opening the door to leave, noticed the faint line of her panties through the tight-fitting jeans. His thoughts started to run wild. She certainly had grown up into a real cracker, he thought to himself.

She lay in bed that night feeling so terribly lonely. Since her mother had died and Mary had gone to London, she had not made any new friends.

Chapter Six

The phone rang in the Rev. Peters's study. Mrs Davidson rushed in to answer it as the vicar was over at the church. The old lady was somewhat startled to hear David Freeman's voice. In his usual cold and supercilious way he asked to speak to the Rev. Peters.

After explaining that he was out and wouldn't be back for an hour, Mrs Davidson asked how Mary was.

'She's not too good, but better than she was.' His reply was curt and without feeling.

'Could I have a quick word with Mary?' Mrs Davidson asked excitedly.

'Tell Reverend Peters I'll call him later,' he said ignoring her request.

'But Mr Freeman, shall I ask Reverend Peters to call you?'

She was getting a little irritated by his tone but, before she could say any more, he repeated, 'I'll call him.' The click sounded in the old lady's ear as he put the phone down.

Her hand was shaking as she replaced the receiver. She knew it was the result of that man's voice. He had a knack of somehow reminding her that she was just the housekeeper.

On his return the Rev. Peters did not wait for him to call back. He began dialling David Freeman's number before he'd even removed his coat.

The grave look on the vicar's face, as he stood listening while the phone rang the other end, gave Mrs Davidson cause for concern.

Not wanting to appear nosy she quietly left the room and went into the kitchen. For the first time in her life, the old housekeeper left the door open with the full intention of eavesdropping.

'Hello, David. How are you? Sorry I wasn't here when you called. I've been trying to get in touch with you for weeks.'

'What! Are you sure?'

'Well, yes, of course I'm pleased. I just never expected this quite so soon.'

'How is she? Can you get her to the phone?'

'Oh dear, poor girl.'

'No, no. I understand.'

'Well, don't worry about that. I think it better to wait a little while before I make an announcement. Let's wait until she's feeling better and then maybe she can come down for a visit. The country air might do her good.'

'Oh, and tell her not to worry about Anne. She's fine. Her father's moved back in with her and, by all accounts, they're getting on really well.'

'Yes. Okay, David. But do tell her to write or phone as soon as she's feeling a little better.'

'Thanks for the call. Tell Mary everyone sends their love. Goodbye.'

Mrs Davidson could not see that the colour had drained from the vicar's face and his hand trembled as he replaced the receiver.

On entering the kitchen the Rev. Peters was more composed and feigned a smile. Pulling a chair out from under the kitchen table he said, 'Poor Mary. She's still very much under the weather but sends her love and promises to be in touch soon. David says this illness has left her somewhat depressed but that we're not to worry and she will be in touch soon.'

Mary sat in the lounge, her feet up on a stool. In her hands she held the Holy Bible open at the Old Testament. For one hour each evening David had insisted she study the Holy Book. In order not to incur his wrath, Mary now did almost everything she was told. Each evening she sat pretending to read but instead merely stared at the open pages.

David entered the room and sat down beside her. Without saying a word he took the Bible from her and placed it on the floor. Fear took hold of her, as it did whenever he came near. She was about to conjure up the black shadows to hide behind when he suddenly said, 'I've just spoken to your father.'

This jolted her back to reality. Her face took on an expression of excitement as she asked, 'How is he? Did he ask for me?'

'Of course he did.' He reached out and took her hand in his. 'I told him you were resting. Mary, we have to be very careful how we handle this. I want him to get used to the idea of his precious daughter being pregnant before you speak to him.'

She made no response other than to look up at the ceiling with the vacant look in her eyes that he had become quite accustomed to. Irritated by her vagueness, he placed his hands either side of her face and forced her to look at him.

'Your father asked us to go and visit him.' Lowering his voice almost to a whisper he went on, 'But I'm afraid Mary, that because of what I have just learned, it will not be possible.' He pulled her face close to his. She could smell alcohol on his breath. 'The man who raped you. You remember him, don't you Mary? He's back living with his daughter. Your best friend is living with the man who raped you. From what I understand, they're getting on really well.'

His sinister voice went round and round in her head. The man who raped you! The man who raped you! The smell of alcohol brought it all flashing back.

Removing his hands from her face, he shook her, shouting, 'I will not have you upset by that evil devil or anyone related to him.'

Letting go of her, he began to pace the floor, shouting, 'I will arrange for all connections with your past to be severed in as nice a way as possible.' He did not look at her when he announced, 'I am afraid that includes your father.'

In a change of voice that was full of compassion he went on, 'Mary, now you are over four months pregnant I will not be coming to your room at night until after the baby is born.'

No relief showed on Mary's face. She was already hiding behind her black shadows.

Chapter Seven

Mrs Davidson stood looking out of the kitchen window. Either side of the old wooden gates the yellow gorse swayed in the late spring breeze. The chimes of the old kitchen clock interrupted her daydreams. Glancing up to verify the time she wondered what had happened to the vicar. It was unlike him not to be bustling around at 7.30 in the morning, getting in her way. It was now eight o'clock.

One of the things that gave her great satisfaction was watching him eat a big hearty breakfast. It had not been easy in the early days to get him to accept that breakfast was the most important meal of the day.

The kettle was boiled, the frying pan warmed. Bacon, eggs and tomatoes lay on a chopping board beside the stove.

Deciding to find him before she made the tea, the old lady went and tapped gently on his study door. Not receiving any acknowledgement, she pushed the door open but found the room empty.

Standing at the bottom of the stairs, she called him several times before making her way up to knock on his bedroom door. Receiving no answer she gently opened it a fraction and popped her head round.

She noticed his clothes draped over an old pine box that stood at the end of his unmade bed.

Thinking it a little strange that his clothes were seemingly where he had left them the night before, she entered the room and made her way to the old iron framed window with the intention of opening the curtains.

It was as she walked around the side of the bed that she saw him slumped in the corner between the large pine chest of drawers and the door. His face was drained of all colour. One corner of his mouth drooped and saliva dripped down his chin on to the front of his pyjamas. One of his grey eyes was open and staring blankly ahead while the other one was closed.

The scream from Mrs Davidson echoed through the Vicarage, as she stood transfixed at the gruesome sight.

It was several minutes before she could compose herself enough to ring for the emergency services.

That same morning Mary could only sit and listen to the constant chilling sound of the telephone ringing in David's locked room. By eleven o'clock it had become more than she could bear and she went to her bedroom to cover her ears with a pillow.

'Stop it! Stop it!' she screamed out loud and began to sob until the black shadows engulfed her once again.

David arrived home at lunchtime, bringing cold meats and fresh salad. Mary was not in the kitchen and the table was not laid. At once he felt agitated and began calling her. Eventually he found her lying face down on the bed, her head covered with a pillow.

'Mary, what on earth do you think you're doing? It's lunch time.' His voiced betrayed his irritation.

Removing the pillow, he rolled her over onto her back. When he saw the look on her tear-stained face he realised that she was in a state of distress.

'It's the phone,' she whimpered. 'It's been ringing all morning. I can't stand it.'

'Goodness me!' His reply still showed some agitation. 'Is that all? I thought something had happened to our baby.'

She shuddered when he used this terminology. In her mind she still thought of this thing growing inside her as a cancer. The bigger her stomach grew, the more repulsive she felt.

He lifted up her head and stared into her face. Then grabbing her by the arm he pulled her off the bed and dragged her down into the kitchen. As he settled her onto a chair, the piercing sound of the telephone started again and she immediately covered her ears with her hands.

Feeling in his pocket for his keys, he hastened upstairs. The sound of him unlocking the bedroom door could just be heard in between the telephone ringing. Mary heard the door slam and the ringing come to an abrupt end. The silence that followed made her shiver.

With the movements of a sleepwalker Mary began laying the table. Two knives, two forks and two large white napkins. It had to be just like he had shown her. He would get very angry if anything was out of place. She was about to reach for the two glasses when he came back into the room.

'Sit down!' he commanded. She left the glasses and immediately sat down. She could sense the irritation in his voice and had no desire to make things worse.

He sat on the opposite side of the table and, taking both her hands in his, said, 'I am sorry my dear, but I have got some rather bad news for you.'

Her face had little expression as she looked at him. Leaning further forward he went on, 'It's your father, my dear. He's had a stroke and has been taken to hospital.'

She jumped up. 'Oh, no! Oh, no! I must go to him.' Her voice trembled. He stood up, walked round the table and pushed her shaking body back down onto the chair. Cupping her chin in his hand he spoke very slowly. 'Now, my dear. I will not have you upset by this. We have got our baby to think of.'

He pulled away and began pacing the floor. 'The best plan is for me to catch the early train in the morning and find out just how serious this is.' He stopped and turned to Mary. 'You will stay here. After all, your father may not have told anyone yet about your pregnancy. We don't want to embarrass him, do we?'

Mary lost control and ran towards him screaming, 'No! I must go to him. You can't keep me here.' She began pulling at his clothes. The slap from the back of his hand sent her reeling and she fell against the cooker. Lifting her up by the arm he dragged her back up to her bedroom, pushed her down on the bed and then said quietly but firmly, 'Mary, I will not have you question my decisions. My lunch break is ruined now so I will go back to the office.' As he left he called over his shoulder, 'I hope you will have settled down by the time I return.'

Mary began to sob. Not only for herself but also for her father. Soon the black shadows rescued her from this nightmare.

Anne sat opposite Mrs Davidson at the kitchen table. The former warmth and cosiness of the Vicarage seemed to have been replaced by a cold, gloomy atmosphere. The old lady had tried to drum up some enthusiasm to make Mary's favourite cake, feeling that the smell drifting through the kitchen would go some way to comfort the poor girl, but after a sleepless night she had neither the energy nor the inclination to bake.

It was three o'clock in the afternoon. Anne kept looking at her watch and glancing through the window.

'Are you sure they gave you no idea what time they would arrive?' she asked Mrs Davidson. The old housekeeper gave her an impatient look.

'I've told you twice, my dear. He said they would arrive sometime today.' The past events and a sleepless night were beginning to tell on her.

'Now, put the kettle on and we'll have yet another cup of tea,' she said. 'There's a good girl.'

Anne, still not satisfied, pushed her chair back angrily, went over to the stove and continued, 'But Davy, I still don't understand why you didn't talk to Mary.'

Mrs Davidson put her head in her hands, 'My dear girl, how many more times do I have to go through it? I asked to speak to her. He went to fetch her, came back and said it was inconvenient and I was to leave a message.' Her voice waivered a little as she said, 'That girl has got too big for her boots since she went to London.'

Anne went across and put her arm around her shoulders. 'So we don't really know whether Mary is coming or not,' Anne whispered.

Mrs Davidson got up from her chair, looked Anne full in the face, and said, 'Of course she'll come. I know she's not behaved in a very considerate manner over the past few months, but this is no time for recriminations.'

Tears began to appear in the old lady's tired eyes. 'I only hope he will recognise her. He doesn't seem to know anybody else.'

'Oh, I am so sorry, Davy.' Anne patted the back of the old lady's hand. 'I came here to comfort you, yet all I seem to be doing is upsetting you.'

'No, my dear. It's alright. Let's make that cup of tea – although I feel like I need a large brandy to cope with that pompous fool our Mary has married.' They both laughed and Anne went to put the kettle on.

Anne stood by the stove with her hands resting on the handle of the big old kettle feeling very gloomy. Her whole life had changed. Her mother had died a painful, miserable death. Her best friend, for all intents and purposes, had run out on her. Her father had taken up with yet another floozy and kept bringing her to the house. Now the Rev. Peters could no longer speak or walk.

Poor Davy had been inconsolable, and although nothing had been discussed, there was a probability that she would have to move from the Vicarage. If Anne had had any faith left in God she would have prayed that the new vicar would be as kind and understanding as the Rev. Peters and let dear old Davy stay on. But since God never seemed to answer her prayers, she decided to put it out of her mind.

Many more cups of tea were drunk and they found themselves saying the same things over and over again. Why hadn't Mary written? Why hadn't she phoned? The old clock struck six and David Freeman and Mary still had not arrived.

Anne looked up at the clock and then at the distraught Mrs Davidson. 'Right, that's it!' she exclaimed. 'I'm going to phone them and maybe give Mary a piece of my mind. How can she do this to her poor father?' She walked purposefully towards the vicar's study.

A few minutes later she returned, shaking her head. 'Well, surprise, surprise! Nobody's answering the phone.'

Trying to reassure her, Mrs Davidson braved a smile and said in the most cheerful voice she could muster, 'There you are, you see. That means they're on their way.'

Anne began shouting. 'It means nothing. When have we ever got an answer from her?' She stopped suddenly as she realised she was losing her temper.

The sound of a taxi coming up the drive took them both racing to the window. 'It's them,' Anne said excitedly.

'Where's Mary?' Mrs Davidson asked, putting an arm around Anne's shoulders. They watched in dismay as David Freeman got out of the taxi alone.

Smoothing the front of her dress, Mrs Davidson composed herself and then walked swiftly to the door. As she opened it she heard him say to the taxi driver, 'I won't be more than twenty minutes. Wait for me.'

'Good evening, Mrs Davidson.' David Freeman's cool manner immediately unnerved the old lady.

'Good evening, Mr Freeman. Where's Mary?' Her voice showed no trace of the nervousness she felt.

'Mary's at the hospital with her father,' he lied. Then, ushering her inside, continued, 'I think we need to have a little chat.'

Mrs Davidson deliberately showed him into the kitchen instead of the study where the Rev. Peters received important guests. I don't want him thinking he's important, she thought to herself.

As soon as David Freeman saw Anne his agitation became apparent. Turning to Mrs Davidson he said, 'I do not have a lot of time and there are certain matters I have to discuss with you that are private.' He turned to Anne. 'Please leave us.'

Anne gave the old lady a questioning look.

Mrs Davidson nodded. ' Give us a few minutes my dear.'

A furious Anne left the room, displaying her annoyance by slamming the door.

Sitting himself down at the kitchen table David glanced round the room, not hiding his disapproval at having been received in the kitchen.

'Now, Mrs Davidson. As I said, I don't have much time so I'll come straight to the point. You may or may not know that Mary is pregnant.'

The shock was a little too much for the old lady. She quickly sat down and tried to compose herself. With great difficulty she forced a smile and said, 'Well, congratulations to you both. I am very happy for you.'

David, ignoring her good wishes went on, 'This has not been an easy pregnancy for Mary. Now perhaps you'll understand why I do not want her subjected to any stress. For this reason I'm making arrangements to move her father to a nursing home in London.'

Mrs Davidson nodded gravely and replied, 'I see. I suppose that will make it more convenient for Mary to visit him.'

Once again he ignored her response.

'Now, this is the difficult part. She's heavily involved in helping me with various charitable organisations and has made many new friends. She now wants to put her life here behind her.'

He got up from his chair and walked across to the window. With his back to her he continued, 'I would be grateful if you and Anne Stacey would stop trying to contact Mary.'

The old lady was stunned. 'But why?' she asked in a trembling voice.

He began pacing the floor. 'That girl comes from a very undesirable family. I've heard all sorts of things about her father, who I now understand is living in the same house as her. Mary asked me to let you know, as nicely as possible, that you do not fit into her way of life any more.' Taking a deep breath he went on, 'Now, if you or that girl have any feelings for Mary at all, you will cooperate with her wishes. She's not finding this easy and has enough to worry about with her father right now.'

Tears welled up in Mrs Davidson's eyes as she stammered, 'B-b-but Mr Freeman, I've known Mary all her life and Anne is her best friend.' The tears were beginning to trickle down her cheeks.

David Freeman shifted uncomfortably. 'Times change. Mary is a bright and intelligent girl and knows what she wants. I can assure you she no longer thinks of Anne as her best friend. Like I said, she's moved on and has a completely new circle of friends.' He turned towards the door. 'I must go. Mary's waiting for me at the hospital. I trust you'll inform Anne Stacey of the situation.' With that he left, slamming the door behind him. Mrs Davidson sat staring into space.

After having related the story to Anne, Mrs Davidson sat resting her face in her hands. Anne looked across at her and said, 'So, she doesn't want to see you either?'

'That's right,' the old lady replied sadly.

In contrast, Anne's face was that of a very indignant and angry young lady.

'How far is the hospital from here?' she shouted. 'Twenty minutes at the most, and after all this time, she couldn't be bothered to come and tell us herself. Stress? I'm afraid our Mary doesn't know the meaning of the word.'

The old lady still sat with her head in her hands.

'Who does she think she is?' Anne was almost screaming

now. 'Whatever would her father say?' She took a deep breath and went on, 'You, Davy, who has not only taken care of her throughout her childhood but have been like a member of the family, looking after her father the way you have.'

Anne stopped shouting. 'My God. It all makes sense now. Never answered the phone. Never gave us an address. She didn't want us to contact her. All that stuff about her being ill.' Then, after thinking for a moment, she went on, 'She's even rejected her own father. The only reason they're taking him to London is because he can't walk or speak and therefore can't be an embarrassment to their, so-called, posh friends.'

Mrs Davidson looked up with a tear-stained face. Anne realised she wasn't helping the distraught lady by her outbursts, but upsetting her even more. She felt like going to the hospital to have it out with Mary and looked up at the clock, but realised they would be long gone by now.

Anne went over and put her arm around the old housekeeper's trembling shoulders. 'I am so sorry. The last thing you needed was me spouting off, but I'm so angry that you, of all people, should be treated in this way. Let me get you that brandy we talked about.' The old lady's only response was a shake of the head.

'Well, let me make you another cup of tea before I go.' Mrs Davidson nodded.

Anne banged the kettle down on the stove. 'You know. I truly hope she never comes to see us again. I hate to think what I might say to her and that pompous husband of hers.'

On her way to work the next morning, Anne's anger had changed into a miserable emptiness. The only person left whom she really loved had walked out on her. It was inconceivable to think that Mary was to become a mother but that her child would never play in the woodlands behind the

Vicarage. The pain and isolation she felt at the thought of never seeing her friend again filled her with despair.

During the afternoon her spirits were somewhat lifted when the store manager called her to his office. He told her that she had been selected for a management course.

The gloom soon returned once she arrived home. She found her father lying on the settee with his girlfriend.

'Hi, princess.' He winked at her as he removed his hand from inside the blonde's half-open blouse.

Anne looked at him in total disgust. The blonde was suitably embarrassed and began fastening her blouse. Ignoring the look he said, 'I've got some good news for you.'

Walking into the kitchen Anne replied sarcastically, 'Oh! Are you moving out?'

'No,' he called after her, 'Sharon's moving in with us.'

Anne stormed back into the living room. 'What did you say?' she asked, glaring at him.

'I said, Sharon's going to move in with us. She'll help with the bills while she's still working.' With an evil grin on his face he went on, 'The good news is that you're going to have a new brother or sister. Yes, old Sharon here is in the club. What do you think of that?' Untangling himself from the blonde he stood up, put his hands on Anne's shoulders and said laughingly, 'This calls for a celebration drink my little princess.'

The heat from his hands on her shoulders made Anne feel sick. Pushing him away she screamed, 'You disgusting pig.' Then, losing total control, she slapped him hard across the face.

John Stacey grabbed his daughter's arm in a vice-like grip and, with the other hand, gave her a resounding slap across the head.

The blonde screamed and cried out, 'Stop it, John. Don't hit her.'

With her head reeling, Anne raced upstairs and threw herself on her bed. She sobbed herself to sleep.

The following morning she was greatly relieved to find her father and Sharon were nowhere to be seen. She made herself some tea and toast but the toast stuck in her throat.

Getting ready for work, she began thinking about the management course. She would be away for about six weeks and then, hopefully, would never have to come back. She gave a long wistful look up at the ceiling and thanked her mother for making sure the house was left to her so if needs be she could sell it, move away and hopefully her father would never find her.

Not for the first time, she wondered how her mother had ever got tied up with her father.

Her grandparents, who had died before she was born, had left the house to her mother on the understanding it should never fall into the hands of John Stacey who they had never approved of.

Four days went by and there was no sign of her father or Sharon. On the Saturday night she ventured into the little boxroom where her father had slept. She had been adamant that he was not be allowed to sleep in her mother's bedroom.

Relief swept over her as she opened the wardrobe and chest of drawers and found them empty. The only tell-tale signs of her father ever having been there were an overflowing ashtray and several empty beer cans. The tears began again but they were the result of release from a nightmare situation.

Chapter Eight

David Freeman arrived back in London only to find Mary still in bed, just as he had left her. He calmed his anger with a large whisky.

Mary was woken by the noise in the kitchen and immediately jumped out of bed and went to find him. He glanced at her over his shoulder, annoyed that she looked such a mess.

'David, I'm so sorry for my outburst. How is my father?' she asked.

His reply was curt and without feeling. 'Go and tidy yourself up and put on some clean clothes.' Mary immediately raced from the room and, after brushing her hair and putting on a new maternity dress that David had bought for her, sheepishly returned.

'Sit down!' he commanded. He poured himself another large whisky. Obeying his instructions she pulled a chair from under the table and sat down. He came and stood behind her and put his hands on her shoulders. The usual shiver went through her body.

He spoke sympathetically. 'My dear. Your father has had a very serious stroke. He's paralysed down one side and his speech is so impaired it is impossible to understand him. The doctors have tried to get him to communicate by writing things down but, sadly, he's completely lost the use of his hands. I waited at the hospital for the results of a scan that showed severe brain damage. Unfortunately, they hold little hope of a recovery.'

Mary never moved or spoke but just stared down at the table.

Massaging her shoulders, he went on, 'In order to make things easier for you I've made arrangements to have your father transferred to a nursing home in London. This will enable you to visit him without the stress of a long journey.'

His hands moved from her shoulders and down her front where he began massaging her breasts. His breathing became heavier as he continued, 'After all, you do have to be careful. Nothing must harm our baby.' He felt her shudder. Still massaging her breasts in a spiteful and painful way he said, 'Now, go and get your coat and I'll take you out for supper.'

Mary responded with a shake of her head. 'No,' she whispered.

The command was repeated. 'I said, get your coat!' She immediately got up and obeyed.

David Freeman kept his word and took Mary to see her father at St Mary's nursing home in London.

The Rev. Peters lay flat in his bed. His face was grey, one eye half closed and the other now closed completely. One side of his mouth drooped so badly that it made him look grotesque. Several tubes were attached to him and a monitor registered his heartbeat.

David Freeman looked down at him and with a grin on his face whispered, 'You poor unfortunate soul.'

This was more than Mary's very confused mind could take. Something inside her brain snapped and, instead of the emotional outburst that David had expected, she just stared at her father as if she had never known him.

They made several visits to the hospital during the next few weeks and her reaction never changed.

One evening, after returning from the hospital, David told her she was to expect a visitor. Mary looked at him with a vacant expression. She seldom spoke to him now. He lifted her chin with his finger and said with a smile on his face, 'It's only the midwife coming to check you over. It won't be long before we have our baby and we want to make sure everything is alright.' His smile faded as he continued, 'You know, I'm not sure that you look after yourself properly.'

She was a kind and gentle midwife but did not understand the look of disappointment on Mary's face when she announced that everything was fine and that it should be a straightforward birth producing a healthy baby.

As she was leaving she presented David with a card. 'Here's my telephone number. Call me any time if you're worried about anything. I'll see you again in two weeks.'

'Thank you,' said David in his aloof way.

Mary was dozing one evening in her room when a ring on the doorbell startled her. The sound of David unlocking the door was followed by a woman's laughter. Mary got up and opened her bedroom door very slightly just in time to see David taking the woman into his bedroom.

She had badly bleached blonde hair, very heavy make-up, and the shortest of black leather mini skirts. Her very high-heeled shoes and black fishnet stockings completed the picture of a second-rate prostitute.

David ushered her into his bedroom and, as always, locked the door. Mary quietly closed her door comforted by the knowledge that he'd found his pleasures elsewhere. She lay awake in bed for a long time willing the black shadows to take her away.

Chapter Nine

It was the fourth of September, a warm late summer morning when Jennifer Freeman was born. The midwife was amazed at Mary's silence even when the final acute contractions ripped through her body although by now she realised that there was something wrong with her mentally.

The midwife excused many of David Freeman's rude remarks by putting it down to the enormous stress he was under. He had not gone to work that morning but stayed well away from the room during the confinement.

'There we are,' proclaimed the midwife as she tried to hand the baby over to Mary, who immediately turned away and hid under the covers.

'Come along now,' she whispered, 'this is what you've been waiting for this past nine months.'

'No,' Mary screamed. 'Take it away. Please take it away.'

Her screaming brought David rushing into the room. On seeing the baby in the midwife's arms, a smug look came over his face. 'Give the baby to me. As you can see, my wife is very distraught. She's not been well for some time.'

The midwife handed the little bundle to him. 'Here's your daughter Mr Freeman.'

'Don't worry,' he said taking the baby from her. 'I've got a nurse coming to look after my wife and our baby.'

Mary heard the words from under the covers. Our baby, our baby. She immediately set her mind to find the peace of the dark shadows.

That evening Bridget Connors arrived to take charge of David Freeman's wife and baby. In spite of Bridget's protests, Mary was moved from her bedroom to the little box room. David had insisted that the boxroom was not big enough for Bridget and the baby.

Mary never once held her child or fed her. Bridget managed from the outset with a bottle.

Although she had been forewarned by David of Mary's depression, she could not help but notice that the girl was much better when he was out of the house.

He had told her that he wanted Jennifer awake when he returned from the office and that dinner should be half an hour later than usual. This would give him time to spend with his daughter.

Life settled into an organised routine. Bridget took constant care of Jennifer. She shopped in the mornings, taking the child with her. On her return she would attend to the laundry and the tidying of the house. David had not relented on his obsessive tidiness. In fact he became even fussier, constantly worrying that Jennifer could be in danger of picking up germs. The baby was always awake and dressed in pretty clothes when he returned home from work.

Jennifer was nine weeks old and, since she had been born, Mary had not been taken to see her father. Not wanting to irritate David, she asked Bridget if she would take her to the hospital when she went shopping.

'I don't see why not,' Bridget replied, giving Mary a sympathetic smile. 'In fact, why don't we do it tomorrow?' Mary nodded, her face showing no expression, just the vacant look that was about her most of the time now.

David Freeman appeared to be in a cheerful mood that night as he sat down for dinner with Bridget and Mary. He had just returned from saying goodnight to Jennifer and had a half smile on his face.

'Have you ever seen such a beautiful child?' he asked Bridget. 'I really am blessed.'

In an effort to bring Mary into the conversation Bridget said, 'Rosy cheeks and big brown eyes. Like a little doll, don't you think, Mary?'

David quickly interrupted, 'That's all credit to you Bridget, making sure the child gets plenty of fresh air.'

'Well,' she replied, 'We're going to get Mary some fresh air tomorrow. I plan to drop her off at the hospital to see her father while Jennifer and I go shopping. Isn't that so, Mary?'

Mary lowered her head as she saw David's face change and take on a steely, scary look. Staring down at the table, she could feel his eyes boring into her.

Bridget broke the silence. 'Mr Freeman, do you have a problem with me taking Mary out?'

David was silent for a few seconds before answering quietly. 'We'll talk about this later Bridget.' The remainder of the meal was eaten in silence.

Mary helped Bridget wash the dishes and then, pleading a headache, went to her room.

Later that evening, after preparing the baby's bottle, Bridget went in search of David. She found him sitting in the lounge.

'Come in Bridget. Come and sit down. I need to talk to you,' he said in a soft weary voice.

He explained that Mary was not a well girl and seeing her father in the condition he was in always upset her so badly that the doctors had recommended she stay away.

Bridget nodded. 'Mr Freeman. I do understand. I'm truly sorry. I realise I've overstepped the mark. It will not happen again I can assure you.' Hesitating, she could not help making a final comment. 'But I do get a little concerned by the fact that Mary never leaves the house.'

Nodding his head in agreement he replied, 'Yes, I worry

about it too. I'll see how she is tomorrow. I might try and take her out to dinner. She used to enjoy that.' He got up from his chair and walked towards the door. Bridget took this as her cue to leave but he stopped and turned round to face her. 'You must understand. You must never take her out without my prior permission.'

Bridget couldn't be sure, but she thought she saw a faint tear in the corner of his eye. Her heart went out to the poor man.

She now walked towards the door, and as he opened it for her he repeated, 'Now you do understand, Bridget, Mary's not a well girl. I, as her husband and counsellor, have to tread very carefully with her.'

Mary was on her knees by the side of her bed deep in prayer. She did not hear David enter her room. The first realisation that he was there was when the wide sticking plaster was strapped across her mouth. David pulled her up and turned her round to face him. The fear in her large blue eyes excited him.

Holding her arms in a steely grip, his face very close to hers, he whispered, 'Mary, you were making plans behind my back. You know full well that is a sin.' She shook her head from side to side and closed her eyes.

'God has sent me to punish you,' he proclaimed. He sat on the edge of the bed and pulled her across his knees. Removing her panties and producing a thin cane from inside his jacket he began thrashing her bare buttocks. The pain was excruciating. The plaster stuck firmly across her mouth prevented her from crying out. After what seemed like an eternity, he threw her on the bed and satisfied his bizarre sexual needs. Before retiring to bed that night, David poured himself a large whisky. He had a satisfied look on his face and a gleam in his eyes.

The Rev. Peters died the following year. To David's surprise, Mary took it all in her stride. She showed no emotion save for a few silent tears. He arranged a quiet funeral where just he and Mary were in attendance.

On the way home, Mary said quietly, 'It would have been nice if some of his friends had come. Did he have any friends? He was a vicar you know.' David made no reply.

Mary lay in bed that night, desperately trying to sort out her mind. She felt someone was trying to comfort her and called out for Mrs Davidson, but in her muddled mind realised it couldn't have been her father's funeral because the old lady would have been there. No matter how hard she tried everything became more and more confused. Sitting up and resting against the pillows, she tried to think of her father. She knew he was a vicar, but she couldn't see his face. Now someone had told her he was dead. Was that his funeral she had been to, she wondered? She gave up, finding it impossible to focus on anything.

From that day on, Mary Freeman lost the will to live. Like a robot, she did everything she was told. When David came to her room at night she slipped behind the black shadows as her body was subjected to his depraved demands.

Chapter Ten

Anne Stacey did her best to get her life back to normal. After the death of her mother, the disappearance of her best friend and the antics of her father, she felt as if the whole world was against her. The management course went very well. She was now back at the supermarket where she had to work for a year as a supervisor before taking stage two of the course.

Mrs Davidson was offered the chance of continuing as housekeeper to the new vicar but declined. 'Too many sad memories,' she said.

Anne suggested that she should come and live with her but the old lady decided to rent a little cottage in the village. 'I know it's only small, but it will do until another suitable position for a housekeeper comes up,' she said as Anne poured her another cup of tea.

Anne looked at her wistfully, knowing full well that she had no intention of taking on another housekeeping job.

'The last thing you need, my dear, is an old woman under your feet. It's time you found yourself a nice young man. Besides, I thought you had decided to sell the house.' The old lady's voice trembled a little.

Anne, trying hard to control her impatience said, 'Davy, you were the one who persuaded me not to leave the village until I had completed the management course.'

'I know that, my dear. I still think that's for the best and, after all, I am only five minutes' walk away.' Picking up her bag from the chair she continued, 'Now I really must go. I've got some bits of shopping to pick up on my way home. I only popped in for a quick cup of tea.'

During the next six months Anne worked very hard at the supermarket. Most of her evenings were spent studying. She was determined to make something of her life. Her only recreation was if Mrs Davidson popped in or she went to the old lady's cottage for dinner after work. Lonely as it was at times, she felt settled and had no desire to make new friends, male or female.

It was a Friday evening, about 9.30, when her life was thrown into turmoil again.

Settling herself in the armchair she began scanning the 'Cars for Sale' advertisements in the local paper. She had passed her test the previous month and was saving hard to buy a small car.

A ring on the doorbell interrupted her. She looked at her watch and wondered who it could be at this hour. She knew for certain it wouldn't be Mrs Davidson.

Her stomach lurched as the thought went through her mind that it could be her father. Gingerly, she opened the door. She was horrified to find Sharon standing on the doorstep. It was pouring with rain and her soaking wet hair hung limply around her face. It was a few seconds before Anne realised that the bundle Sharon had in her arms was a baby.

'Anne. Can I come in for a minute?' she whispered as she put her foot in the door.

Anne surprised herself at the venom in her own voice. 'No, you can't come in. I don't ever want to see you or my father again.'

'Please, Anne. Just for a minute,' Sharon begged. 'You won't ever see your father again. At least not with me, anyway.'

'Will you please go away or I'll call the police,' Anne screamed.

The child, awakened by the shouting, began to cry.

'Please, Anne.' Sharon was almost in tears now. 'If I can't come in, will you please take the baby? Just for tonight. We have nowhere to go.'

Anne looked down at the crying baby. 'Where's my father?'

Sharon shook her head. 'If I knew that, I wouldn't be here. This is your brother, Anne. Please take us in, just for tonight. I promise we'll be gone by the morning.'

Sure that she would regret it, Anne stood aside and let the rain-sodden woman into the house.

Without even removing her wet coat, Sharon collapsed onto the settee, laying the baby down beside her. Anne shuddered as she remembered the last time she had seen this woman draped over her settee.

Timidly, Sharon asked, 'I don't suppose you have a drink in the house? I've been walking the streets all day.'

'I'll make you a cup of tea,' replied Anne, knowing full well it wasn't tea this woman was after. She looked down at the baby who had stopped crying and fallen asleep. 'What about the baby? Can I get him something to drink?'

Sharon looked over at the sleeping child and said, 'His name is Trevor. Some milk would be good. I've got his plastic beaker in the bag.'

Looking perturbed, Anne asked, 'Shouldn't he have a bottle?'

Sharon's face hardened as she rummaged through the dirty old bag. 'Your father hurled that through the kitchen window before he left us a month ago. We've not seen him since.' She looked up and gave a weary smile.

Anne made no reply. Taking the beaker, she went into the kitchen to put the kettle on. She stood with both hands clasped around the handle of the kettle, trying to pluck up courage to go back in there and send this awful woman packing. How she despised her father for getting her mixed up in his sordid life.

Returning to the living room with the tea, she was confronted by the sight of Sharon sprawled out on the settee, inhaling deeply on a cigarette. The thought immediately flashed through Anne's mind that she could afford cigarettes, but not a bottle for the baby.

Mustering up a little courage Anne said curtly, 'Would you mind not smoking in here, please?'

'Sorry,' replied Sharon, 'I've just got to finish this one.'

Then, to Anne's disgust, she leant forward and flicked her ash in her saucer. Anne left the room and returned with the child's milk. She looked questioningly at Sharon.

She replied with a wave of her hand, 'Oh stick it anywhere, he's asleep now. I'll give it to the little perisher when he wakes up.'

Anne flinched at the poor little mite being called by such a name.

Sharon noticed this and remarked, 'He's not as cute as he looks. When he's awake he drives me up the bloody wall.'

Anne placed the beaker of milk on the coffee table and said, 'You can sleep on the settee for tonight. I'm going up now. But don't go getting any ideas. This is just for tonight. I want you out of here by tomorrow.'

'Now wait a minute,' said Sharon removing her feet from the settee. 'Why don't you go and get yourself a cup of tea and I'll tell you what your father did to us?'

'I don't want to hear what happened,' Anne replied angrily, 'and I certainly don't want to hear anything about my father.' With that she turned and went up to her room.

She sat on the edge of her bed and stared at her reflection in the mirror. 'Oh my God. What have I done?' she said out loud. Her eyes focused on the little silver frame that held a photograph of her mother. Reaching out she picked up the photograph and kissed it. Holding it in front of her she whispered, 'Oh, Mum. What shall I do? If only you were here to talk to me.'

She tiptoed to the bathroom, feeling a sense of relief when she was back in the sanctity of her bedroom. Although she was very tired, sleep would not come. She kept listening for any movement or noise from downstairs. Finally she fell into a sleep of fitful dreams. A little boy that everyone knew was her brother was walking around in the rain, crying.

The closing of the front door woke her. She sat up in bed and looked at the clock. It was a quarter past seven. The memory of her unwelcome visitor came rushing into her mind. Slowly she got out of bed, crept towards the door and pulled her dressing gown off the hook. Tightening the belt around her waist she ventured downstairs. Opening the living-room door gently, she found the room empty. Straining her ears to listen, she heard no sound from the kitchen. On entering the living room she at once saw the note under Sharon's unwashed cup. The saucer was full of cigarette butts.

Anne began to tremble as she read the note. 'Take care of your brother. I can't. You won't ever see me again – Ta, Sharon.'

Anne's eyes wandered across to the little bundle curled up fast asleep in the corner of the armchair. She sank to the floor in a state of shock, not knowing what to do next. Nine-month-old Trevor began to stir, and the enormity of the situation she was in began to register.

At 10.30, with the child in her arms, Anne knocked at the door of Mrs Davidson's cottage. The door opened straight onto the country lane and Anne felt conspicuous standing there with a baby in her arms.

The door opened after what seemed an eternity. Mrs Davidson expressed surprise at seeing Anne. 'My dear. What's wrong? Why aren't you at work?' Her voice trailed away as she spotted the baby in Anne's arms.

'Davy, can I come in please?' The weight of the baby was beginning to tell on her.

'Of course,' replied the old lady. 'Come on in and sit down. What, or should I say who, have we here?'

After Anne had related the events of the night before, Davy said, 'Oh, you poor girl.' Taking the baby, she whispered, 'And you poor little boy.'

They both sat in the fireside chairs opposite each other with Mrs Davidson staring down at the child in her arms.

Anne broke the silence. 'Davy, I just don't know what to do or who to phone. I can't possibly look after a baby.'

The old lady rose from her chair and handed the baby back to Anne. Shaking her head she replied, 'Well, the first thing that comes to mind, my dear, is that you must call the authorities.' She moved towards the kitchen, rubbing her hands down the front of the faded pinafore that Anne remembered her wearing at the Vicarage. 'I've got some soup on the go out here. It's gone twelve. Let's have some lunch. Maybe little Trevor would like some too.'

She disappeared into the kitchen and called back, 'Has the poor little mite had anything to eat this morning?'

'No,' Anne replied. 'I didn't have anything suitable, but he has had some milk.' She looked down at the little face looking up at her and found herself saying, 'You have been a good little boy haven't you.' Baby Trevor stretched and gave a smile that melted her heart.

Anne spoon-fed the child with the thick vegetable soup while Mrs Davidson laid the small gateleg table for them. Once the child had finished Anne stood him on the floor, holding him under the armpits. Young Trevor bounced up and down with a cute smile on his face. Once again Anne's heart went out to him. Sitting the child on the floor, surrounded by cushions to stop him from falling, Mrs Davidson and Anne tucked into their soup with lovely fresh bread that the baker had delivered that morning.

'How do we get in touch with the authorities?' Anne asked, tilting her bowl so as to scrape up the last of the soup.

'I'm not really sure,' replied Mrs Davidson, wiping the corners of her mouth with her napkin. 'We can easily find out by ringing the police.'

'The police!' echoed Anne. 'What can they do?'

The old lady's face looked serious. 'Well I should think they'll take young Trevor and get him placed in care, or tell us how to go about it.'

'You mean, like a Doctor Barnardo's home?' Anne asked.

'Somewhere like that, I suppose,' replied Mrs Davidson. Anne felt her stomach lurch, but knew she had to be sensible.

Together they walked back to Anne's house. Not for the first time, she marvelled at the energy of the old lady. Anne had to hurry to keep up with her.

Mrs Davidson took the baby while Anne fumbled for her key. Looking at the bundle in her arms, the old lady said in a child-like voice, 'We've got a phone in this house. We'll soon find you a nice home, sweetie.'

A surprised Anne turned and stared at Mrs Davidson, who gave an embarrassed laugh.

Once inside, they began rummaging through the bag that Sharon had left.

'Look at the colour of these nappies,' exclaimed Mrs Davidson. 'They look like they've been washed in a puddle.' They found a romper suit that needed a wash and a cardigan so matted that it looked like it had been made from a rug.

Anne watched Mrs Davidson give Trevor a bath in the kitchen sink. After dusting the little body with talcum powder she turned and said, 'Now, I'll get these washed and ironed ready for him to wear tomorrow.'

Anne looked at her questioningly. 'Tomorrow? Won't they come for him today?'

Looking agitated, the old lady replied, 'Well, I don't know Anne. You'd better ring and find out. Why don't you leave it until tomorrow?'

'Do you think that's best?' asked Anne.

Mrs Davidson replied, 'I really don't know my dear, but if we are going to leave it until tomorrow, I'd better get back and fetch some of my things.'

Anne did not know what to say. She put her arms around the old lady and hugged her. Mrs Davidson gently pushed her away. 'You can't look after him by yourself all night. Besides, it will give us more time to think.'

Pulling on her old faithful tweed coat and pushing a few grey hairs from her face she asked, 'Now, is there anything we want from the shops for the poor little mite?'

While she was gone, Anne busied herself by putting clean sheets on the bed in the spare room. Looking around, she was comforted by the fact that no trace of her father lingered. The room was newly decorated, with pale yellow emulsioned walls and yellow and white flowered curtains. The new décor had taken place, not only to remove all traces of him, but in the hope that Mrs Davidson would move in when she left the Vicarage. She smiled to herself, wondering how long she would be able to persuade her to stay.

Closing the door behind her she went across to her mother's room. Although it had never been used since her mother had died, Anne cleaned and polished it every weekend when she did the rest of the house. She stared down at the maroon candlewick bedspread. Her eyes moved across to the silver-framed photograph of herself that stood on the table beside her mother's bed. She felt sad, remembering how much her mother had loved her. She had always done her best to shield Anne from the trials and tribulations that her lazy, drunken father had subjected them to. The mahogany dressing table still had her mother's hairbrush with the comb placed in the centre. Two glass candlesticks stood either side on little crocheted mats. The matching wardrobe was empty now. Mrs Davidson had helped her take everything to the Salvation Army.

Anne picked up the hairbrush and recalled her mother's light brown curly hair. Looking in the mirror she wished, as she had often done in the past, that she had hair like her. Her own straight rich dark brown hair and big brown eyes were inherited from her father. Banishing all thoughts of him, she looked around the room. Her imagination began to run wild. If she moved into her mother's bedroom, Trevor could have hers.

Tossing her hair back she said out loud, 'What on earth are you thinking of?' Pulling herself up with a start, she ran downstairs to check on the baby.

He was lying on the floor between cushions. Picking him up and holding him above her head she noticed he had the same large brown eyes as her. Once again her father had left his mark. She held him close and whispered, 'My little brother. I have to let you go to people who can look after you far better than I can.'

Three days had gone by since Trevor's arrival. Mrs Davidson and Anne sat silently, side by side, on the settee. The old lady was knitting and Anne was reading the paper. The baby was fast asleep, upstairs in Anne's room.

She put the newspaper down on her lap, 'So! Do you think I should phone the authorities tomorrow? I must go back to work on Monday.'

The clickety-click of Mrs Davidson's knitting needles did not stop. Neither did she look up as she muttered, 'I suppose so, dear. I'm going to finish this row and then I'm going up.'

Anne frowned. It was obvious that she did not want to talk about it. Ten minutes later the knitting was put away. Mrs Davidson said goodnight and went to bed. Anne heard her check on Trevor before going to her own room.

Flicking through the last few pages of the newspaper, Anne noticed an item on the 'Goods for Sale' page, ringed round in a red pen. Her eyes began to fill with tears as she read, 'For

Sale – Child's Pushchair, Cot, Highchair. All in excellent condition. Any reasonable offer considered.'

Anne dried her eyes with the back of her hand. She sat and thought for a few minutes before venturing up the stairs to the old lady's room. Without knocking, she slowly opened the door. She found her sitting up in bed wearing a pink hairnet and cream flannelette nightdress. Her hands were placed with her palms down on the flowered eiderdown that she had brought with her. She looked worried and was staring into space.

'What is it, my dear?' she asked.

Anne gave a big smile and sat on the edge of the bed. 'What is it, my dear?' she mimicked. Producing the newspaper from behind her back. 'I'll tell you what it is, my dear.' She continued smiling, finding it difficult not to laugh.

Mrs Davidson remained serious. Fidgeting with her hairnet she replied nonchalantly, 'Oh that. I was thinking. If we kept Trevor and I moved in, just for a month's trial, we could see how we coped. We would need things like that. After all, it would be silly to buy new as it's only for a trial period.'

Once again the tears began to well in Anne's eyes. Looking at her dear friend she said, 'You are the kindest person I know. I'm so very, very fond of you.'

'Yes, Yes. That's enough of that,' the old lady snapped. 'Now go and get some sleep. We'll talk in the morning.'

Anne went to bed that night knowing that this was no trial period. She felt quite relieved. Mrs Davidson had made the decision for her.

So began Trevor Stacey's life with his sister Anne and Nanna Davy.

Chapter Eleven

It was late September. One of those damp, overcast days in London. Bridget was getting impatient with Jennifer. The weather did nothing to lift her spirits. She had been trying to put a pair of gloves on the child but to no avail.

She had been in the Freeman household for almost five years and the child's behaviour had grown steadily worse. She was also very upset with Mr Freeman. Her suggestion that Jennifer should invite a couple of children to her fifth birthday party had not been appreciated at all. He was almost rude when she mentioned that she thought it was time his daughter begin mixing with other children.

'She'll have her birthday party as normal with her mother, father and yourself,' he snapped, 'I would remind you, Bridget, that you are here to look after my daughter and wife. You are not employed to decide what's best for them.'

One glove was now on. Bridget picked up the other one only to find that Jennifer had taken off the first and thrown it on the floor. She now lay on the floor screaming, crying and kicking her legs in the air. Quietly and slowly, the door began to open. Mary stood there looking down in horror as the little girl continued to scream.

'Now look what you've done. You've disturbed your mummy,' Bridget shouted.

Jennifer stopped screaming and looked up at her mother. Before Bridget could stop her she was on her feet. She ran across and began kicking her mother hard in the shins. Mary did not respond. This seemed to bring out the worst in the child. Screaming again, she carried on kicking her mother as hard as she could. Bridget finally caught her round the waist and carried her struggling and screaming into her bedroom.

On her return Bridget looked at Mary's badly bruised legs. 'Oh Mary, I am so sorry,' she said shaking her head. 'The sooner that child gets to school the better.'

Staring blankly into space Mary said, 'It's alright. My father's a vicar, you know.'

Chapter Twelve

Grange Lodge was a delightful house. It was black and white, Tudor style, with a lovely old red front door. It stood halfway up a hill in the village of Ramsden. To the side, a garage had been built away from the house. The gardens, a feature of the property, were laid to lawn with pretty flowerbeds and shrubs and surrounded the entire house. Several beech trees swayed in the breeze either side of the main gate.

David Freeman's Jaguar pulled into the drive. He looked at his watch. It was ten minutes to three. The agent was due to meet him here at three.

For some time now he had wrestled with the idea of moving out to the country. Although hating to admit it, he was becoming quite concerned about Mary. He had come up with the idea that a garden might be the answer. She seemed to be in a total trance these days. The only words she ever seemed to say were, 'My father's a vicar you know.'

Jennifer was nearly six. The novelty of being a father was wearing a little thin. He knew the child was badly behaved, and he was getting tired of Bridget's continuous complaining.

He looked up at the outside of the Lodge again with a satisfied smile. The agent arrived on time and showed David around the house. The lounge was at the front with a beautiful bay window overlooking part of the garden. Behind that was the dining room, big enough to house his beloved dining suite. From the front door the hall led to the kitchen, which was suitably equipped and larger than the one in London. The largest bedroom was at the back of the house. This suited him perfectly. Further along the landing were three more good-sized bedrooms. Beige carpeting was fitted throughout the house and good-quality curtains hung at all the windows.

After driving around the village he was more than satisfied. There was a high street of shops, a nice-looking village school and the station was close by with a direct line to London. All this was only a short walk down the hill from the Lodge. Twenty minutes later David had made an offer on the property.

All he had to do now was find a live-in housekeeper. He did not foresee any problem with this as he was prepared to pay an exorbitant wage. He drove back to London feeling very pleased with himself.

Once everyone was in bed he had his usual large whisky and went to Mary's room.

Three weeks and ten interviews later, Dorothy Maitland showed up at David's office. He explained in detail how Mary had become mentally ill after having given birth, but emphasized the fact that she was never violent, just in a daze for most of the time.

Dorothy Maitland was 41. She had been housekeeper and nanny for a doctor for the past five years. Her mousy-coloured hair was drawn back from her face and tied in a bun. David thought she looked more like a schoolteacher than a housekeeper. Her navy blue cardigan and white blouse added to her staid look. Her rosy red cheeks and small blue eyes complemented a warm kindly face. She was leaving her present position due to the fact that the doctor and his family were moving abroad.

Dorothy was taken aback at what she thought was an incredibly large salary. However, it was not only the salary that encouraged her to take the job. Mr Freeman seemed a good man and she could not help feeling sorry for him. A date was agreed when she would go to the house to meet Mary and his daughter.

That same night, David told Bridget that he intended taking his family to the country to live. He went on to say that once the move had taken place, her services would no longer be required.

Bridget was staggered at the news and the coldness in his voice. No thank-you for the past five years. No apologies for putting her out of work.

But in her room that night, she surprised herself by feeling almost relieved. She had been wondering of late how long she would be able to cope with Jennifer. It was Mary she felt really sorry for. David Freeman had paid her well and she had been able to save a substantial amount of money. She decided then and there that a good holiday was what she not only needed but deserved.

The day before Dorothy Maitland was due to come to the house, David sat Mary down to tell her what was about to happen. Her expression turned to one of sheer terror when told of Bridget's imminent departure, believing she was going to be left alone at the mercy of David and the child. Her terror only subsided when he told her of the new housekeeper and garden at the Lodge.

Mary stared up at the ceiling and whispered, 'Garden! Garden!' In her mind she was trying to recall another garden where once she had played amongst the trees. It was no use. Everything got muddled. Once again she gave a faint smile and said, 'My father's a vicar, you know.'

The smile came to an abrupt end as David banged his fist on the table. 'I know your bloody father was a vicar,' he shouted. 'He's dead, Mary. Do you understand? He's bloody dead.' He got up and began to shake her.

The black shadows came and engulfed Mary and so she did not hear David's change of tone. He went on

70

sympathetically to explain what fun she could have in the garden as well as lovely walks around the village.

Eight weeks later, they were all settled in at Grange Lodge. Dorothy had the room next to Jennifer. David had the largest room at the back of the house. He immediately arranged for a locksmith to come and put a new lock on his door. Mary had the smallest room at the end of the landing. From the outset, Mary felt a degree of comfort with the Chelsea Rose curtains that hung at the windows and the little bedroom chair covered in the same fabric.

Even more pleasing to her was the view from the window. She could see the flowerbeds and the tall trees that swayed in the breeze.

Jennifer was soon enrolled in the local school, which meant the house was peaceful for most of the day. Mary would take herself off to her room as soon as she heard the child come home. Her fear of Jennifer was becoming more apparent. The child, noticing this, became even more spiteful to her mother.

Dorothy Maitland soon became used to David Freeman's pedantic rules with regard to mealtimes. Breakfast was at 8.30. He caught the ten o'clock train to London and arrived back at Ramsden station at six o'clock where he picked up his car. A short drive through the village and up the hill got him indoors at 6.15, ready for dinner at seven.

Mary dreaded dinner times. David insisted that Jennifer was now old enough to dine with them each evening. In spite of Dorothy's chastisement, the child continued mocking her mother, pulling faces and kicking her under the table.

Despite David's terrifying visits to her bedroom and her fear of her daughter, Mary found solace in the garden. When time allowed, Dorothy would help with the flowerbeds and the two of them built up a friendly relationship.

As well as sympathising with Mary, Dorothy also felt sorry

for David Freeman. His strange ways had to be the result of the tragedy that had befallen his wife.

It took a while for Mary to realise that David was only kind to her when Dorothy was around. When alone with him, he would be cruel and spiteful. She learnt to avoid him and Jennifer unless Dorothy was present.

Lunchtime became something that Mary looked forward to. Dorothy always prepared lunch for the two of them in the kitchen as opposed to the formal dining room. The garden was usually the topic of conversation although Mary's contribution was no more than an occasional 'Yes' or ' No'.

Dorothy was extremely patient with Mary. She told her stories about the doctor's family she had lived with before coming to Grange Lodge and bought garden magazines, which delighted Mary. They would sit and read them together after lunch.

On one of these occasions, Dorothy asked Mary if she felt well enough to go into the village to do some shopping. Mary looked at the floor and shook her head from side to side vigorously.

Dorothy put an arm around her shoulder saying tenderly, 'I'll take that as a "No" shall I.' Mary nodded. 'Would you like to tell me why?' Dorothy asked quietly.

Mary tried to think. Although her mind was muddled she finally remembered what had happened the last time she had planned to go out with Bridget. The horror of what happened that night began to show in her face. 'Not allowed,' Mary replied in a frightened voice.

Before Dorothy could pursue the matter, Mary grabbed her magazines from the table and, clutching them to her chest, abruptly left and went to her room.

Dorothy sat and stared after her. 'That poor man,' she muttered under her breath. 'What a lot he's got to put up with. No wonder he seems strange at times.'

Dorothy Maitland was by no means a gossip, but she was a

friendly person who soon got acquainted with people in the village. The word soon spread about David Freeman and the tragedy of his wife. Many people had said to her, 'A lesser man would have put her in a nursing home by now. What a good man he must be.' Dorothy would nod in agreement.

Every Sunday morning David would attend the village church. He never got into conversation, but most people knew who he was. They would smile, wish him good morning, or sometimes remark on the weather. David would respond but never stopped to talk.

He would always sit at the back of the church. When he heard the vicar preaching about God's forgiveness, a smirk would spread across his face. His thoughts would run wild. Forgiveness? God had never forgiven him, but had thrown him out of the profession he loved.

By the time he arrived home, he would be angry and full of bitterness and go straight to his room.

It was on one of these Sundays that, on his return home, he found Mary looking happier than he had seen her in a long time. She was kneeling down, weeding her garden. He was out of the car before Mary saw him. Glancing around quickly to make sure no one was around, he rushed over and kicked her so hard that she fell face down in the flowerbed.

'That should make you happy,' he said gritting his teeth as he walked swiftly away into the house.

That evening at dinner, Mary was sporting a badly grazed cheek. Her mouth was swollen and cut where her tooth had penetrated her lip.

As he sat down, David looked across the table and said, 'What on earth have you done to your face, my dear?' Mary responded by lowering her head.

Dorothy interrupted, 'My dear. What happened? Did you have a fall?'

Jennifer piped up, 'I bet she did it on purpose to make us feel sorry for her.'

Dorothy stared at the child and said quietly, 'That's not a nice thing to say.'

Jennifer put on one of her sulky looks. 'Well she's not a very nice mother.'

To avoid a scene, the housekeeper changed the subject.

After dinner, she followed Mary into her room taking with her the first aid kit. She never saw the cuts and bruises on Mary's legs as these were hidden by her calf-length pale blue denim dress. As Dorothy bathed the grazed cheek she noticed, not for the first time, what a pretty girl Mary was with her long blonde, slightly curly hair and large pale blue eyes. She was thinner and paler than she should have been, but was nevertheless a beautiful girl.

'Did you fall?' Dorothy asked. Mary nodded her head.

Later that same week, Dorothy asked David if she could take Mary for a walk in the village. 'I know she gets plenty of fresh air in the garden, but I thought she might like a change of scenery. I suggested a walk to her the other day and she said she was not allowed. Don't you think it would be good for her?'

David shook his head wearily. 'Of course I do. I'll try and speak to her.'

'Why does she say she's not allowed then?' Dorothy asked. 'Is that part of her illness, Mr Freeman?'

David nodded. 'Yes, I suppose it is, although I thought moving to the country would help her in that respect.'

Sadly, Dorothy noticed the worried look on his face and tried to cheer him up by saying, 'Don't you worry about it, Mr Freeman. I'll keep trying. As I said, she gets plenty of fresh air in the garden.'

She went off in search of Jennifer, wishing she had not troubled the poor man.

Chapter Thirteen

Anne Stacey and Mrs Davidson had never mentioned the one-month trial period again.

Mrs Davidson's ability in handling a baby had astounded Anne. The only experience the old lady had had was with a son who had died at the age of six with meningitis. To watch her you would have thought she had been looking after babies all her life. From the time Trevor had arrived, most of Anne's savings had been spent on him. Consequently her dream of owning a car had been put on hold.

For five days, Anne had had to stay in London as part of the management course. She phoned Mrs Davidson every night, and on her return was overwhelmed by the warmth of affection that awaited her. It was so much better than coming home to an empty house. For the first time since her mother had died and her best friend had run out on her, she felt close to a family again.

Mrs Davidson continued to nag her about her social life. 'It's time you found yourself a nice young man,' she would say at every opportunity.

There was no time or inclination on Anne's part to even think about that. She was happy spending her evenings at home. An hour was put aside for her course work and the rest of the time she spent chatting to the old lady about Trevor's activities during the day. At weekends she got enormous pleasure out of spending most of her time with the boy. This also gave Mrs Davidson a much-needed break.

One evening, Anne sat reading a magazine while Mrs Davidson busied herself in the kitchen. The article she was reading was headed, ' I Want My Baby Back.' It described some of the misery that foster parents had to endure when parents took their babies back.

Trevor was nearly five. Anne's love for him was so great she thought she would die if anyone took him away. The thought of him having to go and live with that awful woman who called herself his mother, made her blood run cold.

Closing the magazine she got up and wandered into the kitchen. Mrs Davidson was putting the last of the dinner things away. Hearing Anne come in, she called over her shoulder, 'You're just in time. I've finished here. You can make us a nice cup of tea.'

Minutes later, as they sat drinking their tea, Mrs Davidson looked across at Anne and asked, 'Anything troubling you my dear?'

Not wanting to worry the old lady, Anne jokingly said, 'As a matter of fact, there is. You haven't taken your pinafore off. You always take it off before you sit down for the evening.'

Mrs Davidson looked down at her pinafore and they both laughed. Anne could not remember when she had been this happy.

The following day she received a letter from head office in London. An appointment had been made for her to be interviewed by the marketing director of Andersons, the supermarket chain Anne worked for. Mrs Davidson watched her face as she read the letter at the breakfast table.

Anne's eyes lit up as she put it down and she clasped her hands together in excitement. 'Oh my goodness, I really think this is good news.' She handed the letter to Mrs Davidson to read.

'Of course it's good news. No one deserves it more than you, my dear,' the old lady said.

Anne arrived for the interview ten minutes early. She took

the opportunity to go to the Ladies. Looking in the full-length mirror, she was pleased with what she saw. Her hair hung to her shoulders and shone as it caught the light. She wore a cream light woollen suit that she had purchased for the occasion. The brown sweater underneath brought out the sparkle in her eyes. Her make-up consisted of brown mascara and a light pink lipstick. She had very good skin, never clogged with foundation. Throwing her small brown leather bag over her shoulder, she went to announce her arrival.

The interview went better than Anne could ever have dreamed. She was to be promoted to area inspector. This meant that she would be travelling from store to store ensuring that product promotions were being handled in accordance with the brief from head office. In addition, she was to listen to any problems the store managers put to her, and report back to her area manager.

Anne sat across the desk from Ralph Stevens. 'You look surprised, Anne,' he said in a very cultured voice.

It was a few seconds before Anne could reply. She licked her lips and explained confidently, 'I am surprised. I thought the next step was to manage my own store.'

Ralph Stevens got up from his chair. He went and stood by the huge window and looked down at the busy London traffic.

He was a tall man, over six feet. A mop of unruly blonde hair made him look even taller. He wore a dark grey suit with a pale blue shirt and tie. He turned to face Anne and she noticed the colour of his eyes was almost identical to his shirt. His manner was far friendlier than she had expected.

'You are quite right, Anne,' he said, as he slowly began to pace the floor. 'I have been studying your course work. A lot of people here are very impressed.' He stood and looked at her before continuing. 'I thought you would be better suited to area management, and area inspector is part of the training.'

Anne nodded and replied, 'I understand.'

'Well, Anne, congratulations,' he said, smiling. 'Miss Jamieson is expecting you; her office is at the end of the corridor. She will sort out your salary and car. Oh yes, I forgot to mention, you will have the use of a company car.'

Anne could not believe her ears. 'Where will I be based, Mr Stevens?' she asked.

Giving her a dashing smile, he said, 'Where would you like to be based, Anne?'

'Well, I don't know. This has all come as a bit of a shock,' she replied quietly.

He sat down at his enormous desk. 'How about at home?' he asked. Anne began to think he was teasing her. To her annoyance, she felt herself blush. So as to save her any embarrassment he quickly went on, 'All our area managers and inspectors are allowed to work from home. You will have quite an area to cover. Miss Jamieson will give you the list of our stores. She will also explain in detail what is expected of you and set up a meeting with your area manager.'

'Thank you very much indeed, Mr Stevens,' was all she could think of to say.

Ralph Stevens looked down at the folder on his desk. Anne had already noticed that it had her name on it. 'You're not married, Anne; neither do you have any children.'

'No,' Anne replied.

'Any plans?' he asked.

'If you mean, do I have plans to marry, the answer is no.' She quickly followed this by saying, 'My career is too important to me.' Anne thought that sounded impressive.

He gave a little laugh. 'You have time on your side, Anne. Now off you go and see Miss Jamieson. Work hard for us and you will find the rewards are good.'

As Anne walked to the door, she was hoping that her skirt had not creased at the back where she had been sitting down.

Ralph Stevens took a deep breath. Her perfume lingered in the air.

The discussion with Miss Jamieson went well. She was a humourless woman in her late fifties who said, in a monotone voice, 'You will have a petrol allowance so you must keep a close check on your mileage. All telephone bills will be paid provided they are not overseas calls.' She then handed Anne a written contract. 'Read this carefully when you get home. Your new salary is shown on page two. If you agree with everything I would be grateful if you could sign it and post back to me tomorrow.'

Sitting on the train on her way home, Anne began to reflect on the day. Most of her thoughts were centred on Ralph Stevens. She wondered if he was married. Surprised at her train of thought, she opened the big brown envelope and began to read the contract. When she got to her new salary she had to take a deep breath. It was far more than she had expected. What with this plus the additional perks she felt on top of the world.

By the time she arrived home, Trevor was already in bed. Mrs Davidson was busy laying the table for the two of them.

In her excitement, Anne rushed over, gave her a big hug and kiss on the cheek. This outward show of affection caused the old lady to be somewhat embarrassed.

They both let most of their lamb stew get cold as Anne babbled on and on about her day.

It was nearly two hours later when Anne suddenly realised she had not even enquired about Mrs Davidson's day with Trevor. Quickly trying to make amends she asked, 'And how has our boy been today?'

'Fine,' she replied. 'But you know, Anne, he is turned 5 now, we've got to think about school.'

'School,' said Anne thoughtfully. 'I know. I've been thinking about that. Do you think we'll have any problems? You know, me not being his mother and all that.'

Mrs Davidson got up from the table and began clearing the plates. They looked particularly unappetising, half full of cold stew. She mumbled, 'I don't know. Tomorrow's Saturday so let's talk about it over the weekend. I'm going to wash this lot up and then I'm going to bed. I suggest you do the same dear. You've had a long and tiring day.' As she was about to go into the kitchen she suddenly turned and faced Anne and said, 'Congratulations, my dear. You deserve to do well.'

There proved to be no problem with the local school. Anne simply explained that her mother had died and her father had left them some time ago.

She took Trevor to school by car in the mornings and Mrs Davidson collected him in the afternoon. The house became the hub of a really happy household. Trevor took to school like a duck to water and made friends right from the start, and Mrs Davidson joined a local whist drive.

Anne was really enjoying her job, and the extra money removed a lot of pressure from them both.

It was after a day at a friend's house that Trevor asked the question they had both been dreading. 'Why have I got an auntie and a nanna? My friend Paul has got a mummy and a daddy.'

Anne pulled the boy towards her and sat him on her lap. 'Let me try and explain,' she said, deliberately keeping a smile on her face. 'Our mummy died and our daddy had to go away. Because I'm so much older than you, I thought it better that you called me Auntie.' The boy started to fidget as Anne went on, 'Dear Nanna Davy here came to help me look after you.'

Trevor squirmed off her lap and said, 'So my sister is my mummy, and Nanna is my daddy.' Both Anne and Mrs Davidson laughed out loud. By this time the boy had completely lost interest and went to retrieve his toy car that had got stuck under the settee. Life seemed to be back on its happy course again.

By the time Trevor was eleven years old, he had developed the same rich brown hair and eyes as Anne. Although she was pleased that he looked like her, she was not so pleased that these characteristics were inherited from her father.

Chapter Fourteen

Things were not so harmonious at Grange Lodge. There were constant complaints about Jennifer's behaviour at school. Dorothy had talked to David Freeman about it, but to no avail. He continued spoiling the child.

One morning as Dorothy came out of the post office, she bumped into Jean Saunders, a rather frail-looking woman whose daughter was in Jennifer's class.

'Dorothy, I'm so glad I caught you. Could I have a quick word?' she said nervously.

'Yes of course,' replied Dorothy, knowing full well what was coming. 'But I haven't got a lot of time. I'm in a bit of a hurry this morning.'

'I don't want to make a fuss, but Jennifer is being very unkind to my daughter Valerie. She's saying such cruel things to her and being very spiteful. Valerie came home in tears yesterday. I don't want to go to the school and complain. I thought that if I had a word with you, it could be sorted out.' The poor woman looked desperate.

'I'm so sorry. Leave it to me, Mrs Saunders. 'I'll sort it out. I don't know what gets into that child, I really don't.' Dorothy felt cross and a little embarrassed. This was by no means the first time she had run into one of these encounters.

Walking back up the hill to the Lodge she wondered what, if anything, she could possibly do about it. She knew she could resign, but would never earn the money Mr Freeman paid her anywhere else. More importantly she felt so sorry for

Mary. She promised herself she would have another try at talking to the child. Depending on the outcome, she would make up her mind as to whether to speak to Mr Freeman about Jennifer again.

That evening proved to be the wrong time to speak to either of them. During dinner the telephone rang in David's room. He excused himself from the table and went to answer it. Dorothy looked across at Mary. Her face displayed her nervousness at hearing the telephone ring. David had explained why the only telephone in the house had to be kept in his room. 'It upsets her terribly,' he had said.

A few minutes later, he returned to the table, looking solemn. Picking up his knife and fork he announced that his father had died.

'Oh dear, I'm so sorry,' said Dorothy sympathetically. 'You must leave at once. Don't worry, Mr Freeman, I can take care of things here.'

'No point in going tonight,' he said coldly. 'Not much I can do until the morning.'

'But what about your mother, Mr Freeman? She must be devastated. I'm sure she would appreciate you going.'

'My mother's already dead, Dorothy,' he said, continuing to eat his dinner. 'She died a year ago.'

'Oh I am sorry, Mr Freeman, I didn't know.' The signs of embarrassment showed on Dorothy's face.

David stopped eating, looked up at her, and said, 'No, neither did I until just now.' Dorothy did not know what to say, so said nothing.

David left the following morning – not for Coventry where his father had lived, but London to see his solicitor.

The ageing and rather overweight Mr Cornell, tried to get up as David entered the office. So quick were David's movements that he was only halfway out of his chair by the time his client had sat down in the chair opposite. There were no handshakes or niceties, but Cornell was well used to David's rudeness.

He quickly offered his condolences and went on to inform David that he was the sole beneficiary apart from a small trust fund that had been set up for Jennifer. David gave one of his sinister smirks, and said, 'People are odd. They have never seen the child. I am surprised they knew she existed.'

Before he left, he handed Cornell a business card bearing the name of his financial advisor. 'I want the whole of the estate sold, including the factories. This man will be in touch with you as to what to do with the proceeds.'

David stood up and, looking down at old Cornell, said, 'I would be very grateful if you would get someone to handle the funeral arrangements. No expense spared. You know where to get in touch with me.' He walked towards the door, stopped, turned to the solicitor and said, 'Thank you, Mr Cornell. Good day to you.'

Once his client had left the office, the old solicitor shook his bald head and called for his secretary to get the undertakers on the phone.

David had told Dorothy that he was going to Coventry and would stay overnight as he had the funeral to arrange. Instead he walked around Soho. It was not long before he found a lady to his liking. After a brief conversation they went back to his hotel room.

Dorothy thought Mr Freeman's absence would be a good time for her to have the talk with Jennifer. She waited until she arrived home from school. The girl's milk and biscuits were on the kitchen table waiting for her. She walked into the kitchen, threw her bag onto the floor and shouted, 'I hate school.'

Mary heard her arrive and immediately went to her room.

Jennifer snatched a biscuit from the table. 'I don't want milk, I want lemonade,' she said rudely. So as not to start off on the wrong foot Dorothy immediately replaced the milk with lemonade.

'How was school today, Jennifer?' Dorothy began.

'Boring.'

Dorothy looked at the child. She did not resemble either parent, with her large brown eyes and her rich brown hair.

Dorothy tried again. 'Do you have a girl in your class called Valerie?'

Jennifer stopped drinking her lemonade. 'Yes, and I hate her.'

'Why do you hate her, Jennifer?'

'Because she tells everyone my mother's mad.'

'Your mother is unwell, dear.'

'No she isn't. She's mad, and I hate her as well.'

Exasperated, Dorothy continued. 'Jennifer, I do wish you would be a little kinder to your mother. If you behaved yourself at school instead of being so nasty to everyone, you'd make some friends.

'Where's my father?' Jennifer screamed at the top of her voice. 'He shouldn't leave me here with that mad bitch. I hate her.'

Dorothy tried in vain to calm her down. Taking the lemonade, she grabbed Jennifer's arm and pushed her towards the door. 'Now go to your room. I don't want to see you until dinner time.' Dorothy was doing her best not to shout.

Jennifer ran to her room still screaming, 'I hate her. She should be locked up.'

That evening the three of them sat at the dinner table, Mary not saying anything as usual, and Jennifer obviously sulking.

Half-way through dinner, Mary dropped her napkin on the floor. Bending down to retrieve it, she accidentally touched Jennifer's leg.

Jumping up from the table, the girl started screaming again. 'She pinched my leg. She is always doing that.'

Before Dorothy could stop her, Jennifer lunged towards Mary. She began tugging at her hair with one hand and slapping her face with the other.

Dorothy jumped up. Grabbing hold of Jennifer she gave her a resounding slap across her face.

The screams went through Mary's head. She clasped her hands to her face and trembled.

Dorothy dragged Jennifer, still screaming, off to her room and left her there.

When she arrived back in the dining room, Mary had disappeared. Dorothy sat down at the dining table and put her head in her hands. She dreaded what Mr Freeman's reactions would be when he found out that she had actually slapped his precious daughter.

Dorothy need not have worried. It was Mary who was subjected to the full force of her husband's anger. As expected, Jennifer couldn't wait to tell her father about the incident when he returned the next day. Even the beautifully wrapped gift was left unopened until she had finished her completely fabricated version of events.

David Freeman's response was to give her a hug and a kiss on the cheek. 'Never mind, darling, Daddy's home now.'

Dorothy interrupted. 'Mr Freeman, I'm afraid it wasn't quite like that.'

David held up his hand, 'I am sure it wasn't. Now let's forget all about it shall we.'

'Will you punish her for pinching me?' Jennifer's face portrayed a certain smugness. Dorothy was quite unnerved by the nastiness of the girl.

Later that evening, just before going to bed, Dorothy found David sitting in the lounge, reading. She coughed politely as she went in. He looked up from his newspaper but said nothing.

'Mr Freeman, could I have a quiet word with you?' Dorothy asked nervously.

'What is it?' he replied.

'I would like to put the record straight regarding the incident that took place while you were away,' said Dorothy.

Before she could continue, David dropped the newspaper onto his lap and said, 'Consider the matter closed, Dorothy. I am not condoning your method of chastisement, but I am sure you had your reasons.' He picked up his newspaper again and said, 'Goodnight Dorothy.'

Later that evening, after Dorothy had gone to bed, he downed two large whiskies. He then went quietly upstairs and along the landing to Mary's room. She was fast asleep but woke with a start as the sticking plaster went across her mouth. The sheer terror in her eyes excited him.

'Get out of bed,' he said quietly. Mary obeyed immediately.

'Do you realise, my dear, that when I am not here, you are supposed to look after our daughter.' He kept his voice to a whisper. Mary lifted a hand to remove the plaster in order to answer him. As quick as a flash he caught her wrist, spun her round and tied both hands behind her back.

Pushing his face up close to hers, he whispered, 'Do you know what the duties of a mother are?' Mary nodded. 'Do you think you fulfilled those duties when I was in Coventry arranging my father's funeral?' His face was even closer now. The smell of the alcohol on his breath sent shivers down Mary's spine. She began praying for the black shadows to engulf her, but they would not come.

'Answer me Mary. Do you think you fulfilled your duties?' The excitement in his voice and the gleam in his eyes terrified her. Mary slowly shook her head from side to side.

'Do you think you should be punished for that?' There was now an evil smile on his face and he was breathing heavily. Mary looked at the floor. Stepping forward, he pulled her pyjama bottoms down and she immediately stepped out of them. Pushing her face down onto the bed, he produced the thin cane once more from inside his jacket. He began thrashing her unmercifully.

Mary's prayers were answered when the black shadows began to engulf her. They did not block out the pain completely but blacked out the reality of what was happening. Once the thrashing had stopped, he proceeded to satisfy his bizarre sexual desires.

The following morning at breakfast, Dorothy noticed Mary wriggling around on her chair.

When David arrived he said caringly, 'You really don't look too well this morning, Mary. Why don't you spend the morning in bed?'

Nodding her head in agreement Dorothy said, 'You do seem a little fidgety, dear. A morning in bed might do you good.'

Mary's eyes opened wider than ever as she picked at her fingernails and stared into space.

Jennifer looked at her mother with contempt.

Chapter Fifteen

In London, Anne sat waiting outside Ralph Stevens's office. She had been called to head office for a meeting. She was unsure as to whether the turmoil she felt in her stomach was due to her nervousness of the meeting or excitement about seeing Ralph Stevens again.

Crossing her legs, Anne admired her black patent high-heeled shoes. She knew she looked nice. She had taken special care with her appearance this morning. Her black light wool suit fitted her like a glove. The collar of her pink silk blouse was turned down over the collarless jacket. The high heels complemented her slim shapely legs.

The door opened and Ralph Stevens walked towards her. 'Hello, Anne.' He greeted her with a beaming smile. 'Do come in, it's lovely to see you again.' Following him into the office, Anne noticed a strange look on his secretary's face. What she didn't know was that it was highly unusual for Ralph Stevens to come out of his office to greet anyone. It was his secretary's job to take visitors in. He closed the door and gestured Anne to sit down. He did not sit behind his desk as she had expected, but in an armchair near the window facing her.

'Well now,' he began. 'It must be three years since we last met.' He stared at Anne. 'You haven't changed much.' She tried her hardest not to blush.

Ralph Stevens leant back in his chair and said, 'I've had such good reports about you. I am very impressed by both your ability and your enthusiasm.'

'Well thank you. I do my best,' she replied, blushing.

'Your best has paid off Anne.'

He got up from his chair, walked over to his desk and picked up her file. As he passed he noticed just the faintest hint of perfume.

Returning to his chair he asked, 'Are you aware of your area manager's plans to go overseas?'

She nodded. 'I'll be sorry to see him go. I've learnt so much from him.' Plucking up courage she asked, 'Do you know who my new manager will be?'

With a half smile on his face he asked if she was interested in the position. Ralph Stevens watched Anne's face light up and did his best to conceal the effect this girl had on him.

It was gone seven by the time they had finished discussing her new position. He explained that area managers did not come under the jurisdiction of Mrs Jamieson. This was a much more senior post and she would be reporting directly to him.

Looking at his watch, he exclaimed, 'My goodness me! Look at the time. Have you a train to catch?'

Anne replied, 'Oh, it's quite alright Mr Stevens. I'm staying in a small hotel in London tonight. I hope to get some shopping done before I leave in the morning.'

'That's very sensible,' he said, walking back to his desk. 'Do you have plans for dinner tonight?'

Anne's heart skipped a beat, as she replied, 'Yes, thank you. I shall have something to eat at my hotel.'

Ralph Stevens never dated employees. He had strict principles regarding this. He amazed himself by saying, 'You're eating alone in a strange hotel. I am eating alone in a little restaurant down the road. Seems a little daft don't you think?'

Anne did not know what she thought, so did not reply.

Like a man used to having his orders obeyed, he walked towards the door, opened it and said, 'Right, you go and powder your nose. We'll meet down in Reception in ten minutes.'

Anne began to protest but he simply ushered her out of the door saying, 'Off you go. See you in ten minutes.'

They walked to a little Italian restaurant about 200 yards down the street. It was quite obvious that Ralph Stevens was well known here.

'Your usual table, Mr Stevens?' the headwaiter enquired.

Ralph Stevens nodded and, with his hand on her back, guided Anne to a table at the back of the restaurant. The meal was an absolute delight and she began to feel at ease in his company. He told her that he had been married for two years. It had not worked out and he was now divorced.

'Do you live alone, Anne?' he asked.

'No, I have a housekeeper, more of a good friend really. She helps me look after my young brother.'

'So how old is your young brother?' he asked.

'He's fourteen and quite a handful at the moment. I don't know what I would do without dear Mrs Davidson.'

Anne did not want this conversation to go on. She looked at her watch. 'I'm sorry, Mr Stevens. I don't want to be rude, but I really must be going. You see, I always ring Mrs Davidson when I'm away. She'll be getting anxious.'

'Yes of course,' he replied. 'How thoughtless of me.' Nodding to the waiter to bring the bill he went on, 'I will see you back to your hotel.'

Anne hoped the panic did not sound in her voice. 'No thank you. It really isn't necessary. It's only five minutes away.'

'Well, let me put you safely in a taxi.' He reached across the table and patted her hand. 'I can see I am making you nervous,' he said with a smile.

Back on the street Anne spotted a taxi immediately. Before she could stop herself she blurted out, 'There's one!' like a schoolgirl.

Ralph Stevens grinned as he hailed the taxi.

'I'm not going to eat you, my dear.'

Anne felt stupid. Here she was at the age of 34 behaving like a 16-year-old on her first date.

As she got into the taxi, Ralph took her arm and kissed the back of her hand.

Back at the hotel, she phoned Mrs Davidson but there was no reply. She checked her watch. It was 11.30, and she smiled to herself. It was way past Mrs Davidson's bedtime – the old lady would be fast asleep by now. The chances of Trevor getting up and answering the phone were remote.

Her thoughts wandered to Trevor. He was growing up to be a really spoiled and selfish boy. Many times she'd had to chastise him for being rude, not only to her, but to Mrs Davidson as well. Deep down, she knew she had spoiled him. The thing that worried Anne more than anything was his likeness to her father. Not only in appearance but, more worryingly, his behaviour.

Banishing all thoughts of Mrs Davidson and Trevor from her mind, Anne lay on the bed and thought about Ralph Stevens. How she wished she had not behaved so stupidly. She began to wonder how many other women at the age of 34 had never had a relationship with a man. 'Old spinster, that's what you are,' she said out loud. Jumping up from the bed, Anne looked at herself in the full-length mirror. She took comfort from the fact that she did not look a day over 25.

Next morning, she decided to abort her shopping expedition. The earlier train would get her home before lunch. The need to tell Mrs Davidson about her huge pay increase was far more important than shopping, she would also be delighted to hear about her dinner date.

As the train chugged along, she made pretence at reading the newspaper, but her thoughts were all over the place. Anne Stacey promoted to area manager. She still found it hard to believe. Closing her eyes, she whispered to herself, 'I did it, Mum. If only you were here, I know you'd be so proud of me.'

Reaching her destination, Anne went straight to the flower stall. She bought Mrs Davidson a huge bunch of flowers. It was beginning to drizzle as Anne walked through the car park to her company car. She tutted to herself. Her windscreen wipers were not working as well as they should. So many times she had put off taking the car to the garage to get them fixed. A sudden warm glow went through her body as the realisation set in that, with her new job, her car would be upgraded.

She was singing along to the car radio as she pulled up outside the house. Mrs Davidson was going to be surprised to see her so early. Anne was also a little relieved that Trevor would be at school. This meant that she could give her all the good news in private. They had never discussed money in front of the boy, and she certainly couldn't discuss Ralph Stevens with him there.

Inserting the key in the door, it was Anne who got the surprise.

Trevor confronted her. He was sprawled over the settee. The television was on full blast. For one moment, it reminded her of her father sprawling over the furniture.

'Trevor, what are you doing here? Why aren't you at school? There's nothing wrong, is there?' Her voice trembled a little over her last words.

'Hi! I thought you were going shopping,' he said in a nonchalant manner.

'Never mind that. Why aren't you at school, and where is your Nanna?' Her annoyance was showing. She walked over to the television and turned it off.

Trevor got up from the settee and said, 'What are you doing? I was watching that.'

Anne moved towards him, and, getting hold of his arm asked, 'Where is your Nanna?'

Trevor sighed and said, 'She went to hospital in an ambulance.'

'What!' she screamed. Lowering her voice and letting go of his arm she went on, 'Oh Trevor. What happened?'

He raised his arms above his head and stretched as if he had just woken up. 'I wondered where she was this morning. No breakfast was ready or anything. So I went to her room, but I couldn't wake her up. I went to get the milk off the doorstep so I could have some cereal. That nosy old woman from next door asked me to give Nanna a message and I told her I couldn't wake her up. Before I could stop her, the nosy old bitch was in here and up the stairs. The next thing I knew, she was calling an ambulance.'

'Trevor, what is wrong with you? Why didn't you phone me? Don't you ever think of anyone but yourself? Which hospital is she in?' Anne was frantic.

Trevor, raising his voice, said, 'I don't know what hospital she's in. Why are you getting yourself in such a state? The old woman is not related to us. Why can't she clear off and live with her own relatives? Can I have some toast now?'

Anne's hand came out of nowhere and slapped the boy hard across the face. 'How could you say such things?' She was shaking now at the realisation of what she had done. It reminded her of the night she had lost her temper and slapped her father. At that point the boy looked so much like his father she disliked him.

After checking with her neighbour, Anne drove at break-neck speed to the hospital. She was directed to Cavell Ward and sprinted down the long corridor. It was a small ward, with only six beds. One bed was curtained off. After looking around at the other five patients, Anne knew that this must be Mrs Davidson.

Nervously pulling the curtain to one side, Anne peeped in. The nurse, who was holding Mrs Davidson's hand, looked up. 'Are you a relative?'

94

'Yes. Anne lied.'

'Are you Anne?' Anne nodded.

'She's been asking for you,' the nurse said, and motioned Anne to come in and hold the old lady's hand.

Removing the oxygen mask from Davy's face, the nurse bent down, and whispered in her ear. 'Anne is here now. Can you hear me, Mrs Davidson?'

The tired old eyes flickered, but did not open. The grip on Anne's hand tightened a little as Mrs Davidson gasped, 'I called you last night.'

The grip on Anne's hand weakened. Anne put her arm around the old lady and kissed her on the cheek. 'Don't talk any more. You must rest,' she whispered.

Mrs Davidson did not try to talk any more but slowly passed away.

Anne did not know how long she had been sitting by the bedside when the nurse came back. She felt for a pulse and lifted the old lady's eyelids. 'I am so sorry,' she said, 'I'm afraid she's gone.'

For a minute Anne thought she was going to pass out. She stood up and bent over the bed. Cradling her dear Davy in her arms she sobbed uncontrollably.

Eventually two nurses had to pull her away.

In the hospital car park Anne sat in her car with tears streaming down her face. She tried to insert the key into the ignition but her hand was shaking too much. Slumping forward and resting her head on the steering wheel, she felt lonelier than she had ever felt in her life. She had lost her mother and her best friend. Now she had lost her soulmate. There was no one she could turn to.

The thought of confronting Trevor filled her with dread. What a thoughtless and selfish boy he had grown into.

On the slow drive home, tears blocked her vision on several occasions and she had to stop. Finally, she pulled up outside the house. The thought of going in and not having Mrs Davidson to greet her filled her body with such pain.

Polly, her next-door neighbour, came rushing out to the car. Trevor had been right about one thing. Polly really was a busybody, but she had a heart of gold. After a lot of protesting, Anne succumbed to Polly's invitation to go and have a cup of tea. They went through to Polly's spotlessly clean and tidy living room. Anne slumped gratefully into an armchair feeling as though her legs would not hold out much longer. She began to cry uncontrollably. Polly poured her a cup of strong tea, pulled across a dining chair and sat down next to her.

Anne pulled herself together and sipped her tea. She looked at Polly and said, between sniffles, 'It was a massive heart attack. They could do nothing for her.'

'Brought on by that brother of yours,' Polly snapped.

'Please, Polly, this is no time for recriminations,' Anne whispered.

'No, you're right. I'm so sorry, that was thoughtless of me. You have enough on your plate right now.' She put her arm around Anne's shoulder and gave her a squeeze.

'You just let me know if there is anything I can do for you.' Anne nodded. She could not bear to think about life without her dear Davy.

After she had finished her tea Anne stood up. 'Thanks Polly. Now I had better go and see where that brother of mine is.' The way she felt at that moment, she could not really have cared less where he was.

It was two days later that Anne got to hear of the commotion that had gone on while she was in London.

Apparently Mrs Davidson had been very worried about Trevor. He was usually home from school at about five o'clock. At nine o'clock that evening the old housekeeper tried to ring Anne at her hotel. The receptionist told her that Anne was out. She was about to ring the police when she heard a commotion outside. Trevor had arrived home just before ten, with a gang of unsavoury-looking boys who appeared somewhat older than him. Feeling intimidated, Mrs Davidson would not let Trevor bring them into the house. They reacted by throwing stones at the front door and shouting abuse through the letterbox.

Trevor was heard shouting, 'It's not your house, you just sponge off my sister. You've no right to stop me bringing my mates home.'

The shouting went on for about half an hour before they left, kicking beer cans up and down the street.

Anne now realised that she had her father's double on her hands. She had no idea how to handle it. More worryingly, she had no one to turn to now for advice. Why hadn't she made more friends, she wondered? Deep down, she knew it was due to the hurt she had suffered when Mary so cruelly ran out on her. Anne did not ever want to go through that again.

Chapter Sixteen

For many years Mary endured the cruelty of her husband and daughter. The shelter of her room gave her some protection from Jennifer, but in the evening it felt like a prison, where she would lie trembling waiting for David's footsteps on the stairs. Relief only came by hiding behind the black shadows, which engulfed her more and more.

Occasionally, with David's permission, Dorothy would take her for a walk through the village.

Jennifer was outraged that her mother was going into the village where people could see her. 'Now all my friends know that my mother's mad,' she screamed at Dorothy.

David overheard the commotion and decided he would have to do something about it. Jennifer was now 17 and he did not want her to suffer the embarrassment caused by Mary's outings. He wished now that he had never given permission. It was too late to put a stop to it and he could not think of a reason that would sound feasible to Dorothy.

The problem was solved for him when Jennifer came into the lounge one evening and sat on the floor by the side of her father's chair. She had grown into a very attractive young lady. She lifted her large brown eyes to look up at her father, and tossed her long hair back.

'Daddy,' she began, ' May I talk to you for a minute?'

He took a sip of whisky and said, 'Of course. As long as you are not going to complain about your mother again.'

'No, it has nothing to do with that. I want to talk about college.'

He put his whisky glass down on the table beside him and looked down at his beautiful daughter. She was wearing a pair of black leather trousers and a bright red T-shirt. She always had as many clothes as her heart desired, David made sure of that. In fact there was not one single thing she had ever asked for that wasn't forthcoming.

Her appearance sometimes disturbed him. It was on these occasions that he wished Jennifer was his real daughter, then perhaps he would not feel the way he did when she pranced around in front of him.

'What about college?' he asked.

'Well, as I have been struggling with my O-levels and there is not the slightest possibility of me getting to university, I wondered if you would be prepared to pay for me to go to a private art college? There is a girl in my class called Amanda who is going to one near Cambridge, and I wondered whether I could go too.' She put her hand on his arm and looked up at him with a childlike expression on her face.

He smiled. 'We could certainly look into it, my dear. But Cambridge is quite a distance. You realise you will have to live away from home.'

'I know that, Daddy. Everyone who goes there boards at the college. You see, they don't take day students. I would miss you terribly, but I would be home at weekends.'

'Find out the name and address of the college and I will send for a prospectus. I can't make a decision until I know more about it,' he replied.

Back in her room Jennifer felt triumphant. 'Yippee,' she shouted as she threw herself on to her bed. She was well aware that her father always gave in to her, but had been doubtful that he would agree to her living away from home.

How she wished she had access to a telephone like any normal family. Amanda would be longing to hear how she had got on, but she knew that the phone in her father's locked room was totally out of bounds. 'The telephone frightens your mother,' he told her each time she brought the subject up.

Quite often Amanda would invite Jennifer to her house, but she could never reciprocate because of her mother's insanity. 'How I hate that woman,' she said out loud. Stretching out on her bed, she began to think about how that mad woman had ruined her childhood. It had been impossible to bring girlfriends home and, whenever a boyfriend found out about her mother, the relationship came to an end abruptly.

She got up from the bed and looked at herself in the mirror. A smile lit up her face. Things were going to be different now. Jennifer knew she was attractive and, once at college, no one would know about her mother. She giggled at the thought of the fun ahead of her – taking boys back to her room for sex. She giggled again, then picked up her hairbrush and began brushing her hair.

Hearing footsteps outside, Jennifer quietly opened her door. She caught a glimpse of her father creeping towards her mother's room. She closed the door and looked at her watch. It was nearly eleven o'clock. 'Surely not,' she whispered to herself.

Once in bed, Jennifer tried hard to think of another explanation as to why her father would be creeping along to her mother's room at this time of night. She fell asleep convinced it was for sex, and the thought of it repulsed her.

The next morning, at breakfast, Mary kept staring at Jennifer. The long brown hair was disturbing her, and she wondered who she had known in the past that had the same colour hair. As usual, the more she tried to think the more muddled her mind became.

'Shall we do some gardening together today, Mary?' Dorothy asked.

Mary looked at the ceiling and replied, 'My father's a vicar, you know.'

The disappointment showed on Dorothy's face. It was obvious this was not going to be one of Mary's better days.

Jennifer jumped up from the table, looked at her father and said in a loud spiteful voice, 'I can't stand this. Why don't you put her in a home or something?'

'Now Jennifer, please. You'll be off to college in a few weeks. You must understand. I need your mother here. She would be very unhappy in a home,' David said quietly. The thought of not having Mary whenever he desired filled him with dread.

In temper, Jennifer pushed her chair back and David watched the shapely body, clad in tight jeans and white sweater, swagger out of the kitchen. Dorothy gave a sigh and started to clear the breakfast things.

It was apparent to David Freeman that Dorothy was coming to the end of her tether with his daughter.

'Dorothy, sit down for a minute.' She carried on clearing the table. Piling the plates together, she said, 'Don't worry Mr Freeman, I'm used to her tantrums.'

'Dorothy! Will you please sit down? There is something you ought to know,' David said, his irritation showing.

Dorothy sat down and listened as David told her of his plans to send Jennifer away to college.

Trying not to let the relief show on her face, she said, 'I think that's an excellent idea.'

He got up from his chair, and walking to the door, said, 'How do you see your position here without Jennifer to look after?' His hand was on the doorknob and his back to Dorothy as he waited for an answer.

'I don't really know,' she replied. 'That really is up to you, Mr Freeman. I suppose it depends on whether you need me to help look after Mary.'

He turned round to look at her. 'I can't really answer that question at the moment. I need some time to think about it.' With a cold smile he left the room.

'What a strange man,' thought Dorothy, shaking her head. Faced with the opportunity of leaving without too much fuss, she was not sure whether that, indeed, was what she wanted. She had grown very fond of Mary over the years and could not help but worry about what would become of her if she left.

That night David decided to tell Mary of his plan to send Jennifer to college. It was eleven o'clock, after he had drunk his second whisky, when he crept along to her room.

Mary was not asleep. She heard the dreaded footsteps on the stairs and prayed that he would go to his own room, but she heard him coming along the landing. Knowing exactly what was in store for her, she closed her eyes and hid behind the black shadows. Already having removed her pyjamas for him, she kneeled naked by the side of her bed.

He walked swiftly towards her, pulled her to a standing position and whispered in her ear, 'You disgusting little tart. You've been waiting for me haven't you? I only wanted to talk to you, but you make me do these exciting things to you because you like it.' He was shaking her violently. 'Ask me to fuck you,' he panted. 'Say please. Go on, beg me.'

There was no sticky tape tonight, so she whispered in a terrified voice, 'Please.'

Once his bizarre needs had been satisfied, he told her that Jennifer was being sent away to college. 'It's for the girl's own safety. She's terrified of you.'

Mary could only hear him in the distance, but replied, 'My father's a vicar, you know.'

He slapped her several times as hard as he could across her bare buttocks before he left the room.

Chapter Seventeen

Anne's new position took up a lot of time. She had to visit head office in London quite frequently. This meant she had less time for Trevor. At first this presented no problem. His behaviour had improved somewhat. But things began to deteriorate when he was 17. She heard of crowds of boys going to the house during lunchtime. Anne really began to worry when she had a letter from the school complaining about Trevor's absenteeism. She had persuaded him to stay on at school in order to qualify for a computer course at college.

The thought occurred to her that Polly might help out by keeping an eye on the boy. She mentioned this to Trevor, who threw a tantrum. 'For Christ's sake, I'm seventeen,' he shouted. 'I don't need babysitting. Were you going to pay her?'

'Of course,' replied Anne. 'She could probably do with the extra money.'

'Well, give me the money and I'll look after myself.'

Anne glared at him. 'I'll do no such thing. You have quite enough pocket money as it is.'

On reflection, Anne wondered whether Polly would have helped. She had no time for the boy at all.

Anne was always there to see him off in the mornings. He refused to let her drive him to school. The real worries for her were the evenings. There were times when she had to go to London, which meant that it was quite late by the time she arrived home.

On several occasions Ralph Stevens had invited her out to dinner. She really wanted to go, but for fear of what Trevor would get up to, she had politely refused.

After a meeting one evening in London, he asked her to stay behind as he had a few things to discuss. He noticed her hesitancy. Once the other members of staff had left, he said, 'I'm sorry Anne, have you got a dinner date?'

'No,' she replied. 'But I do have a train to catch.'

'Oh, you're not staying in town tonight?' he said, sounding surprised.

She had not told him about the death of Mrs Davidson. She did not want him to think that looking after Trevor would impede her work.

'It's not a problem, Mr Stevens. I can easily catch the next one,' she said efficiently. He walked towards her. 'No. I don't want to make you late unnecessarily. Perhaps we could get together for lunch next week?'

'That would be very nice,' she replied. ' Shall I arrange it with your secretary?'

'Laughing, he replied, 'No, that won't be necessary. Does next Wednesday fit in with your schedule?'

She checked her diary, trying hard to keep her hand steady. 'Yes, that's fine,' she replied.

Before she could say any more, he rubbed his hands together and said; 'Right. I'll see you at one o'clock at our little Italian restaurant down the road.' Holding her elbow, he steered her towards the door. 'Run along now and catch your train.'

They met the following Wednesday as planned. He was already seated at the table when she arrived. She was immediately ushered over to where Ralph was sitting. He stood up as the waiter pulled out the chair for her. With a grin on his face he said, 'You look stunning, Anne.'

She smiled and said, 'Oh, I bet you say that to all the girls.'

He had already ordered a bottle of Sancerre. When the

waiter came to pour it, she quickly put her hand over her glass. 'No, thank you. I have my car at the station.'

Ralph looked disappointed. 'I promise I'm not trying to get you drunk,' he teased.

She poured herself a glass of water before replying, 'I've never been drunk in my life.'

They both ordered the pasta of the day. While waiting for it to arrive, she asked, 'What is it we have to discuss, or shall we wait until the meal is over?' Giggling, she went on, 'You can tell I'm not used to business lunches. I don't know when to eat and when to discuss business.'

He laughed out loud. 'Anne, I'm always going to be honest with you. I do not have any business to discuss other than why you keep turning my dinner invitations down.'

She looked at him with a twinkle in her eye. 'Perhaps it's because I prefer lunch.'

He laughed again and said, 'Smarty pants.'

As he saw their food arrive he smiled, leant forward and whispered, 'By the way. We'll talk business while we eat.'

She in turn leant forward and whispered, 'Suppose I've got my mouth full. What do I do then?' They both laughed.

While sipping their coffee he asked, 'Why do you think that I can't stop thinking about you?'

Anne blushed. 'I really don't know.'

'Will you come out to dinner with me again?' he pleaded.

Anne spent the next 20 minutes telling him about Mrs Davidson's tragic death. She went on to explain the difficulties she was having with Trevor. Ralph was very understanding.

'There is an easy answer to all this, Anne. You could either move to London or I'll drive out to see you in Denton, wherever that is,' he said as he looked at her longingly.

Sitting in the train on her way home, Anne felt a warm glow. She had thoroughly enjoyed her lunch with Ralph. He made her laugh and she felt completely at ease in his company. It was difficult for her to understand why he, a director of such a large organisation, was interested in her.

The train pulled into Denton station. It was 4.30 in the afternoon and her diary was clear. She thought it would be nice to get home early for a change. Most of the time Trevor came home to an empty house, and she always felt guilty about that. Walking down the steps to the car park she rummaged in her bag for her keys. She hurried towards the car thinking she would have a nice meal ready for when Trevor got in.

Anne gasped as she looked at the space where she had left the car. It wasn't there.

She began walking to the telephone box on the platform. There was no point in phoning Trevor because he would not be home yet. The only thing she could think of was to phone for a taxi. Once indoors, she would phone the police.

Anne was looking inside her bag for a minicab number when she heard the screech of tyres. Looking up, she was amazed to see her car being driven into the car park. Rooted to the spot, she watched as it was driven into the parking space where she had left it that morning.

To her horror she saw Trevor and a young girl get out of the car. He slammed the door, called something to the girl, and the pair ran off.

Shaken by what she had seen, Anne walked slowly across to her car and climbed in. Driving home, she tried to think about how she would handle the situation.

Once indoors, she went straight to the little pot in her bedroom where she kept her spare set of keys. Just as she expected, the pot was empty.

Half an hour later Trevor arrived home. Anne was standing in the kitchen when she heard his key in the lock.

'Hi!' he shouted, and went straight across and turned on the television. Slumping into an armchair he called out, 'You're early. I thought you were going up to London.'

Anne was dreading the argument that she knew had to come. 'How was school?' she called out.

'Same as ever. Why?'

'Did you take my car to school?' she asked, as she entered the room.

'Don't be daft,' he said, without taking his eyes off the television.

'Did you go to school today, or go joyriding in my car?' she asked sarcastically.

'What is this? Some sort of inquisition?' he asked rudely.

'Give me the car keys at once, you stupid boy,' she screamed.

'What are you getting in a state for? I only borrowed it. I knew you were in London.'

Anne was beginning to lose her temper. 'You have no driving licence. No insurance. More importantly, do you realise it was stealing? I almost phoned the police.'

With a hateful look on his face he replied, 'Well, isn't that typical. No wonder our father ditched you.'

'For your information, our father didn't ditch me. I ditched him. That's what I intend to do with you unless you mend your ways.'

The argument went on for some time. Anne was near to tears. 'How could you behave like this after all I've done for you?'

He got up from the chair and threw the keys at Anne. 'Keep your precious car,' he snarled. He picked up his coat from where he had thrown it down on the settee and said, 'I'm off.'

He slammed the front door behind him. Anne stood motionless not knowing what to do. For the rest of the evening she tried to read, but could not concentrate.

At ten o'clock the phone rang. Expecting it to be Trevor she answered curtly, 'Yes!' and was taken aback to hear Ralph's voice.

'My. We do sound officious, don't we?'

'Ralph,' she blurted out, 'Whatever are you doing calling me at this hour?'

'Just wanted to say goodnight and wondered what your plans were for the weekend,' he said jovially.

'Well, other than visiting a store in Chelmsford early on Saturday morning, I don't have any.' Her heart was racing.

'Good,' he replied. 'If I can ever find Denton, I'll pick you up about seven for dinner. You must know where the good restaurants are in the area.'

Anne swallowed. She did not want him to come to her little terraced house. Although it had been completely refurbished and looked very nice, she felt somewhat embarrassed, knowing that he must live in a much grander place. Stalling for time she said, 'Can I call you tomorrow to confirm?'

'Of course,' he replied. 'You know I won't take no for an answer.' She feigned a laugh. His voice was so warm when he said, 'Goodnight, Anne.'

'Goodnight, Ralph,' she replied. It sounded strange. She had never called him by his Christian name before.

It was eleven o'clock. Anne decided she was not going to wait up any longer for Trevor. After making her usual hot drink she went to bed.

Expecting to be kept awake worrying about her wayward brother she was surprised to find that all she could think about was Ralph.

The next morning she did begin to worry about Trevor. His bed had not been slept in. It was obvious he had not been home. Calling two of his friends, she found out that he had not been to school for weeks. 'What is that boy up to?' she said out loud.

On leaving the house for work she was convinced he would be home that evening. She was about to get in the car but suddenly turned and went back into the house. Up in her bedroom she opened the little pot and took out the spare set of keys. 'Just in case,' she said to herself.

When she arrived home that evening, Trevor was nowhere to be seen. There were tell-tale crumbs on the kitchen table where he had made himself a sandwich. At least she knew he had been home. Feeling a little weary, Anne decided to go up and have a shower before making herself something to eat.

As she got to the top of the stairs she saw it. Lying open on the landing was her jewellery box. The only jewellery she owned was what Mrs Davidson and her mother had left her. She had always kept it in the right-hand drawer of her dressing table. Opening her bedroom door she was filled with dismay. The drawer was open and photographs and hairbrushes were strewn across the floor.

The string of pearls and ring that Davy had left her, as well as the gold locket her mother had bought her on her eighteenth birthday had gone. The large St Christopher pendant that had been her grandmother's was also missing. Her mother had given her that before she went into hospital. Realising it could only have been Trevor who had taken these treasured possessions, her dismay turned to rage.

Normally she dreaded confrontations with him. Tonight she couldn't wait for him to come home, almost looking forward to hearing his key in the lock. She wanted to see his face when she told him the police had been informed.

Forgetting about her shower and certainly in no mood to eat, she decided to watch the news, the contents of which did nothing to lift her spirits. Another 16-year-old girl had been raped. Anne was startled to hear where the attack had taken place. It was only five minutes away from the woodlands behind the vicarage. The pictures that were now being transmitted were of a part of the woodland where she and Mary had spent so much time together. I wonder how she is now, she thought. It had been 17 years and not a word.

109

The telephone rang. Quickly she turned off the television before answering it. It was Trevor.

'Hi, thought I'd give you a ring to let you know I've had enough and I'm not coming back.'

'What do you mean, you're not coming back?' she said angrily. 'Where do you think you're going to live?'

'None of your business,' he replied. 'I'm eighteen now and I can do as I like.'

'I think you'll find it is my business. I'll call the police and report you unless you give back everything that you stole from my jewel box. How could you do such a thing Trevor?' she asked.

'I don't know what you're talking about,' he snarled. 'And I don't think you'll go to the police either. Those posh bosses of yours in London wouldn't be very impressed with all the bad publicity.'

Anne was stunned by his threats. 'Look, Trevor. Why don't you come home and let's talk about this like adults.' Her voice wavered.

'Listen, don't go reporting me to the police. You'll never hear from me again. I'm only phoning because I know I can't be reported missing once I've told you I was leaving.'

'Trevor, what about your computer course? You only have six months to do. Don't ruin it all now,' she pleaded.

He laughed. 'I've got a job. Don't you worry. Bye big sister.' The phone went dead.

Anne stood staring into the mouthpiece.

Chapter Eighteen

Dorothy waited a few days before she tackled David Freeman about her future employment. She knew the best time to talk to him was after dinner when he disappeared into the lounge with his whisky and newspaper. She tapped on the door quietly and went in.

Looking up he gave a half smile. 'What is it, Dorothy?'

She cleared her throat. 'Mr Freeman. I wondered if you'd given any more thought to my position of employment now Jennifer is going off to college.'

'Yes, I have.' He gestured to Dorothy to sit down on the chesterfield opposite him.

'I am not a young man, Dorothy. If you were to leave I would have to give up counselling. I have not got the energy, mentally or physically, to cope with the job and Mary.' He folded his newspaper in half, stood up and leaned against the mantelpiece.

'I don't think Mary's getting any better and I don't really think she will now. She has made a friend of you. I fear that if I were to bring someone new in to look after her, it could have disastrous effects. The only other alternative is to put her in a home.' He looked at Dorothy. 'I've thought about that long and hard, but just can't bring myself to do it. Does that answer your question?'

Dorothy smiled. ' I think so Mr Freeman.'

'What are your thoughts on the matter?' he asked. 'Are you prepared to stay on and look after Mary, or had you thought of moving on?'

'Of course I'm prepared to stay. I've grown very fond of Mary. Once Jennifer's away at college I'll have more time to spend with her.'

'Yes indeed you will,' he said. 'Of course your salary will stay the same. In fact it might even be time for a review.'

As she closed the door behind her, she felt nothing but compassion for her employer. 'What a good man he is,' she thought to herself. 'Strange, but a good man nevertheless.'

A week later Jennifer along with her friend Amanda Saunders left for Caxton Art College in Cambridge.

After registration, both she and Amanda were shown to their rooms, which, to their delight, were next to each other. They were allowed two days to settle in, after which, they had been told, it was heads down and hard work. Jennifer was a bright girl and her poor results at school had simply been due to lack of effort. She had no intention of settling down to hard work, however, her main priority being to enjoy her newly found freedom.

Fascinated by the hoards of students riding around on bicycles, she immediately telephoned her father and a brand new bike was delivered to her in three days. Amanda used what little savings she had to buy a second hand one.

It did not take long for Jennifer to make new friends. She soon realised that the male students found her attractive. Compared with Jennifer, Amanda was a plain girl with fair hair and grey eyes, and was a little on the plump side.

James Brandon, who had once lived locally, offered to show both girls around Cambridge. He was about 6 feet tall with curly blond hair. Jennifer immediately found him attractive and did her best, during the next two days, to persuade Amanda to plead a headache so she could be alone with him. Amanda was not very happy about this and the two girls had their first falling out. As usual, Jennifer got her way.

After riding around Cambridge on their bicycles for an hour with James pointing out various places of interest,

Jennifer suddenly brought her bicycle to a halt. 'I think I've seen enough historical buildings for one day,' she said.

'Are you getting bored?' he asked.

'No, just a little tired,' she replied.

Flashing a smile James said, 'OK. Let's go and have a drink by the river. There's a great pub there and we can sit outside.'

Jennifer sat on the grass while he went to get two glasses of beer. It was the end of October and there was a chill in the air. Despite this, she removed her sweater. The T-shirt she had on underneath was low cut and showed off a very attractive cleavage. She lay back on the grass and began posing for when James returned.

As they drunk their beer Jennifer shivered in the breeze.

'Why don't you put your sweater back on?' he asked.

'Why don't you cuddle up to me and keep me warm?' she replied.

He quickly moved towards her and grabbed her in his arms. His mouth closed over hers with such urgency, it sent shivers down her spine. His tongue was soon exploring the inside of her mouth. After a while she had to push him away in order to breathe.

'I'm sorry,' he said. 'You looked so beautiful that I couldn't help myself.'

'You tiger,' she said, laughing as she pulled her sweater back on.

'What are you doing tonight?' he asked.

Placing her hands either side of his face she said, 'Finishing off what we just started, I hope.'

He gave a meaningful smile. 'That sounds good to me.'

They cycled back to college with Jennifer making sure she rode in front in order for him to see her backside moving sexily from side to side.

Back at the cycle shed he took her in his arms again. His hand went straight up her sweater, under her T-shirt and rested inside her bra. She allowed him to leave it there for a few seconds while he massaged her breast.

Suddenly, he pulled his hand away. 'Someone's coming,' he whispered breathlessly.

'Room seven. Be there at nine,' she said, before putting her bike away and wandering off to her room.

Amanda's door was open as she went by and so she popped her head in.

'Hello. How's the headache?' she teased.

'Very funny,' replied Amanda sulkily. She did not bother to look up.

'Coming for a cup of tea?' Jennifer asked.

Amanda reluctantly got off her bed. 'I suppose so. I've been stuck here all afternoon.'

Downstairs in the canteen she complained bitterly to Jennifer about her behaviour. 'I thought you said we'd stick together.'

'For God's sake, Amanda. That doesn't mean we can't ever go out on our own,' said Jennifer raising her voice loud enough to attract attention.

'That's right, start shouting so everyone can hear,' Amanda whispered.

Jennifer sighed. 'Do you want to know what happened this afternoon or not?'

'Not now. You can tell me all about it tonight. I suppose we are going for a drink tonight?' Amanda said, stirring her tea vigorously.

'I can't,' replied Jennifer. James is coming to my room tonight. With a bit of luck I'm going to have my first experience of proper sex. Now you wouldn't begrudge me that, would you?'

Amanda glared. Knocking against the table in her haste to leave, tea spilled all over the floor. 'No. I wouldn't begrudge you that Jennifer. If this is your way of sticking together I don't think much of it. I thought we'd be going out in foursomes.' Angrily, she strode away leaving Jennifer at the table.

James was the first of many who went to Jennifer's room for sex. Word soon got around that she was not only an easy lay, but also a good one.

Two days before end of term Amanda was in a pub in the middle of Cambridge with fellow students. She spotted a tall good-looking man standing at the bar. He had thick dark brown hair with eyes to match. He was dressed in tight-fitting jeans and black T-shirt. Around his neck hung a large St Christopher. Bored with the conversation around her, she wandered across to the bar and ordered a glass of beer. He smiled, and she smiled back.

'All alone?' he called across.

'Looks that way,' she called back.

He strolled over. 'Would you believe, I've been stood up?'

'So have I,' she lied. She was looking her best. Her curly fair hair was newly washed and the long pale pink smock that she wore over the top of her tight jeans hid her slightly bulging midriff. Her pale pink lipstick matched the top and, for once, she could not have been described as plain.

She knew he was not a student by the way he was dressed but, in order to make conversation, still asked the question.

'No, I'm not,' he replied. 'I wouldn't normally be in this pub but I had a date with a girl who said to meet her in the Red Lion for a drink. Then we were going for a Chinese. So here I am! I've been waiting for an hour and she hasn't shown up.' He shrugged his shoulders.

'Oh dear,' was all she could think of to say.

He smiled at her again. 'Still, if she had turned up I wouldn't have met you. My name's Trevor Stacey.'

'And I'm Amanda Saunders,' she replied.

'I'm glad we've got that out of the way. Are you hungry? Would you like a Chinese?'

Amanda was not the slightest bit hungry, but was not about to turn this opportunity down. 'Starving,' she said.

'Good. Let's finish our drinks. I know a fabulous little Chinese restaurant just a walk away.'

As they sat enjoying their meal, Amanda suddenly looked up in horror as she saw Jennifer, with yet another new boyfriend, enter the restaurant. Jennifer spotted them immediately and walked straight over to their table. She looked absolutely ravishing as usual. Her black leather trouser suit clung to her slim figure. Amanda suddenly felt her pink smock was cheap and nasty. She also knew that her pink lipstick had disappeared and had been replaced by the grease from her chop suey.

'Hello, Amanda. What a surprise seeing you here,' Jennifer said with a big smile on her face. Amanda did not look up but Trevor was already staring at the vision of loveliness before him. Seeing that her friend was not going to respond, Jennifer turned to Trevor, held out her hand and said, 'I'm Jennifer, Amanda's best friend.'

Much to Amanda's annoyance Trevor stood up. 'Nice to meet you.'

The boy with Jennifer stretched out his hand. 'Hi, I'm Alan Elwood.'

Amanda already knew who he was, so gave a disgruntled, 'Hi Alan.' She was furious and wanted to say, 'How dare you introduce yourself as my best friend? We haven't spoken for weeks.' Knowing she would only make a fool of herself, she kept quiet.

'Why don't you join us? We've only just started our meal,' said Trevor.

Amanda interrupted, 'Don't be silly. I'm sure Jennifer and Alan want to be alone.' It was too late. Jennifer was already squeezing behind Trevor's chair. Alan followed, and sat himself down next to Amanda.

The conversation covered a variety of topics to which Amanda contributed little. Jennifer held court as normal.

As they were drinking their coffee, Trevor said, 'Do you students really find it that hard with regard to money?'

'You wouldn't believe how hard,' replied Amanda. 'My parents pay my fees of course. They also send me money for books. Anything else I have to pay myself. Next term I plan to get a job at weekends.'

'Poor Amanda,' said Jennifer. 'She's always crying poverty.' She put her hand on top of Trevor's. 'It really isn't that bad, although it's true my father's a lot more generous than Amanda's. Fortunately, I only have three months to wait before I inherit a sizeable trust fund left to me by my grandparents.'

Amanda had no idea whether this was true or not.

Alan suggested it was time to make a move. He could see Jennifer only had eyes for Trevor and was beginning to feel embarrassed.

'You two go on ahead. We're going to have another coffee,' said Trevor, turning his attention back to Amanda.

Jennifer's disappointment was apparent, but Alan grabbed her hand and said, 'Bye. See you again I hope.'

'Now you can tell me why you don't like your best friend.' said Trevor jokingly.

'Oh, it's not that I dislike her,' Amanda replied. ' It's just that when we arrived at college together, we were going to look out for each other. It didn't work out that way.'

'You mean you drifted apart.'

She began fiddling with the salt pot. 'Something like that.'

'Well, perhaps next term things will be better,' he said, as he leaned across the table and held her hand.

'Enough about me,' she said. 'So. As you're not a student, what do you do?'

'I work for a computer company. I hope one day to be able to write programs.' He stopped as the waiter brought the bill. 'That's the trouble with dating a student, I can't even ask you to go Dutch.'

117

Amanda blushed. He patted her hand again and said laughing, 'I'm only teasing.'

He walked her back to college. Taking her face in his hands, he kissed her full on the lips. 'I'll phone when you get back. I take it you're going home for the holidays?'

'Yes. Though it won't be much fun. Ramsden has to be one of the most boring places on earth,' she replied.

He pulled her towards him and kissed her passionately. 'I must go,' he said. 'I'll see you in a few weeks.'

With both arms around his neck she asked, 'No chance of seeing you before that?'

'Wish I could,' he replied. 'Some of us have to earn a living, you know. You enjoy your break. Get some work done so that when you come back to Cambridge we can spend time together.'

He pinched her nose and left.

Chapter Nineteen

The day that Jennifer left for college, Mary watched at the window. David helped his daughter into the car and her friend Amanda jumped in beside her. Dorothy told her that David was taking them to the station where they would get the train to Cambridge.

As Mary watched, she tried to recall a train journey that had taken her somewhere. Who had driven her to the station, and where was she going? Trying to remember became too much, and her head began throbbing. Mary chose to go to bed and hide behind her black shadows.

The tapping on the door woke her. 'Mary, are you awake?' Dorothy called out. She jumped off the bed and opened the door. 'Mr Freeman and Jennifer have gone. I wondered if you would like to walk down to the village with me. Your gardening magazine is due in today.'

Mary's only reply was a nod.

'Shall I do your hair for you before we go?', Dorothy asked. Again Mary just nodded. Brushing her hair she went on, 'Mary, you'll be able to sit on your hair soon, it's got so long. Would you like to have it trimmed? Of course I'll ask Mr Freeman's permission and then we'll go to the hairdressers in the village. I might even get mine trimmed while we're at it.'

When Dorothy had mentioned David's name, Mary started shaking her head from side to side. She stared at Dorothy for several seconds before whispering, 'No. Not allowed.'

Dorothy was confused. The poor dear had been quite

happy to go for a walk in the village to get the magazine, but the mention of getting permission from her husband had upset her. Try as she might, Mary would not be persuaded to come out of her room until lunchtime.

Instead of her usual routine of going to her room after lunch, Dorothy suggested they watch television for a while. She had to be careful, as the only things Mr Freeman allowed Mary to watch were gardening programmes. After turning on the television Dorothy went into the kitchen in search of the paper.

Mary sat staring at the screen. The news had just started. The newsreader was relating the story of yet another rape. 'It is believed to be connected to the rape incident in Denton last month when a young girl was attacked.' The accompanying pictures showed an area around an old tree trunk.

Mary stiffened as she continued staring at the television. In her mind she was there, in the woodland, running for her life. Suddenly, she screamed so loud, it brought Dorothy running back into the room. She went on screaming and shaking, and it took a while for Dorothy to calm her down.

'Whatever's the matter, dear?' she asked. It was too late. She recognised the vacant look on Mary's face as she slipped behind her shadows.

Dorothy had decided not to mention the incident to Mr Freeman. There is no need to worry him unduly she thought to herself. Furthermore, he might well blame her for letting Mary watch the news. She glanced up at the clock. He was late. This had never happened before in all the time she had lived there. When he was an hour late she began to worry. Not having access to a telephone had never bothered her before, but him being late brought home to her the need of one in case of emergency.

She was about to go and check on Mary when she heard his key in the door. Running into the hall she gasped, 'Oh, thank goodness you're home!'

He gave her a blank look and said, 'Something wrong?'

'No,' Dorothy answered feeling a little embarrassed. 'I just wondered where you had got to. I thought you might have had an accident or something.'

'I had to attend to something on my way home,' he said as he hung up his coat. He then went straight to his room.

He was there longer than usual. When he came out into the kitchen he told Dorothy that he would not be dining with them.

'But Mary and I have waited for you, and you must eat,' she grumbled.

'How has Mary been today?' he asked, changing the subject.

'She's been fine. Is there anything wrong, Mr Freeman?'

'No,' he replied. 'I just feel gloomy about Jennifer. I'm going into the lounge to have my whisky and read the paper. See that I'm not disturbed, please.' He closed the door behind him.

Dorothy sighed as she looked at the overdone lamb cutlets she had prepared for dinner. So as not to disturb him she went upstairs to fetch Mary instead of calling her for the evening meal.

Mary seemed uncomfortable that David was not there for dinner. Dorothy had noticed before that any changes to a normal routine made Mary feel disorientated.

'We might just as well be eating shoe leather,' she joked as she prodded her lamb chop.

On her way to bed Dorothy passed the lounge and noticed the door was slightly open. David Freeman was sitting in his usual chair with his head in his hands. Wondering whether to go in she remembered he had particularly asked not to be disturbed. Quietly she walked by and went upstairs to bed.

It was an hour later when David went upstairs and along the landing to Mary's room. He quietly opened the door, went in and sat on her bed. Mary was fast asleep. He sat staring at her, thinking how pale and thin she looked. He cleared his throat and moved beside her. As he slid one arm under her neck, she opened her eyes. They had the same terrified look that had always excited him. He continued staring at her. Without warning he pulled the covers off, picked her up and sat her on his lap. Cuddling her, he began rocking backwards and forwards.

'My dear Mary,' he said. 'You're all I've got and I'm all you've got. What on earth is going to happen to you when I'm not here?' He was holding her so close she could hardly breathe. 'You have given me so much pleasure. You do understand don't you?'

Mary felt his tears drop on to her arm. She was so scared of what was coming next that she closed her eyes and called for her black shadows. David sat for more than an hour, rocking backwards and forwards, cuddling her. Then he gently put her into bed and left.

The following morning Mary knew something strange had happened but did not know what. She remembered David coming to her room but could not understand why she was not suffering the usual pain that she had become accustomed to after his visits. She thought that she may have been dreaming but Mary's brain was now so muddled she could not tell the difference between that and reality.

At times certain things flashed into her mind that she wanted to hold onto, but to no avail. One recurring vision was of a girl with long brown hair and brown eyes. She felt extremely close to this girl. Once the vision had disappeared, she was left scared and confused. The images she had seen were like Jennifer, the cruel girl everyone referred to as her daughter.

The most treasured vision she found behind the black shadows was of a large farmhouse kitchen. An old lady bustled around. God was always there wearing his white collar. She found the place full of love and protection but, however hard she tried, could not hang on to it.

A week before Jennifer was due home, Dorothy suggested she might take Mary to the hairdressers. David agreed but insisted that if Mary became upset she was to be brought straight home.

The following evening at dinner, David asked Mary if she would like to go to the hairdressers with Dorothy.

She began touching her hair and a faint smile played across her lips. Shaking her head she whispered, 'No.'

'Oh, Mary, I thought you'd like to,' Dorothy said, sounding disappointed. 'Jennifer's coming home next week and you want to look nice for her, don't you?'

Mary stared at David, waiting for him to respond and was surprised to hear him say, 'I think it would be a good idea. You've got beautiful hair but I agree with Dorothy. It does need a trim.' He switched his glance to Dorothy and said firmly, 'Make an appointment for her.'

Mary got quite excited about the visit to the hairdresser. On the morning of the appointment she came down to breakfast wearing a white polo neck sweater with a pair of navy blue trousers, new clothes that Dorothy had bought her the previous week. David was very generous with his wife and daughter. 'Buy whatever you think she needs,' he had said on several occasions.

'Don't let them cut it too short,' he said, pushing his chair back from the table. As he stood up Dorothy thought he was a little unsteady on his feet. For a few days now she had thought he looked a little tired and pale.

After lunch, she suggested gently to Mary that it might be better to wear an old sweater for her haircut. 'You can put the new one back on when we come home,' she said as she followed her into the bedroom.

They left in plenty of time taking a slow, leisurely walk down the hill. Dorothy wanted Mary to be calm and relaxed when they arrived.

The salon was owned by a Mrs French who, knowing of

Mary's problems, had agreed to make certain that they would not be kept waiting. There were two clients already there having their hair done by other hairdressers. Dorothy recognised one, a girl who had attended the same school as Jennifer.

Mary seemed quite unperturbed as she was led to a chair. She even gave a faint smile as the towel was put around her. All was going well until her head was tilted back over the basin. A look of terror came into her eyes and she tried to get up. Gently, Mrs French tried to stop her by putting her arm under Mary's chin.

Something snapped in Mary's mind. Suddenly she could smell the dirty old mattress and feel the arm under her chin forcing her head back. Screaming, she sent Mrs French flying across the salon. Jumping up from the chair Mary ran to Dorothy. 'Help me,' she sobbed. 'Please help me.'

The other hairdressers and customers looked on in horror. Mary stopped crying and appeared to go into a trance with the vacant look on her face that Dorothy knew only too well.

After apologising to Mrs French, Dorothy took Mary by the hand and began to walk slowly home. She made no attempt at conversation, knowing Mary was in one of her dreams. Feeling gloomy over her failure to cheer the poor girl up, she did not protest when Mary went straight to her room.

Chapter Twenty

Ralph Stevens felt a mixture of disappointment and anger as he made himself a vodka and tonic. Anne had called him early that morning to tell him that she had a problem with her brother and unfortunately could not meet him for dinner. Try as he might he could not get her to tell him what the problem was. After his third vodka he began wondering whether there was a problem at all. Perhaps she just didn't want to see him.

He had never met this brother of hers, but was beginning to dislike him. He must be 18 by now. How could she let him run her life? He switched on the television and tried to watch the news. The three vodkas were beginning to have an effect. He was too tired to make himself anything to eat and began to nod off in the chair.

The ringing of the telephone woke him. He looked at his watch. It was 9.15. Stretching, he leant over to answer it. It was Anne. He cleared his throat, wishing he had not drunk the vodka.

'Anne. What a lovely surprise. Have you changed your mind?'

'No, not exactly,' she replied. 'I was wondering whether we could have lunch tomorrow instead.'

'Of course. Where would you like to go?' he said, unable to hide the excitement in his voice.

'Well, I don't mind coming up to London. I've got a few things to sort out with personnel. I could stay in town and do that first thing Monday morning.'

125

'Wow! Does that mean we can have lunch and dinner?' he said mischievously.

She laughed. 'No, it does not. I'll catch up on some work in the evening ready for Personnel.'

They agreed to meet at Liverpool Street station. There was a train that got in at 12.30.

Ralph stared at the telephone once he had replaced the receiver. What was it about this girl that made his heart skip a beat? Feeling on top of the world he went into the kitchen to prepare something to eat. Settling for smoked salmon and scrambled eggs, he began to sing as he got to work.

It was almost seven years since his divorce. He had dated many women but most resulted in being one-night stands. He had never brought a girl back to his apartment but here he was trying to imagine Anne sitting opposite him at the table.

He started to wonder what she would think of the apartment. He strolled back into the lounge and looked out of the huge bay window. It had a glorious view over Hyde Park, and even at this time of night, there was something magical about it. Closing the curtains he made up his mind that her first visit would be during the day. It was far more impressive then.

Looking around he began to realise how masculine the room looked. The black leather couch with chairs to match stood on a polished wood block floor. The mahogany bookshelves and large coffee table looked very plain and uninteresting. There were two expensive rugs that he had bought when he was on holiday in India.

The only things he had taken any real interest in were his paintings. Part of the divorce settlement was that he would keep his art collection. The thought that he would have to brighten up the apartment with vases of flowers made him laugh out loud. He went to bed that night knowing he was falling in love.

Arriving 20 minutes early at the station, he managed to

park his Mercedes sports car along a side street. He found out which platform the train was arriving at, purchased a huge bouquet from the flower stall and stood like an excited schoolboy waiting for her to arrive.

His stomach turned over as he saw her stepping down from the carriage. She wore a bright red baggy sweater over tight denim jeans. Ralph had never seen her in casual clothes before, it had always been smart business suits. The long brown hair fell over her face as she wrestled with her suitcase. She spotted him immediately. As he rushed to help her he saw she was laughing.

'What's so funny?' he asked.

'It's you,' she replied. 'You looked so funny the way you were standing there holding those flowers.'

'That not a very gracious thing to say,' he said as he handed her the bouquet. 'I feel as though I should kiss you. Isn't that what people do when they meet someone at a train station?'

She offered him her cheek and he kissed it lightly. When they arrived at his car she pulled a face and said, 'My, my. I am impressed.' After putting her flowers in the boot they drove to a little chophouse in Soho where they both ate huge pork chops and salad.

Two and a half hours later while on their third cup of coffee Anne mentioned that everyone else had gone.

He looked around. 'Hmm, I think they're waiting to close.' Holding both her hands across the table he went on, 'I don't want this to end. Can we go for a stroll? It's quite a nice afternoon.'

An hour later, strolling through Hyde Park, Ralph said, 'You can see my apartment from here.' With his arm round her shoulders he pointed to the top of a huge building where you could just about see his window.

She looked up in awe and said, 'I bet you could put my whole house into one of your rooms.'

He spun her round to face him and, holding her by the

shoulders jokingly said, 'That's very kind of you, but I don't want to put your house in one of my rooms.' Lowering his voice, he continued, 'But Anne, I do hope that one day I'll have you in one of my rooms.'

She surprised herself by replying, 'I hope so too.'

Letting go of her shoulders they walked hand in hand to a café for some tea. There she found herself telling Ralph all about her problems with Trevor.

Back in the hotel she began pulling papers out of her briefcase. Several members of her staff were complaining that they had been promised a review and it was way overdue. That was the first thing she wanted Personnel to look at. She began by listing their names and writing her assessment by the side of each one.

Her second task was to get her expenses up to date. With a look of satisfaction she glanced around the room. Her position as an area manager entitled her to stay at five-star hotels. This was somewhat different from the hotel she had stayed in when she came for her last interview.

She looked at the pile of receipts on the desk and wondered what Ralph's expenses were each month. A warm glow engulfed her as she thought of him. At last she had found someone she could talk to. Deep down Anne knew it was more than that. She began wishing they were going to have dinner together that night.

Ten minutes later she found herself dialling his number. She told herself all she wanted to do was thank him for a nice lunch. When he suggested he come over to her hotel for a late supper she readily agreed. Humming to herself she put the receipts back in her briefcase.

Ralph arrived at 8.30 and they ate steak and salad in the hotel restaurant. He ordered a bottle of red wine, which they drank between them. When he suggested they go to the bar for a nightcap she asked if he had his car with him. 'No,' he replied, 'I came by taxi, so let's go and relax.'

Anne was not really a drinker and, what with wine followed by a large brandy, found she was talking non-stop. It seemed as though in one hour she had told him her whole life story.

He was intrigued with the disappearance of Mary. Moving closer to her on the couch he asked, ' You never tried to find her?'

'No,' she replied, 'I didn't really know where to start looking. I was very upset at the way she walked out on, not only me, but her father and dear old Davy as well.'

'Where do you think your father is now?' he asked.

'I really have no idea and I don't care,' she answered, as she rested her head on his shoulder.

'Do you think Trevor may have gone to find his father?'

I hope so. They deserve each other,' she said, as her head slid forward off his shoulder.

He looked at her and smiled. 'I think it's time you went to bed young lady. You're falling asleep.' He put his arm around her shoulders.

They went up in the lift with Ralph holding her close to him. When they reached her room he took her in his arms and kissed her passionately. 'Goodnight, my darling. I hope you don't have a headache in the morning.'

She looked up into his eyes. 'Why don't you come in? We can have another drink.'

He took her in his arms and kissed her again. 'No, my darling. When I come into your hotel room I want you to be sober. I will never take advantage of you.' He opened the door and patted her bottom. ' Sleep tight my love, and don't be late for Personnel.'

The following morning, as she came out of her meeting, she bumped right into him. 'Good morning Anne. What brings you up to London today?'

She felt herself blushing as she replied, 'Oh, just some staff reviews that needed sorting out.'

129

'Meet me for lunch,' he whispered out of the corner of his mouth.

'No, I can't. I have to go home,' she whispered back.

'Right,' he said, with a twinkle in his eye, 'I'll see you at one o'clock in the little Italian down the road.' Before she could protest, he was gone. She watched him as he strode back towards his office and knew she had fallen in love.

Over the next few weeks they saw each other whenever work allowed. Eventually they planned to spend a full weekend together. He was coming to Denton for the first time and Anne was cooking dinner. She had cleaned the house from top to bottom and, that very week, had bought a small polished dining table and chairs that she had put in the corner of the small lounge. It looked a little overcrowded but rather that than the embarrassment of having to entertain him in the kitchen on the pine table and bench where she normally ate.

The fragrance of fresh flowers filled the room. The night before she had cooked a pork casserole. All she had to do now was prepare the vegetables and get changed. She surveyed the room once more, moved the flowers from the windowsill and put them on a table.

Her stomach was churning as she slipped into a black silk trouser suit. She put her hair into a ponytail, twisted it up on top of her head and secured it with a diamante clip. As she placed the two little pearl studs in her ears she wished she had bought some new earrings.

After all, she could afford it nowadays – her savings were growing every month. The bank manager was continuously trying to persuade Anne to make new investments. It was amazing how little money she spent, now that Trevor had gone, and she practically lived on expenses.

The sound of a car sent her scurrying to the window. Her heart skipped a beat as she saw Ralph getting out of the Mercedes. He was halfway up the path carrying red roses and champagne when she opened the door.

A big smile spread across his face as he entered the room. 'So this is your little house,' he said.

After placing the champagne and roses on the table, he held out his arms. 'Come here,' he said. Pulling her to him, he kissed her so passionately she thought she would pass out.

'What time would you like to eat?' Anne asked breathlessly.

'When we've had a glass of champagne and I've told you how beautiful you look. I don't know whether to tell you the other news before or after dinner.'

Anne went to get the crystal champagne glasses that she had bought only the day before. When she arrived back in the lounge, Ralph was sitting in the armchair.

'You look very pleased with yourself,' she teased. 'It must be good news.'

He poured the champagne, handed her a glass and said, 'Now, are you sure you want to hear this before dinner?'

She laughed. 'Why? Will it put me off my food?'

'I hope not,' Ralph replied.

'Okay, tell me now,' she said inquisitively.

She sat in the chair opposite him and waited as he took a deep breath. 'Anne. I've fallen hopelessly in love with you.' A shiver went down her spine and tears began to well in her eyes.

Jumping from the chair, he pulled her up into his arms again. 'I love you so much, Anne. I can't bear to be apart from you,' he said tenderly. She began to feel an ache in her loins that she had never experienced before. Ralph kissed her again, this time his tongue exploring the inside of her mouth. His hand slid round and pressed her buttocks so that her whole body was entwined into his. She could feel his aroused manhood pressing against her. No matter how hard she tried, Anne could not bring herself to push him away. She clung to him, her thighs throbbing and her breath coming in short gasps.

Eventually, when he let her go, she stammered, 'I think I should put the vegetables on, don't you?'

'No, Anne, let's eat later. I've waited so long for this. Let's make love now.'

They went upstairs and, as they got into bed, Ralph noticed the brand new sheets. Thank God, he thought to himself. She wanted this as much as me. He made love to her gently and Anne climaxed for the first time in her life.

After Ralph had been downstairs to fetch them another glass of champagne, he made love to her again, this time not so gently, and her response was as demanding and passionate as his.

They lay on the bed together, spent and perspiring. He broke the silence saying, 'Anne, I can't help myself. I love you so much.'

She turned on her side, rested her head on his bare chest and replied, 'I love you too, Ralph, but I'm scared.'

'Darling, what is there to be scared of?' he asked.

'I always seem to lose people I love,' she answered quietly.

He sat up in bed and held her face in his hands. 'Anne, I will never leave you. I will marry you tomorrow if you want me to. You make me so happy.' She snuggled down beside him and they both slept.

At six o'clock in the morning he woke her, saying 'Any chance of dinner now.' They both laughed.

Chapter Twenty-One

Jennifer lay in bed unable to sleep. She had left her door open in order to hear Amanda come in. Imagining her friend romping in bed with that handsome man was driving her crazy. Amanda arrived home much earlier than Jennifer expected. 'I'm awake. Come in and dish the dirt,' she called out

Feeling disappointed that her date had ended so abruptly, Amanda reluctantly went into Jennifer's room. She sat on the end of the bed and smiled at her friend.

'Where did you find him?' Jennifer asked.

'I didn't. He found me,' she replied, still smiling. 'And if you want to know exactly what happened, I'm afraid you're out of luck. All I will tell you is that he's very special and is going to call me when I get back from holiday.'

That satisfied Jennifer. It would be easy to arrange a foursome next term. She was determined not to let that tall dark stranger get away.

'Talking of holidays, what are we going to do with ourselves in Ramsden?' Jennifer asked.

'Well, I know it sounds boring but I think I'll use the time to get some studying done,' Amanda replied. 'Don't forget, about a month after we're back, it's exam time and I know I won't be able to study here as I'll be spending all my spare time with Trevor.'

'You're very optimistic after only one date,' Jennifer said playfully.

They didn't speak very much on the train journey back to Ramsden. Neither of them was looking forward to three weeks at home with their parents. Jennifer had already made up her mind that she would try and persuade Dorothy that a home was the best place for her mother. There was no use bringing it up with her father again. She knew what his answer would be.

He was waiting at the station for her. She gave him a peck on the cheek but, as usual, there was little response. He greeted Amanda in a cool but polite way.

She noticed he was looking pale and tired. After they had dropped her friend off she asked, 'Are you alright, Father?'

'Yes, I'm fine, my dear,' he replied.

Sitting next to him, as they drove up the hill, Jennifer thought he sounded out of breath. As they arrived at the lodge Dorothy was already at the door. She went out to help with the luggage. It was quite noticeable that David Freeman made no attempt to get out of the car and assist. Instead he watched Jennifer as she leaned inside to retrieve a book. She had on a dark green blouse with the top buttons open. Her breasts were bulging above her bra. He tried to look away but couldn't.

Mary, hearing them arrive, was on her way to her room when she heard Jennifer say, 'I suppose the mad bitch is still here or have you put her away?'

'No,' her father replied 'Your mother is still at home. I've told you before. I need her here.' As he spoke, it occurred to him that he had not been to Mary's room for a week.

'I've cooked your favourite meal, Jennifer. Braised pork chops with crispy roast potatoes,' Dorothy said cheerfully.

'It isn't my favourite meal any more,' replied Jennifer rudely. 'In fact I really only eat Indian or Chinese now.'

As Dorothy laid the table for dinner, Jennifer came into the dining room. Looking at the place settings she remarked, 'Oh, does that mad woman have to eat with us?'

134

'Please don't call her that,' said Dorothy in disgust. 'She is your mother.'

'Well, I try to pretend she isn't. It's so embarrassing,' said Jennifer as she stalked out of the room.

The atmosphere was somewhat strained over dinner. David was not in a good mood even though it was his daughter's first night home. Mary sat in silence as usual, but did not seem to be eating. Jennifer persisted in making rude comments about her and, consequently, Dorothy's nerves were on edge, anticipating a scene.

At one point Jennifer said, 'I don't think I can stand three weeks of this. Why can't she eat in the kitchen? She keeps staring at me. It puts me off my food.' Then, turning to Mary shouted, 'Why can't you say something instead of just staring at me?'

After this outburst David got up from the table and asked Dorothy to serve his coffee in the lounge.

Jennifer went to her room. Ten minutes later the front door slammed as she went out.

Returning an hour later, she went straight to the lounge to find her father. Without looking up he said, 'Jennifer. Don't start. I'm tired.'

'I'm tired too,' she said. 'Tired of that crazy woman making a laughing stock out of me.'

He put his paper down, sipped his whisky and asked, 'What has she done now?'

'I'll tell you what she's done,' Jennifer shouted. 'She went to the hairdressers and had a screaming fit. Not content with that, she pushed Mrs French across the room. For her party piece she then went into one of her dreams where she just stares at everyone. This was all in front of one of my friends from school. Now the whole village will know.

'I can't live here, Father. There's no phone in the house because of her. All my friends have got telephones. They can make arrangements to go out. Why can't I have one? You won't let me go into your room to use yours. I feel like I'm living in a lunatic asylum.'

David stood up and looked thoughtfully down at her for a while before replying. 'Dorothy explained to me the other day that she felt cut off without a phone. Now that you're home I'll tell her to make arrangements at once to have one installed in the hall. As far as the hairdressing incident is concerned, leave it with me. I'll attend to it.'

'You don't understand. It's too late. All my friends will be laughing at me now.' She got up and walked over to the fireplace. 'Father, I just can't live here with her any more.'

He rubbed his cheek with his hand and thought for a minute. 'I've still got the house in London. Do you remember, when you were little, we used to live there? Unfortunately, I've got tenants living there at the moment and so you would have to wait about six months for their lease to run out, but by then you'll have your trust fund and can live where you like.'

'Oh Father, I can't wait six months,' she moaned.

He mopped his brow. 'I'm going to bed now, my dear. We'll talk about it in the morning.'

He felt too tired to go to Mary's room. Jennifer's ranting had worn him out and so he went straight to his own. Before getting into bed he took a little pillbox from his briefcase and, with a glass of water, swallowed two tablets.

On the night he had arrived home late he had been for a check-up. He was diagnosed as having angina. Contrary to his consultant's advice he had not told anyone.

'Always let your family know where your tablets are,' the doctor had said. 'If you have an attack, get them to administer two tablets and you'll be fine. And get them to call me.'

He thought about this as he lay in bed. Maybe he should confide in Dorothy.

The following morning Jennifer refused to come down for

136

breakfast. This gave David the opportunity to speak to Dorothy once Mary had left the room. 'I would like to have a word with you about my health.'

'Oh, Mr Freeman. You're not ill?' Dorothy looked concerned.

Ignoring her remark he went on, 'I've got angina. That means my heart is not in good shape.'

'Yes, I know what angina is. Have you got some medication?' she asked with a tremor in her voice.

'I'll leave some tablets in a pill box in the top drawer of the dresser in here. I don't expect it will be necessary but, should I have an attack, give me two pills and I'll be fine.'

Dorothy looked at him sympathetically. 'Don't worry, Mr Freeman. I know exactly what to do. My father suffered from angina for many years.' She failed to say that he'd died after an attack.

'I am not at all worried, Dorothy. This is just a precaution,' he said in a matter-of-fact voice. 'By the way, I would rather Jennifer didn't know.'

He got up from the table. 'I have also decided to cut down on my workload. I'll only be going to the office twice a week.'

'Very sensible,' said Dorothy.

'Oh! And one other thing. Please ensure there are no more scenes in hairdressing salons.' He left with Dorothy wondering just how much he knew about that. She had told him Mary had got nervous and didn't want her hair cut, but that was all.

David went off to work feeling happier now that he had told Dorothy where his tablets were kept. He decided to deal later with Mary's behaviour in the hairdressing salon.

Soon after he had left, Jennifer appeared in the kitchen. 'Now that the mad woman's gone, I'll have some toast and honey for my breakfast.'

Ignoring her rudeness, Dorothy put bread in the toaster. Eating her toast Jennifer asked, 'Did you get my father's permission before you took her to have her hair cut?'

Dorothy spun round. 'Yes, I did.'

'Well, you won't be taking her again. She's embarrassed my father and me for the last time.'

'How did you know about it?' Dorothy asked crossly.

'How did I know about it? The whole bloody village knows about it.' Finishing the toast while walking out of the door Jennifer remarked, 'By the way, we're going to get a phone!'

Mary sat quietly in her room listening for the sound of the front door closing. This was her indication that David had left for work. He seemed to be taking longer than usual this morning. When at last she heard the slam of the front door she peered through the window. With a sigh of relief she saw that Jennifer was with him. Feeling safe from both of them now, she ventured down into the kitchen.

'I was just going to call you,' Dorothy said. 'I've made a fresh pot of tea. Now sit down. I need to talk to you.' Mary immediately obeyed. Placing the teapot in the middle of the table Dorothy asked, 'How are you today?' Mary sat up straight and smiled.

After pouring the tea and pulling the chair up next to her, she placed her hand over Mary's. 'Now, Mary,' she began, 'I have some rather distressing news. Your husband is not in very good health. In fact he has angina. Do you know what that is?'

Mary nodded.

Dorothy couldn't help but think how much better she was when Mr Freeman and Jennifer were out of the house. 'He doesn't want anyone to know, especially Jennifer. Can you keep a secret Mary?'

Mary nodded again.

Dorothy went on to explain where his pills were kept and what had to be done in the event of an attack. Mary listened intently.

'I'm quite sure that you'll never have to help him, because

I'm always around.' Lowering her voice she continued, 'But I know he sometimes comes to your room to say goodnight. All you have to do is call me.'

A look of horror came over Mary's face. She immediately got up and went to her room and stayed there until lunch-time.

That same evening David arrived home in a much better frame of mind. Jennifer stayed at Amanda's for dinner. Even Mary seemed more awake than usual.

David finished his dinner and went into the lounge with his newspaper.

Dorothy looked across at Mary. 'I hope I didn't upset you this morning.'

To her amazement she smiled and replied, 'Of course not.'

Back in her room Mary struggled with her thoughts. The idea that Dorothy may know what took place when David came to her room at night filled her with shame. She hid behind her black shadows for the first time that day.

It had been over a week since he had visited her room. Consequently she was shocked when he came and pulled the covers off her. 'Get up my dear.' His commanding voice sent a tremor through her. Half asleep, she climbed out of bed.

'Do you know that you have made your daughter very unhappy?' She shook her head.

'Why did you cause such a scene in the hairdressers when you knew Jennifer's friend was there.' She looked at the floor. 'Lift up your head and look at me,' he demanded.

As she raised her head to look at him, the sticky tape was cruelly put across her mouth. 'Take off your pyjamas at once,' he said through gritted teeth. As she did so, he spun her around and tied her hands behind her back, so tight, the cord cut into her flesh. She began to cry. 'That's nice,' he said, with a sinister smile on his face.

He placed a whip on the bed and began removing his

139

trousers. It was at this point that Mary succeeded in finding her black shadows again. They would not take away all the pain but they sheltered her from the humiliation.

The next morning, Dorothy noticed that Mary had gone back into herself. There was no smile today, only constant fidgeting at the table.

David announced that he would not be going to the office. 'I shall be catching up on paperwork in my room. I would appreciate not being disturbed.'

Mary immediately ran off to her room.

'She doesn't seem to be as well as yesterday. What do you think, Mr Freeman?' Dorothy asked.

'Some good days, some bad. That's how it is, I'm afraid.'

'I think I'll go and see if she's alright,' said Dorothy getting up from the table.

'As you wish,' said David.

Without knocking, she entered Mary's bedroom and saw her pulling on a sweater. As she hastily pulled it over her head, Dorothy thought she saw weals on her back.

'What have you done to your back, my dear?'

Mary stared at her. 'Please go.'

Dorothy could see that she was about to go into one of her dreams and decided it would be best to leave her alone.

Chapter Twenty-Two

Trevor Stacy had not, for one minute, regretted leaving home. Initially he stayed with Gary Johnson, a friend from school, and his newly widowed mother. He was delighted when he was accepted for the first job he applied for. It would mean travelling to Cambridge and so he decided to find a flat there.

He was shocked at the cost of renting in Cambridge but was pleased and surprised at the salary the computer company had offered him. He found a small flat in a less attractive part of Cambridge that he could afford, telling himself it would only be until he got some money behind him. All he had to do now was find the money for the deposit.

The day before Trevor was to leave for Cambridge, Trevor and Gary came home to find Mrs Johnson in tears. Trying to compose herself, she explained that the house had been burgled and all her jewellery taken. The wallet containing her credit cards had gone and the police had informed her that a total of £1,000 had already been withdrawn from various cashpoints.

On arriving in Cambridge, Trevor set about selling Mrs Johnson's jewellery. This proved to be much easier than he had anticipated. After paying the deposit on the flat, he was still flush with funds. He decided to buy new clothes and began dating girls.

He was amazed at how easy it was to persuade a girl to have sex on the first date, but found it far more satisfying when the odd one refused and he had to force himself upon them. His next step was to get himself a car. As this was out of his reach for the time being, he decided to find a girl who had money and a car. He intended keeping in touch with Amanda in order to try his luck with her attractive friend Jennifer who was about to come into a substantial amount of money.

Standing in front of a full-length mirror he admired his appearance. Remembering Jennifer's brown hair and eyes, he smiled as he thought how alike they were.

It was a very small flat. It consisted of one living room with a sofa bed, a kitchen that served as a dining area and a small toilet with a shower cubicle. If he missed anything at all, it was his sister Anne doing his washing and keeping the place tidy.

Stealing jewellery was proving to be a way of making money fast. Despite the fact that he enjoyed his job and computers fascinated him, he had no intention of working eight hours a day for very long.

He walked across and sat on the unmade bed. He had an hour to kill before meeting his date for tonight. Flicking through the newspaper he stopped suddenly as he read, 'Denton rapist arrested!' There was a picture of a man with large eyes and a mop of thick brown hair. Beneath the photograph it said that John Stacey had been taken into police custody for questioning. Trevor jumped off the bed and got himself a beer before reading on. Apparently a total of 21 women had been raped over the past 19 years, in and around Denton. He studied the picture again. This could easily be a relative of his, although he didn't know of any living in Denton apart from his sister Anne. Come to think of it, he didn't know of any other relatives at all.

A strange feeling came over him as he wondered whether this man could possibly be his father. He sat staring at the picture. Slowly, a grin spread across his face. 'Dirty old sod,' he thought to himself. 'Not surprising my stuck-up sister didn't want anything to do with him.'

He wondered whether Anne had read the story.

Chapter Twenty-Three

Anne lay in bed with her head resting on Ralph's chest. It was a blissful Sunday morning, the birds were singing and the curtains of her bedroom were half open. Ralph was reading the paper and every time he turned a page she jokingly complained.

They had fallen into a routine where she stayed at his apartment during the week and they both returned to Denton on Friday nights.

Suddenly, Anne felt his body stiffen. Moving up to a better sitting position he said, 'I hope this isn't a relative of yours.' She laughed and snuggled closer to him.

'They've caught that rapist that used to hang around here and, guess what? His name is Stacey. I think you look a bit like him,' he said teasingly as he pulled her closer. 'Why don't you rape me?'

'Oh no! I think we should get out and enjoy some of this sunshine.'

'Later,' he replied, before closing his mouth around her nipple.

It was lunchtime before they finally got out of bed and showered. It was a late spring day and, as the sun was still shining, they decided to go for a long walk. As they passed the Vicarage, Anne pointed to where she and Mary had played together. They walked through the woodlands and sat on the old log. Looking around at the bluebells she felt a tug at her heartstrings. What happy memories she had.

Ralph had taught her to appreciate the past but not to dwell on it.

'Are you going back to London tonight?' she asked.

'I think it would make sense if I did. I've got an eight o'clock meeting in the morning.'

'I know,' she said, resting her head on his shoulder. 'I've got to be in Royston at eight thirty. Do you think you can get through the night without me?'

'You know I can't bear being away from you for one minute, but duty calls.'

'I'm so happy, Ralph,' she said and kissed him on the cheek.

He left at six o'clock and Anne began tidying the house. 'Better change those sheets,' she thought to herself. She smiled at the realisation that they had spent most of the weekend between them.

Ralph was not the tidiest of people and he had left the newspaper strewn over the floor. Picking it up, she began putting the pages back in order.

The colour drained from her face as she looked at the picture staring up at her. It was her father. This was the story Ralph had been teasing her about. With shaking hands she read the article. Her father a rapist? Surely not. A thief and drunkard, but not this. There must be some mistake.

She never finished tidying the house. Instead she sat wondering what she should do. There was no point in trying to contact Trevor. She had no idea where he was anyway.

Once again, she found herself alone. Her relationship with Ralph was close and she had told him everything about her father's disgusting behaviour of the past. He had looked horrified when she explained how he had walked out on Trevor and she remembered him saying that he must be a real bastard. But how would he take this? She was now the daughter of a rapist.

The following day she drove into the Royston store devoid

144

of her usual enthusiasm. 'Are you alright, Miss Stacey?' the store manager enquired.

'Just a headache. I don't think I'll be stopping long,' she replied. By lunchtime she made her excuses and left. Anne drove home slowly, feeling confused.

As she was making a cup of tea, the phone rang. For the very first time she hoped it wouldn't be Ralph.

But there was no mistaking his cheerful voice. 'Hello, darling. What's up? I just rang the store at Royston and they said you'd gone home feeling unwell.'

'Oh it's nothing,' she replied. 'I've got an awful headache. I'm going to take some aspirin and lie down.'

'Oh you poor thing. I'd come down but this wretched meeting is going to resume at six o'clock. Are you sure you'll be alright?' His voice was full of concern. 'I'll ring you when I finish.'

'No Ralph,' she said quickly. 'I think I need some sleep. I'll call you in the morning.'

She'd had very little sleep the night before, and spent the rest of the afternoon dozing in a chair. When she woke up and glanced at her watch she was surprised to see it was 6.30.

The telephone rang. She knew it wouldn't be Ralph as he had just started his meeting. It must be work, she thought to herself, and promptly picked up a pen and pad before answering.

'Hello, Auntie Anne.' The colour drained from her face as she recognised the voice. Determined to remain calm, she asked, 'What do you want, Trevor?'

'Money,' he said coolly. 'I want you to sell the house and give me half. I think I'm entitled to that, don't you?'

'Trevor, let me assure you that you're entitled to nothing. My mother left this house to me.'

He interrupted, 'Don't you mean our mother?'

'No, I don't. I should have told you before. Your mother was a drunken floozie that your father picked up. Once you

145

were born he cleared off and your mother dumped you on me. So, just you understand, Trevor. All I did for you was out of the goodness of my heart. You're not even my real brother and your way of repaying me is to try and steal part of my house.' She was losing control as she rambled on, 'Don't think I don't know who stole the jewellery from Mrs Johnson. How could you do that to a woman who had just buried her husband?'

Sounding not at all fazed by her outburst, Trevor replied, 'Well I know you've got plenty of money in the bank, so I think four thousand pounds will solve your problem.'

'Solve my problem?' she shouted down the phone. 'I don't have a problem.'

'Don't you think your stuffy boyfriend will think it a problem when he finds out your father's a rapist?'

'Goodbye, Trevor.' Her voice trembled as she slammed the receiver down.

Knowing she had no option now but to tell Ralph, she began to cry.

Chapter Twenty-Four

It was very unnerving for Mary knowing that David was going to be in the house all day. Every little sound sent her into a panic thinking he was coming to her room. It was a great relief when Dorothy came and asked if she would like to go shopping.

Walking down to the village, Dorothy mentioned the marks on Mary's back.

'I fell,' Mary said softly.

'Into a bush?' Dorothy asked.

Mary nodded.

Not wanting to upset her, Dorothy dropped the subject. As they reached the bottom of the hill they saw three girls standing outside the post office. One of them was Jennifer. Mary stopped in her tracks and would go no further. Reluctantly Dorothy turned around and they walked back home. Once inside, Mary went straight to her room.

Dorothy tapped gently on David's door. He opened it with a look of irritation on his face. She explained what had happened and asked if he would keep an eye on Mary while she popped to the village.

'I'm trying to work, Dorothy. I pay you to look after Mary. Off you go, but don't make a habit of this, and don't be long,' he said curtly.

Dorothy hurried down the hill wondering why he had to be so rude. She knew he didn't really mind.

In her room Mary heard the front door close and assumed it was David going out. Peering out of the window she was horrified to see Dorothy disappearing down the drive. Her heart sank and she began to tremble.

It had only been ten minutes when she suddenly heard a noise on the landing. It was David's door opening, followed by a loud thump. She waited, ready to escape behind her black shadows. After what seemed an eternity she crept towards the door.

It was then that she heard him calling. 'Mary! Help! Tablets!' He sounded breathless.

Opening the door gingerly, she saw him sprawled across the landing. He called out again. 'Mary! Ge … get … tablets.'

Walking towards him she noticed his lips were blue and his face an ashen grey. She was reminded of another ashen grey face. He was in a hospital bed and she had loved him so much, it hurt.

David had stopped asking for help. His eyes were now closed and he lay motionless. Mary looked down on him and smiled. Walking back into her room she wondered how long Dorothy was going to be. She turned to look at him again. 'Die before Dorothy comes back.' Mary was surprised by the sound of her own voice. She spoke so little now that the noise seemed strange to her.

David's arm twitched and his eyes opened. He was trying to say something, but she couldn't make out what it was. She walked back towards him and stood over his helpless body.

'Phone,' he gasped.

Not knowing where the words came from, Mary said, 'You poor unfortunate soul.'

'Phone,' he gasped again, sounding much weaker.

Mary smiled down at him. 'No!'

Noticing that his bedroom door was open, Mary stepped over him and went in. The first thing she noticed was the cane hanging on his bedpost. Purposefully, she grabbed it, walked back to David and began thrashing him. He felt nothing, as he had already drawn his last breath.

Mary's head was aching by the time she had replaced the cane and gone back into her own room. She tried in vain to hide behind her black shadows, but they would not come.

She heard the front door open and close, and footsteps coming up the stairs. The scream that followed made Mary's blood run cold. The next thing she heard was Dorothy on the phone asking for an ambulance in a panic stricken voice.

Replacing the receiver Dorothy put her hand to her head and said, 'Oh my God! Mary.'

She ran out of David's room, stepped over his body, and barged into Mary's bedroom. Mary was standing by the side of her bed. Dorothy grabbed her and held her close, saying, 'Don't worry my darling, are you alright?'

Instead of the usual nod, Mary replied, 'Yes, I'm alright.'

While waiting for the ambulance Dorothy sat with her arm around Mary on the edge of the bed. 'Don't upset yourself, my dear. Once they get him to hospital I'm sure he'll be alright.'

To Dorothy's surprise Mary replied, 'No he won't. He's dead!'

The sound of the front door slamming prevented Dorothy from responding. 'Stay here and keep your door closed,' she said in a commanding voice.

Dorothy met Jennifer halfway up the stairs. Taking her arm she said firmly, 'Don't go up there, dear. I have some bad news I'm afraid.'

Back down in the kitchen Dorothy explained, as best she could, what had happened.

'You left my father alone in the house with that mad woman,' Jennifer screamed.

'Please calm down,' Dorothy begged. 'The ambulance will be here soon.'

'Where is he?' Jennifer asked.

'It's better you don't see him until the ambulance gets here. They'll probably want you to go with him.'

Jennifer's face paled. 'I don't want to see him and I'm not going in the ambulance,' she replied. A loud banging at the door interrupted them.

David's body was carried out with a blanket covering him from head to toe. His daughter reluctantly went with him.

Mary remained in her room while Dorothy sat in the kitchen drinking endless cups of tea, waiting for the phone to ring.

It was 10.30, and still no word from Jennifer. Finally, Dorothy called Amanda's house and found that she was there and staying the night.

'You could have let me know, dear. I've been worried sick waiting for some news.' Dorothy did her best to hide her annoyance.

'What news were you waiting for? You knew he was dead. Did you think they were going to bring him back to life?' said Jennifer sarcastically.

Somewhat stunned by her coldness, Dorothy replaced the receiver and went to bed.

Because of the marks found on David's body, the police arrived the following day. But after discovering all sorts of sexual implements in his room they came rapidly to the conclusion that his wounds were self-inflicted.

Jennifer arrived home just as the police were trying to persuade Dorothy to go to the station to make a statement.

'There you are,' said the friendly policewoman, 'Her daughter's home now.' Glancing at Jennifer she went on, 'I need Dorothy down at the station for half an hour. Can you stay with your mother?' Jennifer nodded.

Dorothy was uneasy about leaving Mary with Jennifer but, under the circumstances, had little option.

As she heard the car drive away, Jennifer went straight to the kitchen and found the scissors. With a sinister look on her face she went in search of her mother.

Chapter Twenty-Five

Ralph left for the office at 9.15. He had not heard from Anne, but decided not to call in case she was asleep. He parked his car in the space reserved for him and made his way to the lift.

On entering the office he found his secretary in a flap. 'Mr Stevens. Thank goodness you're here,' she said breathlessly.

'What is it?' he enquired.

'I've had Mr Chandler's secretary on the phone twice – Apparently he's getting quite agitated and wants you to call him immediately.'

Ralph smiled. It didn't take much for Chandler to get agitated. Chairman of the board he might be, thought Ralph, but he can wait until I've had my coffee.

Twenty minutes later he called Oliver Chandler.

The unmistakeable booming voice came on the line. 'Stevens. Have you got an employee by the name of Stacey?'

'Yes I have, and she's very nice too.'

Chandler was not amused. ' What are you doing for lunch today?'

'Well, I was planning to have it with Miss Stacey.'

'Cancel it. Meet me at my club at twelve o'clock. I need to talk to you.'

Ralph was becoming irritated. 'If this is about what I think it is, I don't think it's anyone's business but mine.'

'Don't play games with me Stevens. Be there!' Chandler roared and slammed the phone down.

Ralph tried several times to contact Anne before leaving

for his meeting with Chandler, but to no avail. He was comforted by the fact that she wasn't at home. This meant she must be feeling better and was back at work.

Oliver Chandler's club was on St. James's street. Ralph had met him there before and knew exactly where he would be. The aroma of leather furniture and cigar smoke filled the air. Chandler was sitting in his usual chair, facing the door, waiting anxiously.

He was a short man and overweight, largely due to business dinners and lunches. His face was ruddy, with purple veins beginning to show in his cheeks. His thin balding hair was black and Ralph often wondered whether he dyed it.

He walked over and joined Chandler. 'Good morning.' He pulled out a chair and sat down.

Chandler grunted and signalled for the waiter to bring Ralph a drink. 'Straight to the point, my boy. This employee of yours, Stacey. Tell me about her,' he snapped.

'What do you want to know? She's in her middle thirties with long dark brown hair and eyes to match and is more conscientious than anyone I know,' Ralph said with a smile.

'Her background Ralph. I want to know where she's from. How long has she been with the company?' Chandler was getting irritated. He knew he was being played with.

Ralph leaned towards him. 'She came straight from school to work in our Ramsden store and, after taking the normal course, was promoted to supervisor. She's very bright and her ambition was to manage her own store. An opening came in area management. We had applicants with university degrees but as always, none had the personality required for this senior position. I had several recommendations from internal management to interview Anne Stacey and decided to give her a crack at the job. I've never regretted it for one moment. While we're on the subject,' Ralph went on, 'I should tell you that I've fallen in love and plan to marry her.'

Chandler reached into his inside pocket, produced a

newspaper cutting and handed it to Ralph. 'Read that and then fire her. Pay her off handsomely so there are no complications. Then I suggest, my boy, that you forget all about her.'

Ralph turned white with anger as he read the article. It was the same one that he had joked about with Anne. 'So you think this is her father, do you?' he asked sarcastically.

'It's her father alright,' Chandler snapped back. 'We had a call from a chap by the name of Trevor. He's the son of this criminal. Claims he's lost his job because of his father but thought that as we still employed his sister, there may be an opening for him with us.'

'I need some time to sort this out,' said Ralph slowly rising from his chair.

Chandler glared. 'It's already sorted out. All you have to do is fire her. You should know better than to fraternise with members of staff. Now, I've got to go to a business lunch and don't want to waste any more time on your love life.' He got up and walked swiftly towards the door.

Ralph sat down again and ordered himself another drink. Remembering he would have to drive to Anne's that evening, he promptly got up and left the drink untouched.

Arriving back at his office he asked whether Anne had called. He was both disappointed and alarmed to find that she hadn't and immediately began phoning around until finally finding her in the St Albans store. Without mentioning Chandler, he told her that he would be at her house at seven that evening. She seemed reluctant at first, coming up with weak excuses.

'You sound as if you don't want me to come,' he said.

'Don't be silly,' she replied. 'It's just that I've not had much sleep with this headache.'

'Well, I'm coming anyway. We have to talk.'

Anne left the store at five o'clock and drove home feeling as though her world was about to come to an end. She had

154

already made up her mind to confess all to him. The chances were that he would want to bring their relationship to an end, but she could not go on living a lie.

Ralph arrived at 6.45. Anne had not prepared dinner, believing he would most likely want to leave once she had finished explaining the situation.

The care she had taken with her appearance was not wasted. As she opened the door he remarked, 'My God! You look stunning.' Once inside, his plan as to how he was going to handle things went straight out of the window. Not being able to help himself, he took her into his arms and kissed her passionately. She responded and pushed her body up close to him.

Then Anne felt him pull his body away. His kiss came to an abrupt end as he grabbed her shoulders. 'I need to talk to you.' He gently pushed her down onto the armchair and sat opposite.

'Would you like a drink or something?' she asked.

'No thanks,' he replied. Leaning back in the chair he rubbed the palms of his hands together.

'Anne,' he began. 'Are you the daughter of this rapist who has just been arrested?' She looked at him in horror.

'I'm sorry, darling. I didn't mean it to sound quite like that, but I had to ask you,' he whispered.

Her voice trembled. 'He is my father, but in no way do I think of myself as his daughter.'

Ralph looked crestfallen. 'Anne. Please tell me this isn't true,' he said closing his eyes.

'I'm afraid it is. I don't know how you found out, but believe me, Ralph, I was going to tell you tonight,' she replied.

'That wretched brother of yours telephoned the chairman's office on the pretext of looking for a job. He followed that up by sending that newspaper cutting to him.' Ralph looked down at the floor as he spoke. He lifted his head and looked into her eyes. 'Why didn't you tell me when I mentioned it to you on Sunday.'

'I didn't really see it until after you'd gone,' she explained.

The disbelief on his face was apparent. 'I've had instructions from the chairman to fire you,' he said.

Anne was shocked. She half expected to lose the man she loved but it had never occurred to her that her job would be in jeopardy.

Sounding impatient, he said, 'Oh, Anne, use your head. A large company like Andersons can't afford to employ the daughter of a criminal. It won't be long before the newspapers start hounding you for stories of your father. Once that happens you'll be involved up to your neck.'

She saw in his face an expression she had never seen before. One of anger and disappointment.

'Don't worry, Ralph,' Anne said, trying to keep her voice steady. 'You'll have my resignation on your desk by tomorrow. You won't have to fire me.'

He got up from the chair and walked towards the window. 'Have you any idea how embarrassing this is for me?' he said, his back towards her. 'Don't you realise that, if I had married you, this could have cost me my job as well?'

Doing her best to hold back the tears, Anne said, 'I think you'd better go now, Ralph. It's quite apparent that your job is far more important to you than our love for each other.'

He spun round and shouted angrily, 'Anne, what do you think we would live on? I love you as much as ever, but love doesn't pay the bills.'

'Ralph, please go now.' She could hardly see for the tears welling up in her eyes.

Without saying goodbye, he left. She heard the screech of tyres as he pulled away.

Shaking, she collapsed into the armchair. 'Here I am again,' she thought to herself. 'Alone. No mother. No Davy. No Mary. No brother. No Ralph and, this time, no job.'

Chapter Twenty-Six

Arriving back at the Lodge, Dorothy thanked the police-woman and hurried back into the house. She went straight to Mary's room. Nothing could have prepared her for the shock of seeing Mary huddled up in a corner of the bed. Her hair had been cut so close to her head she looked like a convict. Her face was tear-stained and she was shaking violently.

She rushed over and took Mary in her arms. 'Oh, my dear. Whatever have you done to your hair?' The look on her face told Dorothy that she was in one of her trances. It was obvious that she was going to have to wait for an explanation.

Mary stayed in her room for the rest of the day. Jennifer was nowhere to be seen.

The death of Mr Freeman had left Dorothy in an awkward position. She knew the correct thing to do was phone social services and have Mary taken to hospital where she could get proper psychiatric treatment. She also knew that it was only a matter of time before she herself would be forced to leave

Mr Cornell called the day after David Freeman had died. He informed Dorothy that he, as Mr Freeman's solicitor, had been instructed to take care of the funeral. Dorothy was shocked to learn that it was David Freeman's wish that no one attend. He also informed her that there was to be a reading of the will the day after the funeral at his office.

David had left a very detailed will. To Jennifer, a substantial lump sum, the mews cottage in London and an increased monthly allowance from the trust fund.

For Dorothy, he had provided for her salary to be doubled and paid until such time as Mary no longer needed her.

For Mary, his wife, he left the remainder of his estate. This included the Lodge and all of his investments, some of which were substantial.

Mr Cornell showed them to the door of his office. 'You are a very wealthy woman Mrs Freeman,' he said. 'I want you to know that I am always here to help you in anyway I can.' Mary looked at him and smiled.

'That goes for you too, Miss Freeman,' he said as he patted Jennifer's arm. Her only response was to glare angrily at the old solicitor.

As he watched them leave the building he couldn't help wondering why Mrs Freeman had held on to her hat continuously throughout the meeting.

On the way home in the taxi, Dorothy asked Jennifer if she was coming back to the Lodge with them.

'It's not my home any more, is it?' she replied sarcastically.

'Oh Jennifer. Let's not fall out,' pleaded Dorothy. 'The house belongs to your mother and I'm sure she wants you to think of it as your home.' Looking at Mary she went on, 'You want Jennifer to come home, don't you?'

Mary didn't nod or shake her head but said, very clearly, 'No!'

Jennifer stared angrily at her mother and said, 'I hate you!'

Mary did not respond and, for fear of starting an argument, neither did Dorothy.

As the taxi approached Amanda's house, Mary was relieved to hear Jennifer ask the driver to drop her off there. Mary and Dorothy carried on up to the Lodge in silence.

Once inside, Mary surprised Dorothy by not going straight to her room as usual. Instead she went into the kitchen, pulled out a chair and sat staring at the woman she thought of as her true friend.

Dorothy had done a lot of thinking during the journey back from London. The task David Freeman had set for her in his will concerned her greatly. Realising the responsibility it entailed, she was unsure as to what she should do.

Mary suddenly asked, 'Will you stay?'

The fact that Mary was not only speaking, but had taken in everything that had been said in Mr Cornell's office shocked Dorothy.

'For the time being,' she replied. 'Now, would you like some tea?'

Jennifer continued pestering Mr Cornell about the unfairness of her father's will but to no avail. Deciding she no longer wanted to study for a career, she did not return to college. Although she had been bitterly disappointed by the contents of the will, she still had enough money to live well without ever having to earn a living. Her real disappointment was that she was not in a position to throw her mother out of the house and have her committed.

The day before Amanda's return to college, Mr Cornell called Jennifer and told her the house in London was now empty and that she could move in whenever she liked. Amanda's mother breathed a sigh of relief. She was truly tired of Jennifer staying there.

Saying goodbye to Amanda at the station, Jennifer promised to let her know when the house-warming party was going to be.

Looking around her new home, she was more than pleased. The solicitor had told her that the outgoing tenants were going to Canada and wished to sell all their furniture. It was all very modern but of extremely good quality and Jennifer smiled to herself recognising what a good deal old Cornell had done.

Within a week she was on the phone to Amanda, giving her the date of the party. 'Bring as many people as you can,' she said. 'I haven't made many friends in London yet.'

Ignoring the request, Amanda said that Trevor had called and she had been out with him twice.

'Oh, that's great. Bring him along to the party,' said Jennifer trying to hide the excitement in her voice.

Twenty people showed up for the party. Apart from a couple of neighbours and Trevor, the rest were all friends from college.

Jennifer looked stunning in white denim trousers and a green silk top. Most of the students bought bottles with them and she had ordered two cases of champagne. An outside caterer had prepared the buffet.

Amanda, dressed in a long white linen shirt and jeans that made her look slimmer than she was, never left Trevor's side.

It was around eleven o'clock before Jennifer got the opportunity she had been waiting for. Someone had grabbed hold of Amanda and pulled her up to dance. She moved in on Trevor like a spider catching a fly. Without either of them saying a word they went into each other's arms and began dancing slowly to the Righteous Brothers singing 'Unchained Melody'.

After the second dance Jennifer said, 'Come into the kitchen and I'll get you a drink.' Another couple were already there locked in each other's arms. Recognising the girl from college, Jennifer whispered, 'There's a bed upstairs.' Within seconds they had disappeared.

'Well, you seem to have settled in nicely,' said Trevor.

Not wanting to waste time with niceties Jennifer filled two glasses with champagne. 'Do you know anyone who could help me choose a car and teach me to drive?' she asked.

Trevor gave one of his dashing smiles that made Jennifer's thighs throb. She was aching to get this man in bed.

'Come here,' he said, pulling her towards him. His arms went around her and his tongue traced the outline of her lips. She responded by trying to trap his tongue in her

160

mouth. His hand was inside her blouse when a very drunk Amanda appeared at the door.

'You bitch!' she screamed as they broke away from each other.

'Oh, come on, Amanda. It's a party for Christ's sake.'

'Is it?' Amanda staggered towards her. 'I suppose anything goes at a party so try this.' She hurled a full glass of red wine over her so-called friend. Jennifer did not see it coming. Her face caught the worst of it with the rest soaking the front of her green silk top. Jennifer stood with her mouth wide open while Trevor leaned against the worktop with a half smile on his face.

After Amanda had staggered out, Trevor said 'I'd better get you upstairs and change those clothes for you.' Jennifer walked towards him and whispered, 'I think a shower is in order, don't you?'

It was four o'clock in the morning when Trevor awoke. They had fallen asleep after having made passionate love for hours. Raising himself up on his elbow he looked down at Jennifer. There were beads of perspiration on her top lip and forehead. He lowered his head and licked them dry. Realising his own body was soaked in sweat he got up, opened the window and leaned out.

He had not been that impressed with this sex session. She was game for anything he had wanted to do. He much preferred having to use force. However this was a minor detail. He needed this girl for her money. After pulling on his underpants, he crept downstairs to see if anyone was still there. The place was empty and had the usual mess that a wild party leaves.

Trevor poked around and found the coffee. As he arrived back upstairs with two cups, Jennifer stirred. 'Everyone's gone, so drink this and I'll show you how to make love when you're sober,' he said.

She sat up in bed and said sleepily, 'I'll have the coffee but no more lovemaking. I've got an awful headache.'

He paid no attention to her protests and, without letting her finish her coffee, forced himself upon her.

She slept for another two hours before he woke her. 'I really should go now,' he said.

'Will you come back tonight?'

'Try keeping me away,' he replied.

The relationship blossomed, and not only in the bed department. Two weeks later he moved in and after three weeks could tell she had fallen hopelessly in love with him. He had given up his job and flat and was running out of money. It was time to put part two of his plan into action.

They were sitting in a small Chinese restaurant in Soho when he went in for the kill. 'I've got something to confess,' he said as he looked at her longingly.

'Don't tell me you're married.'

'No, it's worse than that.'

Jennifer sat stunned as he told her that his father was in prison on a rape charge and his sister had thrown him out on the street. 'I didn't tell you before because I knew you wouldn't have anything to do with me.' He reached for her hand across the table. 'It was stupid of me. I knew it would only be a matter of time before you found out. I can't teach you to drive either because I haven't taken a test myself so I suppose this will be our last supper. I hope you'll let me stay for a couple of days until I get myself sorted out.'

'Why did your sister throw you out?'

'Anne is both dull and sensible. Selfish too. I'm a free spirit. I like to have fun and take risks. I think I was an embarrassment to her,' he replied.

She smiled as she imagined his dull, staid sister trying to control this gorgeous man. 'How long has your father been in prison?' she asked.

'I don't know. I've never met him and have no desire to,' he replied.

He then told her the story that Anne had related to him about a woman dumping him on the doorstep.

'So you don't really know if it is your father in prison?' she asked.

'I saw his picture in the paper and believe me, there's no doubt about it. I look like his fucking double,' he replied.

Jennifer sat staring at him. 'My, my!' she said. ' You are a dark horse. Now, you think that because your father's in prison and your sister's got no time for you, we should split up. Is that what you're saying?'

'It's not just that Jennifer. You don't understand. I'm broke.'

'I'm not, Trevor. I've got enough money for both of us. We're good for each other. It could be quite exciting living with the son of a rapist. Now, let's get the bill and get out of here and I'll tell you about the skeletons in my cupboard. No more talk of separation now,' she said, getting up from the table.

Trevor left the restaurant triumphant. His plan had worked much quicker and better than he had ever expected.

They took a taxi back to the house. Once inside Trevor said, 'I'll fix us a drink. You make yourself comfy and get ready to tell me about your murky past.'

Jennifer laughed and settled herself in the armchair with her feet tucked up underneath her. She felt happy that Trevor had no money. In her mind she thought this gave her total control over him.

'So,' she began. 'Your father's in prison. My mother should be in a lunatic asylum. She's as mad as a hatter. I hate her with a passion and she hates me. My father was the strangest man you ever did meet. He never mixed with anyone. His family were incredibly wealthy and he inherited the lot. The silly old fool died and left most of his fortune to my mad mother. He claimed to be a counsellor by profession and, for that reason, never put her away where she belonged. I don't

163

think he loved her because he was quite cruel to her at times. But I did see him creeping into her room at night on more than one occasion.'

She went on to tell him about Dorothy and the part she played in looking after her mother. 'So you see,' she concluded, 'I grew up never being able to take my friends home for fear of how the mad bitch would behave.'

Pouring another drink he raised his glass. 'Goodbye to the past, and here's to our future.'

Jennifer, raising her glass, replied, 'To fun, laughter, sex and living.'

Later in bed that night, after he was asleep, Jennifer lay awake. This was a brand new feeling she was experiencing. Recognising that she would be devastated should he ever leave made her feel vulnerable. Is this what they call love she wondered? If it was she didn't like it.

The following morning they sat in bed eating scrambled eggs and drinking champagne. Trevor had bought a car magazine to help them decide what sort of car to buy. They had already arranged to have driving lessons with the hope that at least one of them would pass. They finished their breakfast, made love and set about looking through the magazine.

'My father changed his car every year,' Jennifer said. 'His last car was a Jaguar. I liked that.'

'You have expensive tastes,' Trevor joked. He thought for a minute. 'What happened to your father's car?'

'I have no idea,' she replied. 'My mother doesn't drive. Dorothy can't drive. I expect it's still in the garage.'

Realising what he was thinking, she exclaimed 'No! We'll buy our own car.'

By lunchtime he had persuaded her that it would be in their interest to make amends with her mother and Dorothy. 'Think of the champagne suppers we can have with what it costs to buy a Jag,' he said.

The following day Jennifer reluctantly called Dorothy and asked if she could come and talk to her. They agreed to meet in the village coffee shop so as not to upset Mary. Apart from Jennifer, who was sitting waiting, Dorothy was relieved to see the place was empty.

The two women looked at each other. Jennifer noticed for the first time that Dorothy was beginning to go grey. The cream raincoat she wore was the only coat she ever remembered seeing her in. Underneath that Jennifer knew she would be wearing a white blouse and one of her cardigans. What a sad case, Jennifer thought to herself.

'How are you?' she asked. Dorothy was somewhat taken aback. She couldn't remember a single time when Jennifer had enquired after her well-being. She was even more surprised when she asked, 'And how is my mother?'

They were interrupted by the man behind the counter calling out, 'What can I get you two ladies?'

Jennifer looked questioningly at Dorothy. 'Coffee?'

Dorothy nodded. 'Your mother is making very good progress. But I'm sure you're not here to enquire after her well-being or mine. Why don't you get straight to the point?'

Jennifer sighed. 'I'm trying to make amends. I've no one else to talk to and thought you might give me some advice.' After trying to convince Dorothy she really cared about her mother she told her about Trevor.

'The only advice I would give you, my dear, is get rid of him as quickly as you can. This Trevor Stacey of yours sounds like a bad lot to me. A penniless son of a rapist teaching you to drive! Why don't you go to a driving school like everyone else?'

The conversation was not going according to plan. Trying another tack, Jennifer said, 'I don't want to buy a car until I've learned to drive and I thought that if Trevor taught me, it would be a way of helping him earn some money until he finds a job. He's had a very unfortunate childhood and his half-sister, Anne, has no time for him at all. She threw him out and swindled him out of his share of a house. If you met Trevor, I think you'd like him.'

'Why do you suddenly care what I think?' Dorothy asked.

'Because, since my father died, I feel vulnerable and admit my judgement of people sometimes leaves a lot to be desired.

'Well, at last you've learned something,' said Dorothy. 'Now, is there anything else? Only I really must go.'

'Yes there is. I'd like you to ask my mother if Trevor could use father's car to teach me to drive.'

'Do you intend ever seeing your mother again?'

'Of course I do. But it will have to wait until you think the time is right. I know I haven't been the perfect daughter and I don't know whether she will ever forgive me. Will you help?' she pleaded.

'I'll see,' Dorothy replied.

'And will you meet Trevor?'

'I'll see,' Dorothy repeated. 'Now I must go. Call me in a week.'

She walked back to the Lodge, wondering what Jennifer was up to. Perhaps she had changed. Dorothy doubted it but, on the other hand, why would she go to all this trouble just to borrow a car when she could easily afford to buy one?

As she let herself in she called out, 'Mary.'

A feeling of happiness swept over her as Mary called back, 'I'm in the kitchen.'

Mary no longer spent most of her time in her room. She was beginning to speak quite a lot now. Dorothy was well aware that she was far from normal but the signs of improvement were encouraging. She still went into trances, but these were getting less and less.

Chapter Twenty-Seven

Anne slept very little during the next two days. Several times she tried writing her resignation letter, but her melancholic mood affected her concentration. Knowing there was no use putting it off any longer, she made up her mind to get it done. It was difficult for her to write to the man she loved and address him as Mr Stevens.

As she sat chewing the end of her pen the doorbell rang. Praying with all her heart that it would be Ralph, she walked through the lounge to open the door. Her heart sank when confronted by a complete stranger.

'Good morning! Are you Anne Stacey?' the man enquired.

'Yes. How can I help you?' she replied.

'I wondered if we could have a few words about your father. He goes on trial tomorrow and I wondered how you felt about it.'

'What do you mean, how I feel about it?' Anne's irritation was obvious.

'You know. Just a few questions, like, was he a good father? I understand he walked out on you and your mother. Is it true that you brought up his illegitimate son?'

Too late it dawned on Anne that he was a newspaper reporter. A second man had walked up the path and a flash bulb went off in front of her face.

'Please go away,' she shouted as she tried to close the door.

The reporter had his foot in the way. 'Did you know your father was systematically raping young girls?' he asked.

'If you don't take your foot out of this doorway I shall call the police.' Anne was getting hysterical.

The reporter obliged by removing his foot. 'Could you just tell us where your half-brother lives?' he asked, notebook at the ready.

Anne slammed the door shut and, trembling, went back to the table where she was writing her resignation letter. Resting her head in her hands she moaned out loud, 'What a nightmare! What a nightmare!'

Later in the day, as she was returning from posting the letter, she encountered a group of women gathered together in earnest conversation. One of them she recognised as Jill, a girl who had worked for her in the local supermarket. Expecting to be shunned, Anne was surprised when they began walking towards her.

Jill waved a wad of banknotes for her to see. 'Anne, look what a newspaper reporter's just given me. I hope you don't mind but I answered some questions about you.'

Anne felt sick. 'What did you tell him?' she asked, trying hard to conceal her anger.

'Well, that's just it,' the excitable Jill said. 'All I said was that I had known you since you were a little girl. I told him how I used to sit on the tree trunk with you and your best friend Mary. You remember Mary, don't you? I told him it was near the place where some of those poor girls were raped. He asked if I knew where your best friend lived, but of course I couldn't tell him because I don't know. He wanted to know where Trevor was, but I couldn't tell him that either. Look, Anne, he gave me twenty-five pounds.'

Worried that she was about to lose her temper Anne promptly walked away.

Feeling totally depressed she walked the long way home. Passing the Vicarage she stopped and stared up at the old oak door. Memories of dear Davy came flooding back. She pictured the old lady standing at the door with arms outstretched, ready to comfort her when the loss of her mother was more than she could bear.

Walking through the woodland at the back of the Vicarage, a lump came into her throat. There was the old tree trunk, looking as welcome as ever. It was hard to imagine that her father had raped innocent girls in this treasured spot.

Sitting down on the old trunk she looked up into the sky and thought of Mary. A rustle in the bushes disturbed her thoughts. The flashlight went off as she heard the click of the camera. Spinning around she saw the back of the photographer as he ran into the bushes.

Back home she felt positively drained. It was an effort to find the energy just to make a sandwich and cup of tea. Not wanting to put the television on for fear of news of the trial she had a hot bath and went to bed at 9.30. Although restless until about two in the morning, she finally fell asleep until awakened by the paper coming through the letterbox.

Realising how late it was she jumped out of bed and went down to make some coffee. The paper was lying on the floor where it had fallen. Anne was only halfway down the stairs when she saw the picture of herself staring up at her.

Picking it up with trembling hands she read: 'Anne Stacey Played with Best Friend at the Spot where Father Raped Victims.' Below the headlines was a picture of her sitting on the old log.

At the same time, Trevor Stacey was lying in bed staring at the picture of his sister on the front page. He prodded Jennifer to wake her up. 'You've got to see this.'

Jennifer stirred. They had been at a club until three in the morning and she was feeling the effects of the amount of alcohol she had drunk. 'Later,' she slurred.

'No, now,' he said as he pulled the covers off her.

Reluctantly Jennifer sat up and looked at the paper. 'Wow!' she said, still bleary eyed. 'This is spooky. Your sister looks a bit like me. 'Do you think they'll come looking for you?'

'They already have,' he replied. 'I sold my story to make some money.'

She moved her naked body close to him. 'How many times do I have to tell you that you don't need to worry about money?'

'But I do. It gets a bit tiring having to keep asking you for money every time I want something.' He moved away and jumped out of bed.

After Jennifer said she would transfer £10,000 into an account that he could draw on whenever he needed, he jumped back into bed. They made passionate love for the next hour.

Once they were up, showered and dressed, Jennifer suggested that they go and look for a Jaguar.

'I think it would make much more sense if you phoned old Dorothy. It's been a week now. Let's see what she has to say before we do anything. Besides, we should make up with your mother. You don't want her dying and leaving the estate to the old lady do you?' he said, winking at her.

Jennifer felt uneasy with his continuous remarks about making amends with her mother, and she knew the motivation behind it was money. Aware that a week had gone by since her conversation with Dorothy, she reluctantly agreed to call her.

'I'm going round the corner to get some cigarettes,' he called over his shoulder as he went downstairs.

Picking up the newspaper from the floor, Jennifer looked at the picture of Anne Stacey again. Out of curiosity, she felt she would like to meet Trevor's sister. When the time was right, she decided that she would find out where she lived and pay her a visit.

Checking her watch she realised Trevor had been gone for 45 minutes. It took less than five minutes to walk to the shop.

Her heart began to beat faster. She hated being away from him for even one minute. She was forever worrying about what she would do if he left her. The thought of him having sex with someone else made her feel ill, and just seeing him chatting to another attractive female sent her into a panic.

They made a handsome couple. Girls gazed at Trevor admiringly and it appeared to Jennifer that he enjoyed every minute of it. This made her feel very insecure.

Returning with a cigarette between his fingers, Trevor asked, 'Did you phone Dorothy?'

'Yes,' she lied. ' There was no answer.'

'Shit,' he said. 'Do we have to phone her first? I think we should just turn up.'

'I don't think that's a good idea.'

'Look, if we arrive by train and have to walk from the station to the house, she's bound to take pity on us and let us use the car to get home.'

Jennifer shook her head. 'My so-called mother is not the sort you just call on. In any case, Dorothy wouldn't let you see her. She guards my mother against any surprises or upsets. In any case, had you forgotten you can't drive? We don't take our tests until next week.'

'You sound just like my sister. She went mad when I borrowed her car one day while she was in London. She went on and on reminding me that I had no licence and hadn't passed my test. She drove me nuts.' Trevor was now getting irritated.

'Don't get grumpy. I'll phone Dorothy again in an hour.' She playfully grabbed his crotch.

The two of them fell back on the bed, laughing. 'So we've got an hour to kill,' he said, as his hand slid up between her legs.

Chapter Twenty-Eight

Dorothy sat at the kitchen table with a cup of coffee and a newspaper. It was 11.30 in the morning.

Mary had gone to do some weeding in the garden. Three months had passed since David had died and, although her mind continued to blank out her past, she felt more relaxed knowing David would never come to her room again and Jennifer was no longer there to terrify her.

Dorothy looked at Mary through the kitchen window and smiled. Puzzled as to why she had made such good progress since her husband had died, she picked up the newspaper and began to read.

Her stomach lurched when she saw the headlines. Reading on, she discovered that Jennifer's story about Trevor's unhappy childhood was true. Studying the picture of his sister, it was hard to imagine that she was the sort of girl who would throw him out and cheat him out of his share of the house.

'Never judge a book by its cover,' she said to herself.

Not wanting to upset Mary, she had decided not to mention her meeting with Jennifer. A week had passed and she had not called, so Dorothy had decided to forget all about it.

She had noticed that Mary would go off into one of her trances whenever David Freeman's name came up in conversation and so for that reason she now never mentioned either of them. Dorothy was determined that nothing should interfere with the amazing progress Mary was making.

But, after reading the story in the newspaper, she realised that Jennifer had been telling the truth about Trevor. So, could it possibly be that this awful girl had really changed for the better and was genuine about wanting to make amends with her mother? Her thoughts were interrupted by the back door closing.

Mary came in from the garden and sat down at the table. 'I think I've done enough for one morning.'

'Time for a coffee break,' said Dorothy. She got up to put the kettle on and with her back to Mary said, 'By the way, I forgot to tell you. Jennifer called. She wants to come and see you.'

She turned swiftly to see the expression on Mary's face. 'She's got a boyfriend and wants us to meet him.' Mary showed no sign of going into a trance and so Dorothy continued. 'She wants to make amends.'

Mary stared at her and, after a long silence, said, 'No!'

'That's alright, my dear. You don't have to do anything that upsets you. Now you drink your coffee. I'm going to tidy my bedroom, and after lunch perhaps, we'll go for a walk.'

Left alone in the kitchen Mary leaned across the table and pulled the newspaper towards her. She enjoyed reading tips on gardening.

The face of Anne Stacey stared up at her. With trembling hands she raised her cup to her lips. Coffee spilled down her blouse and over the table. She was back in the restaurant with David. She had spilled her coffee when he asked her to marry him. About to hide behind her black shadows, she suddenly recognised the girl in the paper and murmured, 'Anne.'

Her face took on a vacant expression. She was safe now, hiding behind the dark shadows.

Dorothy returned to find Mary in a trance. Immediately thinking that this was the result of her mentioning Jennifer, she took Mary's arm and led her to her bedroom.

It was late afternoon before Mary ventured from her room. Dorothy was walking around the garden.

Entering the kitchen, Mary saw the newspaper still lying on the table. With unsteady hands she picked it up, sat down and read the rest of the article. It was difficult for her to absorb, but of one thing she was certain. Anne now knew her father was a rapist.

Trying to understand why she had not seen her friend all these years brought tears to her eyes. When, in her mind, she began confusing Anne with Jennifer, she got up and went into the garden to find Dorothy.

'I'm starving,' she called out.

Dorothy looked round and smiled. 'I bet you are,' she said, walking towards Mary. 'I let you sleep through lunch. Come along, let's go indoors and get you something to eat.'

While Dorothy was preparing a sandwich Mary said, 'That's my friend's picture in the paper.'

Giving her a puzzled look, Dorothy placed a plate of sandwiches on the table. To her knowledge, Mary didn't have a friend in the world.

'Look!' Mary thrust the newspaper in front of Dorothy's face.

'I don't think so, dear. But I can tell you who she is.' Dorothy gulped. 'That's the sister of Jennifer's boyfriend. You know, the one she wanted you to meet. The poor boy has had a terrible time and is trying to start a new life with her.'

'That's Anne,' Mary whispered.

'That's right, dear.' Worried that this kind of article would upset her, Dorothy asked gently, 'Did you read the whole story?'

Ignoring the question, Mary repeated, 'That's Anne, my dearest friend. Do you know where she is?'

Dorothy was troubled. She knew how to handle Mary when she went into a trance but had never heard her talk nonsense before.

'No, I'm afraid I don't. Now, why don't you finish your sandwich and we'll go down to the village.'

Mary dutifully finished eating and went to get her coat.

Much to Dorothy's relief, Mary made no further mention of the newspaper story.

On their way back they commented on the beautiful trees and stopped to admire people's front gardens.

'Do you think we should make our flower beds wider?' Mary asked enthusiastically.

'If we do, we'll have to get someone in to do the digging,' Dorothy replied, glad that Mary had stopped talking non-sense.

Chapter Twenty-Nine

Jennifer pretended that she had called Dorothy several times and could get no answer. 'Perhaps they've gone on holiday,' she said when Trevor kept on about it. The pressure he was putting on her to make amends with her mother was beginning to get on her nerves. She had successfully passed her driving test and could see no reason not to go out and buy a car.

To his annoyance Trevor had failed. When Jennifer suggested he put in for another test right away, he snapped, 'I don't need to. I can drive and that's good enough for me.'

'Well, why don't we go and get a car?' she asked impatiently.

'Because I don't want to waste money buying one when you've got a brand new Jaguar sitting outside your mother's house.'

'It's not my car,' Jennifer screamed at him. 'You must think I'm daft. I know why you want me to make up with my mother. You want to wheedle money out of her as well as me.'

He walked over and slapped her hard across the face. 'I don't want yours or your mother's money,' he snarled.

Jennifer was stunned. 'You bastard,' she screamed at him. 'Why don't you go back to your sister and see if she'll keep you in the same lifestyle that I do.'

'I'll do just that,' he shouted. Putting on his coat he walked towards the door. 'You bitch,' he said with venom and slammed the door behind him.

Three hours later when he had not returned Jennifer

176

decided to go and look for him. She knew there was a train station at Denton and had made a note of his sister's address from the newspaper.

With plenty of time to think while on the train, she made up her mind to apologise and take him to pick up her father's car. She smiled to herself as the train pulled into Denton station. She had never apologised to anyone in her life, but she knew how to play a part. The one thing she knew for certain was that this man was for her, and she would do anything to keep him.

Jennifer looked at Anne's house with contempt as the taxi came to a standstill. After replenishing her lipstick she told the taxi driver to wait for an hour.

'Cost you, darling,' he replied, eyeing the long legs exposed by the tight cream mini skirt.

'That's fine. Just wait for me,' Jennifer said rudely.

Preparing to be the hurt and injured party, she rang the doorbell.

For fear of it being more newspaper reporters Anne called out, 'Who is it?'

'My name's Jennifer Freeman. Could I have a word with Trevor, please?'

Anne opened the door slowly. She was surprised to see a young girl with hair identical to her own looking somewhat sheepish. 'I'm sorry,' she said. 'Trevor doesn't live here now.'

'I know. He lives with me. We had an argument and he stormed out saying he was coming back here.'

'You'd better come in for a minute,' said Anne, stepping back to make way for her.

'I don't know why you threw him out,' said Jennifer sipping a cup of tea. 'That's none of my business, but if you do hear from him, will you please give me a call?'

Anne nodded. 'Of course, though I doubt very much if he will contact me. You see, we parted on bad terms.'

Jennifer produced a notebook from her black leather bag

and proceeded to write down her name and telephone number. Handing it to Anne, she said quietly, 'I know about your father. Trevor's taken it very badly.'

Anne stared at the piece of paper and a strange thought crossed her mind. 'Jennifer Freeman!' she exclaimed.

Realising that she must have frightened the girl, she explained, 'I'm sorry. It was a bit of a shock. You see, my best friend from years ago was a Mary Peters and she married a man by the name of Freeman. I never saw her again. It's silly, I know, but I've never really got over it.'

'That's strange,' said Jennifer. 'My mother's name is Mary. Not a very nice person I'm afraid. She's mentally ill and should have been put in a home years ago. My father died earlier this year.'

'Where was your mother born?' Anne asked.

'I've no idea,' replied Jennifer. 'She lives in Ramsden now with her housekeeper.

'I don't suppose you've got a photograph of her?'

'No, I'm afraid not. Look, I must be going. I've got a taxi waiting outside.' Jennifer stood up and made as if to leave.

'I'm sorry you've had a wasted journey. The likelihood of me hearing from Trevor is very remote, but if I do, I'll certainly call you.' Anne showed Jennifer to the door.

The train journey back to London was most uncomfortable. Jennifer had to stand most of the way. This, coupled with her fury at not finding Trevor at his sister's house, put her in bad temper by the time she got home.

There was no sign of Trevor, but the cleaning lady was there. 'Why are you still here?' she snapped. 'You should have been finished half an hour ago.'

The young Spanish girl looked at her with wide eyes. 'I go now?'

'Yes, get out of here,' screamed Jennifer.

Within two minutes of the girl leaving she heard Trevor's key in the lock. All her plans of being apologetic had been forgotten. 'How dare you use the key to come in. You should have knocked. Have you forgotten you don't live here any more?' she said as Trevor entered the bedroom.

'I've come to collect my things,' he replied.

'Where have you been? Out shagging someone else I suppose.'

He walked towards her. 'Jennifer, I thought we were having fun together. Do you really want me to go?'

She responded by walking into the lounge and sinking down into an armchair. Trevor followed and sat on the arm of her chair.

He slid his arm around her shoulders. 'You're right. I was using the car as an excuse to meet your mother. The old girl must be loaded. I can see her leaving it all to old Dorothy or a cat's home. I wanted to see for myself how batty she was. If she's as bad as you say, we can get her committed and you can get power of attorney. That way you get what you want. Your mother will be put away and, the bonus is, she can't leave her money to anyone without your say-so.'

Jennifer felt excited at the thought of having control over her mother. 'Do you really think I could get the mad bitch put away in an asylum?'

'That's where people go when they're mad,' he said laughing.

'I thought you were leaving.'

'Not yet, my darling.' He lifted Jennifer off the chair and carried her into the bedroom.

Chapter Thirty

Ralph Stevens had written a very business-like letter acknowledging Anne's resignation. The handsome settlement was far more than she had expected but did nothing to ease the pain she felt when wondering how he could possibly write such a letter to someone he supposedly loved. Over the next few days she read and reread it, trying to find something that would remind her of the man she had shared her bed with.

Anne made no attempt to look for a new job. She calculated that with her settlement and savings she could live very comfortably for at least three years. Her plan was to sell the house and move away, but she had convinced herself that there was plenty of time before having to make any real decision. In the back of her mind, Anne knew she was only postponing things in case Ralph tried to contact her.

Her father's trial had finished and he had been sent to prison for 11 years. She tried telling herself it was a closed book now and that she had to get on with life. This, however, was proving to be difficult.

Since the visit of Jennifer Freeman she thought a lot about Mary and how strong their relationship had been. She began to wonder whether there was a connection between Jennifer and the David Freeman who had married her best friend. Jennifer looked about 20 and David and Mary's child would be about the same age.

Impulsively she jumped up and rang directory enquiries.

'Do you have a number listed for a David Freeman?' After the operator told her that she couldn't help without an address, Anne decided to put these thoughts out of her mind.

That evening, as she sat watching television, her thoughts started to wander again. Jennifer had said that her mother was mentally ill, but in no way could Anne ever imagine Mary having a mental illness. Oh, how she wished she had asked whether Jennifer's father's Christian name was David. If she hadn't got so much time on her hands then maybe she'd forget about it. She was beginning to feel very lonely. If only Ralph was still around. He was the one person she could talk to. Even now, when she thought of him, tears came to her eyes. She loved him so much.

The need to call Jennifer kept nagging at her, but she was well aware that it would probably put her in touch with Trevor and she was adamant that she wanted nothing more to do with him.

A few days later, Anne was in the process of scrambling eggs when the sound of the telephone ringing interrupted her. Since she no longer got calls from work this was quite an event. She ran to answer it, praying it would be Ralph.

It was Jennifer. 'Hello, Anne. I thought I'd give you a call to let you know Trevor came home safe and sound.'

'Well, I am glad about that,' Anne replied, not really caring.

'I didn't want you to worry.'

Anne could not stop herself saying, 'Oh, I don't think I would have lost any sleep.'

Jennifer then explained the real reason for her call. 'Could I ask you not to mention my visit to Trevor?' She was not sure why she wanted to keep it a secret but her instincts told her it was best he didn't know.

'Don't worry. I'm quite sure I won't be seeing him. In any case your secret's safe with me.' Anne's heart began to race as she went on, 'Jennifer. Tell me more about your father.'

Jennifer laughed. 'I'm not quite sure why you want to

know. There isn't much to tell really. His name was David Freeman. I think he studied to be a vicar but ended up being a counsellor helping down and outs. Charity work. That sort of thing. Pots of money. Do you think you knew him then?'

Anne bit her lip. 'Yes. There's a possibility that I knew him and your mother.'

'Well, I shouldn't dwell on it if I were you. He's dead and she's mental,' said Jennifer callously. 'Must go. Trevor will be back soon. Don't forget, we never met.'

Chapter Thirty-One

Mary and Dorothy were busy in the garden when the phone rang. Removing her gardening shoes, Dorothy sped into the house.

It was Jennifer. 'Hello, Dorothy. I wondered if the time might be right for me to come and see my mother.'

Dorothy, still out of breath from running, replied, 'Jennifer. Your mother does not want to see you. Perhaps another time.' Looking up she saw Mary standing in the open doorway listening.

'Tell her to come tomorrow,' Mary said quietly.

Dorothy put her hand over the mouthpiece. 'Are you sure, dear? You don't have to do this you know.'

'Tell her to come tomorrow,' Mary repeated and went back into the garden.

'What about coming for a cup of tea about three tomorrow?' suggested Dorothy.

'Perfect. Don't worry, Dorothy. I promise not to upset her,' Jennifer replied sweetly.

What Dorothy didn't hear Jennifer say after she'd hung up was, 'I'll upset the mad bitch and get her locked up where she belongs.'

Trevor gave her a peck on the cheek. 'Well done, my darling.'

The following day Dorothy watched closely in case there was any sign of Mary becoming upset. She had already noticed she was wearing her hat indoors. This was something she had not done for some time.

Mary was in her room looking out of the window when they arrived. A taxi pulled into the drive. A tall good-looking young man got out first, followed closely by Jennifer. By the time she got downstairs they were already sitting in the lounge drinking tea with Dorothy.

As she entered the room Jennifer stood up. 'Hello, Mother. I'd like you to meet Trevor.'

Mary looked from one to the other but never said a word. Instead, she walked across the room and sat in the high-backed leather chair by the window.

Jennifer broke the awkward silence that had descended upon the room. 'Trevor was born in a place called Denton. I met him in Cambridge when I was at college.'

Mary just stared at Trevor. The fact that this young man looked so like the creature that had raped her caused her black shadows to surface, but somehow she managed to fight them off.

'How are you, Mrs Freeman?' he asked

Mary said nothing and continued staring at him. She was remembering the newspaper story about Anne and her brother Trevor.

Jennifer was becoming restless. She walked across to her mother. 'I came here to make amends, Mother. Please talk to me.'

Feeling uncomfortable with her daughter standing so close, Mary switched her gaze from Trevor to Jennifer and whispered, 'This is the man in the paper.'

'This is ridiculous!' Jennifer exclaimed. 'What are you talking about?'

Mary hung her head. 'He can't be your boyfriend.'

'Mother. This is Trevor Stacey and he is my boyfriend,' Jennifer shouted.

Mary could no longer keep the black shadows at bay. She closed her eyes saying, 'My father's a vicar you know.'

Jennifer spun round to face Trevor. 'What did I tell you, Trev? She's bloody bonkers.'

Dorothy, who had been sitting quietly, stood up. 'I think you should go now.'

'It will take forever to get a taxi. Can we borrow the car?' Jennifer asked impatiently.

Mary opened her eyes, gave a faint smile and nodded.

Jennifer and Trevor left the room, followed by Dorothy. Mary immediately went and sat in the chair by the open door.

She froze as she heard Trevor say, 'Dorothy, Jennifer's very worried about her mother. We both feel that she would be much better off in a home where she can get proper psychiatric treatment.'

'You said she was getting better,' Jennifer interrupted. 'Well, I don't think she is. My father was qualified to look after her, but you're not.'

Mary heard the anger in Dorothy's voice as she replied, 'How dare you even suggest putting her away. Your father never wanted that to happen. He did everything he could to keep your mother at home. And, in case you have forgotten, young lady, he entrusted me to look after her.'

'Well, my father's dead and I want my mother to go where she will be looked after properly,' Jennifer shouted. 'Trevor's going to seek legal advice. After all, I am her next of kin.' Lowering her voice she continued, 'If you want my advice, Dorothy, you should start thinking about your future, because you won't be living here much longer. Trevor has contacts in the legal profession who will get my mother put away and you evicted.'

Trevor opened the front door. 'Where are the keys to the car?'

Without caring whether they took the car or not, Dorothy snapped, 'In the garage hanging on a hook.'

She watched them walk away and slammed the door so hard it made Mary jump.

Dorothy was relieved that Mary seemed none the worse after Jennifer's visit. Over the next few days she chatted more than ever and there was an improvement in her appearance. Her hair was beginning to grow again and she had begun wearing a little make-up. No further mention had been made of Jennifer or her father. Dorothy decided to leave well alone.

Hunting for her purse she called out, 'I'm going shopping in a minute, Mary. Do you want to come?'

'No thank you,' Mary replied. 'You go. I'm going to read my gardening book.'

'I won't be long. I just need a few bits and my legs need the exercise.' Dorothy was quite comfortable at leaving Mary on her own now for short periods of time.

As soon as she heard the door slam, Mary went upstairs and stood outside David's room. It was several seconds before she gently turned the door handle and went inside. Dorothy cleaned the room once a week and had stored all his old paperwork in a tea chest. Everything else had been left just as it was. Mary's eyes darted to the bedpost where his cane used to hang. It was no longer there. She seemed to remember the police taking it away along with other instruments that he had used to inflict pain upon her.

Walking over to the enormous chest of drawers, she began to tremble. She stood still for a while, fighting against the black shadows that were trying to engulf her. Feeling calmer, she began searching the drawers one by one. Most were full of clothes. The last drawer contained a pile of pornographic magazines. Picking one off the top she opened it. The distasteful subject caused Mary to drop it to the floor.

By the side of the magazines lay several keys. Going through them she found one labelled 'London House'. Mary turned the key over in her hand several times before slipping it into her pocket. Picking the magazine up with her thumb and forefinger she carefully placed it back in the drawer with a look of disgust on her face.

She crept to the top of the stairs to see if there was any sign of Dorothy before entering Jennifer's room. Moving quickly to the dressing table she was pleased to see what she was looking for right under her nose. Picking up the hairbrush she left and went straight to her room.

By the time Dorothy returned, Mary was sitting in the lounge engrossed in her gardening book.

Chapter Thirty-Two

Amanda was home for the summer holidays and was not looking forward to spending six weeks in Ramsden with her parents. She had not seen or spoken to Jennifer since the scene at the party. To Amanda that had been the ultimate betrayal. Although she hated Jennifer for stealing Trevor, she had to admit that life would have been more fun if Jennifer was still around.

Making her way to the bus stop, she spotted Dorothy walking across the road with Jennifer's mother. Waiting for them to catch up she called out, 'Hello Dorothy.' Never knowing how to address Jennifer's mother, she just looked at Mary and smiled.

After exchanging niceties, Dorothy asked, 'Are you on holiday?'

'You could call it that,' replied Amanda. 'But I find Ramsden so boring after Cambridge.'

'You'll have to find yourself a nice young man,' Dorothy teased.

'What? So Jennifer can steal him from me again?' she replied miserably.

Dorothy laughed. 'I think your problems are over in that respect. Jennifer's got herself a boyfriend now and seems very much in love despite the fact that he's from a very dubious background. His father's that rapist from Denton who's been sent to prison. How long he'll stay with her is anybody's guess. I think once her money runs out he'll be off like a shot.'

Amanda cleared her throat. 'You know, Dorothy, I really fell for that guy and I was so sure he liked me. But, as usual, Jennifer did the dirty and was seeing him behind my back.' Raising her eyebrows she went on, 'Still, looks like I had a narrow escape. I might give her a call. Is she still at the same house in London?'

'Yes, she is. Why don't you do that? You might be able to make her see sense.'

'Problem is, if Trevor answers the phone, I'll probably fall in love with him all over again. You know what I'm like.' Amanda saw the bus coming round the bend. 'Must go. Here's my bus.'

Mary remained silent throughout the conversation but had listened attentively.

Dorothy opened the door to the paper shop. 'I cannot believe how much weight that girl's lost.'

'Was she Trevor's girlfriend before Jennifer?' Mary asked.

'It seems so. I wasn't really listening,' Dorothy lied, not wanting to pursue the conversation in case it upset Mary. She had no need to worry. Mary was far from upset. She had understood every word and had a satisfied expression on her face.

That night, Amanda decided to give Jennifer a ring. Trevor answered. Without saying who it was, she asked to speak to her former college friend.

'You could if she was here, but she's gone to see her solicitor. You can chat to me if you want,' he joked.

'No, it's alright. Perhaps you'll tell her I called.'

'I certainly will if you tell me who you are.'

'It's Amanda,' she said reluctantly.

'Amanda! Why on earth didn't you say so? Where are you?'

'I'm at home of course.'

'Listen. Why don't we get together? Are you doing anything tonight?'

'No. Not especially.'

'Well, we're going out for dinner and may end up boogying the night away. Want to come?'

'Trying not to sound too eager she replied, 'That sounds good.'

'Fantastic. We'll pick you up about seven.'

'Are you sure Jennifer will want to drive all the way out here?'

'If she doesn't, I'll come on my own.'

'See you at seven, then.'

'One more thing,' he said quickly. 'Don't let anyone know we're coming out to Ramsden.'

'Understood,' she replied, and hung up.

That evening the silver Jaguar pulled up outside Amanda's house. She was ready and waiting, looking gorgeous in a black tailored trouser suit that fitted her like a glove. The pink lipstick matched the pale pink satin blouse she wore with the collar turned over the lapels of her jacket.

Trevor was stunned when he saw her coming down the pathway. She must have been on a diet, he thought to himself. He was so busy looking that he forgot to get out to open the car door.

She jumped in beside him, delighted to find he was on his own.

'Let's get out of here, you beautiful creature,' he said, unable to take his eyes off her.

Trevor put his foot down hard on the accelerator and roared away. They sped along the country lanes chatting and laughing, and he soon began to realise what a fun girl she was compared to Jennifer, who had become so intense of late. They had been teasing each other for some time when Trevor put his hand on her thigh.

'I told you Jennifer wouldn't want to come,' Amanda said excitedly.

'Perhaps I didn't want her to come,' he replied.

The heat from his hand penetrated her thigh.

They went to a pub in Epping where he told her how fed up he was with Jennifer.

'I feel so trapped,' he moaned. 'She treats me like a pet puppy dog.'

On their way home they stopped in a country lane and indulged in some very heavy petting. Amanda called a halt when Trevor wanted to get in the back seat. After repairing her make-up, she put the top back on the lipstick and, without him seeing, carefully placed it under her seat.

'Can we meet up again?' he asked.

'I don't see why not,' she replied with a smile.

He grabbed her by the back of her hair. 'Amanda. Don't be a tease. I have to make love to you.'

'Next time,' she whispered. 'Now you had better drive me home.'

She went to bed feeling triumphant. At last she had got even.

Jennifer lay in bed becoming angrier by the minute. She expected Trevor to be at home when she returned from the solicitors. It was becoming more and more difficult to keep tabs on him since they had got the car. It was nearly midnight when he eventually staggered into the bedroom.

'Sorry darling,' he slurred, making out to be drunk. 'I met an old mate and had a few drinks too many so I had to get some kip in the car before I could see straight enough to drive home.' He fell backwards onto the bed and pretended to fall asleep.

The following morning after they got up, Jennifer was sulking.

'Are you going to keep this up all day?' he asked, 'or are you going to sit down and tell me what old Cornell had to say about our plan.'

'You'd have known if you'd come with me,' she snapped. 'Drinking yourself silly with a mate was obviously far more important.'

191

'Jennifer, I told you it would be more effective if you went on your own.'

He moved towards her and put his arms around her waist. She could feel his erection pushing against her. The passion she had felt while waiting for him last night had not subsided. Thrusting her pelvis forward she said, 'I'll tell you in bed.'

It took less than a minute for her to tell him that old Cornell said he would make some enquiries and get back to her. The rest of the morning they made passionate love until they were both exhausted.

Late that afternoon Jennifer went to the hairdressers. As soon as she was out of the door, Trevor phoned Amanda and made arrangements to meet her the following night. Once he had done that he phoned a hotel, close to the pub they had been to, and booked a double room.

The following morning Jennifer suggested they go on a champagne picnic. He readily agreed. He wanted to keep her sweet for when he told her he was going out with an old friend again that night.

'I'll drive,' she said. 'Apart from when I go to the hairdressers, I never get the chance.'

They lay on the riverbank for hours. Jennifer drank too much champagne and slept most of the afternoon. By four o'clock, it was beginning to get chilly and he woke her up.

'That was a lovely day,' she said as they packed their things into the boot of the car. 'We must do this more often. You'd better drive though. I've had too much to drink.' As she got into the passenger seat she fell backwards.

'What on earth have you been doing with this seat?' she shrieked.

Trevor walked swiftly round to the passenger side with the intention of adjusting it.

Jennifer was already looking under the seat for the catch. As he got there, she got out and gave him a resounding slap across the face.

'What's this?' she screamed, waving Amanda's lipstick in front of him.

Losing his temper, he slapped her back. 'Don't ever do that again,' he said angrily. Striding round to the driver's seat he shouted, 'Get in, you stupid bitch.'

After adjusting her seat, Jennifer got in and screamed and shouted at him continuously while driving home, repeatedly asking whose lipstick it was.

Trevor never uttered a word. With a face like thunder he drove home recklessly.

Once indoors Jennifer started again. 'Who have you been shagging in my car?' Running towards him she began lashing out. Trevor pushed her away and she fell onto the floor, catching her cheek on the corner of the bedpost. 'You pig,' she screamed, holding her hand to her bruised cheek.

Picking the car keys up from the bed he yelled, 'I'll be back when you've calmed down. There's a perfectly good explanation to all this but it's obvious you're in no mood to listen.'

She heard the front door slam and the car roar away.

He drove towards the pub where he was to meet Amanda. With a smirk on his face he realised things could not have worked out better. Trevor was getting tired of Jennifer's sexual appetite and he looked forward to having sex with someone who would put up some resistance.

Chapter Thirty-Three

Mary sat on her bed with a pile of old newspapers. Slowly and carefully, she cut out from various headlines enough letters to make up the words, ' HE IS SLEEPING WITH AMANDA'.

She had just finished sticking them onto a piece of paper when she heard Dorothy calling her. She quickly slid the finished letter under her mattress.

'Come along, Mary. Your lunch is getting cold.'

Over lunch Mary asked, 'Do you think I'm getting better?'

'I certainly do,' Dorothy replied.

'Do you think I'll be alright to go down to the village and get my magazine on my own this afternoon?'

'Would you like to?'

Mary nodded.

Trying hard to hide her concern, Dorothy suggested that Mary go on ahead and 15 minutes later she would walk down the hill to meet her. Washing the dishes, Dorothy thought what a breakthrough this was. At the same time, she still worried as to how Jennifer's wicked plans to have her mother put away were progressing.

Mary approached the post office with confidence and posted her letter. That was the important part done. She crossed the road to the paper shop and stood outside for a few minutes before plucking up courage to go in.

'Hello, Mary.' The kindly plump lady behind the counter greeted her. 'Have you come for your gardening magazine?'

Mary nodded.

'Nice to see you out on your own.' The plump lady smiled as she handed over the magazine. 'Where's Dorothy today. Is she alright?'

'Yes,' said Mary and quickly walked out of the shop.

Feeling pleased with herself, she began walking home and was almost there when she saw Dorothy coming towards her.

'Well done, Mary! Are you all right?' Dorothy grabbed hold of Mary's hand

Mary smiled. 'Yes, I'm fine.'

Dorothy beamed with happiness. Reaching the front door they looked at each other as they heard the phone ringing.

Mary watched the happiness disappear from Dorothy's face as she said, 'Hello, Jennifer.'

A long silence followed as she listened intently.

'Jennifer. Please don't do this. She's getting on so well,' Dorothy pleaded.

Mary watched as she banged the phone down.

Realising she would have to explain what Jennifer had said, Dorothy strode into the kitchen saying, 'She just wants to come and see you again and, after the last episode, I told her to stop bothering us.'

Mary could see by Dorothy's ashen face that Jennifer had upset her. She also had a very good idea as to what had really been said.

Chapter Thirty-Four

Jennifer's anger showed no sign of diminishing even though she had taken a shower and bathed her cheek. She was angry with herself for letting Trevor monopolise the car and even angrier for stupidly putting money into a joint account where he had complete access to it. Making up her mind to fix the money situation first thing in the morning, she slumped into a chair with a glass of champagne.

The frustration of not knowing where he had gone or what time he would be back was driving her crazy. Knowing she not only loved him but also couldn't live without him, she began to think that the only way forward would be to keep him short of money.

After finishing the bottle of champagne, she sat with her drunken thoughts until eleven o'clock. Staggering over to her handbag she took out the lipstick and wandered upstairs to the bedroom. Removing the top she tested the lipstick on the back of her hand. The only person she knew who wore pink lipstick was Amanda. 'Little dumpy Amanda,' she said out loud. She laughed at the thought of Trevor dating her. She knew he would aim his sights far higher than that. The alcohol was beginning to take effect and she collapsed onto the bed and fell asleep.

She finally woke the next morning at 8.30 and was annoyed that she had slept for so long. When she realised that Trevor had not been home all night, she flew into a rage.

Throwing the empty champagne glass across the room she screamed, 'I'll fix you, you bastard.'

While getting ready to go to the bank, she heard the mail drop through the letterbox. 'More bills that he's incurred,' she mumbled to herself. Looking business-like in a fawn suit, black blouse and with a very expensive black handbag, she made her way to the front door. Picking up the envelopes from the floor she discarded the junk mail. There were two others. The first, just as she thought, was a bill for gents clothing. The second was addressed to her. Checking the postmark she saw it was from Ramsden. Thinking it might be from Dorothy, she tore it open.

The colour drained from her face. It danced before her eyes. 'HE IS SLEEPING WITH AMANDA'. She stood rooted to the spot. 'This has to be some kind of joke,' she muttered out loud. By the time she had retraced her footsteps back to the kitchen, she was not so sure.

After drinking a cup of strong black coffee, she picked up her handbag and made her way to the bank. It started to rain, and by the time Jennifer got there she was completely drenched, something that certainly did nothing to calm her down.

'He's got my bloody car and I'm walking in the rain,' she thought to herself.

It took longer than she had anticipated to close the account. By the time she left the bank it was almost lunchtime. Not wanting to go home yet, she went and sat in a wine bar to think things through.

Opening her handbag she took out the anonymous letter and read it through again. If Trevor were having an affair with Amanda, why would she have sent it? The only other people she could think of in Ramsden who knew both Trevor and herself were Dorothy and her mother. She could not accept that Dorothy would ever do such a thing and knew that it could not possibly have been her mother. She was not even capable of holding a conversation, let alone doing something like this.

Ordering her third glass of wine, she tore the letter into pieces, put them into the ashtray and made up her mind to go and see Amanda. By the time she had consumed her fourth drink the rain had stopped and she made her way to the station.

Arriving at Ramsden station she wished she had not drunk so much. She really wanted a clear head for what lay ahead of her.

Her taxi pulled up outside Amanda's house just in time to see the silver Jaguar disappear round a bend. The taxi driver looked somewhat puzzled as she shouted out, 'You bastard!'

It was 3.30 and she knew Amanda's mother would be at work. Jennifer had to knock three times before Amanda answered the door in her white towelling dressing gown.

'What on earth do you want?' she asked.

Jennifer pushed her to one side and strode into the house.

'Oh! Why don't you come in?' said Amanda sarcastically.

'I thought you were my friend and I could trust you,' said Jennifer through gritted teeth.

'Oh yeah. Like I could trust you,' Amanda snapped back.

'You sent me a poison pen letter, you malicious cow.' Jennifer moved closer.

'I've no idea what you're talking about.' Amanda's voice betrayed her nervousness.

'Whose car just left here?' Jennifer screamed. 'I'll tell you whose it was. It was mine.'

Amanda stepped backwards. 'I think you should leave. You're drunk and I don't want anything to do with you.'

'No, I bet you don't,' said Jennifer quietly as she moved towards Amanda again. 'All you want is for my boyfriend to fuck you when you feel like it.'

Before Amanda could move, Jennifer's hands were around her throat. She tried to scream but only a quiet choking noise came from her lips. She fell to the floor as Jennifer released her. Thinking it was all over, Amanda tried to get to her feet. The resounding slap across her face sent her reeling back against an armchair.

Jennifer stood over her. 'I should kill you,' she snarled as she kicked Amanda hard in the stomach.

Amanda could feel the room spinning and thought she was going to faint when Jennifer pulled her up by the front of her dressing gown and banged her head on the wooden arm of the chair.

Between sobs and screams Amanda pleaded, 'No more, please! No more.'

'Give me one good reason why I shouldn't kill you,' Jennifer demanded, standing over her. 'Believe me, when I get home, I'm going to kill him, so why should I let a dirty little cow like you live?'

Amanda didn't reply. The look in Jennifer's eyes was terrifying.

Chapter Thirty-Five

After Jennifer's telephone call, Mary knew that she had to put her plan into action as soon as possible. In the event of both Trevor and Jennifer being at home, she would pretend the purpose of her visit was to make amends. The train journey would not worry her too much but she was apprehensive about finding her way from the station to the house. It had been about 15 years since she had lived there and as she tried to remember exactly, many things came into her mind. Bridget. What had happened to her? The small room she had been moved into when Jennifer was born. Quickly putting these things out of her mind for fear of the black shadows returning, she went downstairs to find Dorothy bending down at the front door putting out the milk bottles. She watched in horror as a gust of wind caught the front door and it slammed shut, pushing Dorothy forwards flat on her face.

Hurrying to her side, Mary whispered, 'Dorothy, are you alright?'

There was no answer. Dorothy lay face down under the porch.

With great difficulty, she turned her onto her back. Dorothy's face was pale and her eyes were closed. Mary began to panic. Without thinking, she rushed to the phone that had been installed in the hall and dialled 999. By the time the ambulance arrived, Dorothy had opened her eyes and was trying to get up. She caught sight of the ambulance backing up the drive.

'Did you call them?' she asked, looking up at Mary.

Proudly, Mary replied, 'Yes, I did. I couldn't wake you up. I was scared.'

Dorothy smiled and said, 'You clever girl.'

Despite her continuing protests, she reluctantly agreed to get into the ambulance.

'We only want to get you checked out in case of any complications,' explained the fresh-faced ambulance driver.

On arrival at hospital, Dorothy was transferred to a bed in a cubicle. Mary sat by her side looking anxious. A good-looking young doctor, accompanied by a nurse, soon arrived and asked Mary to wait outside.

'We're just going to take a look at your mother,' said the nurse sweetly.

Dorothy and Mary looked questioningly at each other, but neither corrected the nurse.

After what seemed an eternity, the curtain was pulled back and the young doctor came out. 'Well, there doesn't seem to be any harm done but we're going to keep your mother in overnight for observation.'

'Can I see her?' Mary asked.

'Of course. You can go in now, but we'll be moving her upstairs shortly for further tests.'

'You can probably come and pick her up tomorrow morning,' the nurse said kindly as she ushered Mary into the cubicle.

Dorothy was upset about having to stay overnight. 'You can't stay in the house alone, my dear,' she said impatiently.

'And why not?' asked Mary. 'I'm not a child.' A puzzled look came over her face as she tried to remember how old she was.

'What will you have for lunch today?' Dorothy asked.

'Bread and water,' Mary joked.

Dorothy looked at her in amazement. She was not used to Mary making jokes.

'I'm so worried about you being on your own, my dear I feel as though I am letting Mr Freeman down.'

Mary's face changed. She gave a curt, 'Goodbye, Dorothy. I'll be here bright and early in the morning.'

Dorothy wished she had not mentioned David Freeman.

While waiting for a taxi in the hospital reception, it occurred to Mary that this would be an ideal time to put her plan into action.

Not because she was hungry, but almost out of loyalty to Dorothy, Mary made herself a ham sandwich for lunch.

Up in Jennifer's room she searched for a suitable coat. Wondering why she had left so much of her stuff here, Mary pulled a long black raincoat with large pockets out of the wardrobe. Returning to her own bedroom she tried it on. It was far too long but apart from that, it was perfect. Into the pockets she stuffed two pair of plastic gloves, an envelope containing the hair she had removed from Jennifer's hairbrush, two plastic bags with rubber bands and, finally, the keys to the house where Jennifer lived in London.

Just as she was about to leave the telephone rang. Mary stared at it for a long time before gingerly picking it up. The relief showed on her face as she heard Dorothy say, 'Hello dear. Just checking to see if you're alright.'

'I'm fine,' Mary replied. 'Now, will you stop worrying? I'll see you tomorrow.'

Deciding to walk to the station, she set off for London. During the train journey she studied an A–Z street map. Not wanting to leave any evidence of her visit to the house, she made up her mind to get a taxi to Madame Tussauds. Then, with the help of her map, she could walk to Jennifer's.

It was 2.30 when she arrived at Kings Cross station. This was the moment she had been dreading. There were people everywhere. She found the noise deafening. Not having the slightest idea as to where she would find a taxi, Mary walked along the platform to the barrier. The overweight red-cheeked ticket inspector gave her a smile as she walked through.

'You're looking puzzled,' he said.

She turned to him. 'I need a taxi.'

He pointed to a sign with an arrow and in large letters 'Taxis'. She thanked him and began following the signs.

It took her 30 minutes to walk from Madame Tassauds to the top of the mews. Looking down she could see the silver Jaguar parked outside the house. Her heart began to pound. There was no one about as she made her way quickly down to the house.

Slowly and quietly she put the key in the lock. The house was silent. Bending down, she quickly covered her shoes with the plastic bags and put the rubber bands round the top to stop them from slipping. Before moving any further she put on a pair of plastic gloves.

After creeping into the lounge and picking up a heavy brass candlestick she stood still and listened. There was not a sound.

Arriving at the top of the stairs, she saw the door of what used to be David's room was open. Her heart skipped a beat as she saw Trevor lying on his back in a deep sleep. She quickly and quietly checked the other bedrooms. There was no sign of Jennifer. For one moment she tried to remember how she had come to live in this house in the first place. This caused the black shadows to start. Fighting them off she knew there was no time to lose. She rushed in and she smashed the candlestick down on Trevor's face as hard as she could. With all the strength she could muster, Mary continued smashing him about the face and head. Blood spurted everywhere. Trevor made a gurgling sound as blood bubbled from his mouth.

She stood back and surveyed the room. There were splashes of blood on the walls and the cream satin bedspread was turning scarlet. What was left of Trevor's face resembled a piece of raw meat.

Satisfied that part one was now complete, she took the envelope containing the hair from her pocket. This was far more difficult than she had expected, as the gloves, covered in Trevor's blood, were both sticky and slippery. Finally, she somehow managed to place a few strands of Jennifer's hair into each of Trevor's hands.

Knowing it was unnecessary, she picked up a blood-sodden pillow and proceeded to smother him.

'Your father raped me. Your father raped me,' she panted. 'Now you can't put me away in a home.'

She began to tremble and the black shadows started to emerge. She so wanted to hide behind them, but knew she had to keep going. Picking up the candlestick she hurried downstairs. Removing the bloodstained raincoat, she went into the laundry room, opened the washing machine door and threw it inside.

Finally, Mary removed the plastic bags from her feet and placed the blood-stained candlestick on the floor just inside the front door.

Chapter Thirty-Six

Mrs Saunders returned from work at 4.30. Nothing could have prepared her for the horrendous scene she encountered. Her daughter was lying whimpering on the floor. Both eyes were blackened, her lip was split and blood had trickled on to her dressing gown. There was a small bald patch where some of her hair had been yanked out.

She ran to Amanda's side. 'Oh my God! Whatever's happened?'

Through swollen lips Amanda mumbled, 'My chest, Mum. Get help.'

Almost tripping over herself, Amanda's mother ran to the phone and dialled the emergency services. By the time the ambulance arrived, Amanda had lost consciousness.

Mrs Saunders, accompanied by a policewoman, travelled with her daughter in the ambulance. Drifting in and out of consciousness, Amanda explained, as best she could, what had happened.

The policewoman immediately radioed for assistance. 'As fast as you can. It sounds as if she's now on her way to attack a Trevor Stacey.'

Arriving in casualty, both Mrs Saunders and the policewoman were asked to wait in an ante-room while Amanda was wheeled into a cubicle and the curtains drawn.

While they waited, the policewoman went outside and radioed back to headquarters. After a few minutes she returned and asked Amanda's mother if she knew the registration number of Trevor Stacey's car. Mrs Saunders shook her head and dabbed her eyes with a well-sodden handkerchief.

'Do you know the colour or make?'

'No,' replied Amanda's mother as she burst into a flood of tears.

'No joy,' the policewoman reported back.

She walked over to the sobbing woman and put her arm around her shoulders. 'I'll get you a cup of tea.'

It was about an hour before a stout, stony-faced nurse came into the room. 'You can see your daughter now,' she said, looking at Amanda's mother.

The policewoman jumped to her feet, and immediately took out her notebook. 'Not you. Just her mother,' said the nurse, enjoying the control she had over the situation.

'It's very important that I talk to her as soon as possible,' the policewoman pleaded.

'I'll let you know when it's possible.' The nurse gave an artificial smile.

The doctor was at Amanda's bedside as her mother entered. 'Initial examinations show that, apart from superficial wounds, your daughter has a couple of cracked ribs. We'll be keeping her here until we have the results of her x-rays,' he said in a monotone voice.

'Is she going to be alright?' Mrs Saunders asked, holding her daughter's hand tightly.

'I am sure she is,' replied the doctor. He pulled back the curtains and left.

Thirty minutes later the nurse came and asked Amanda if she felt well enough to be questioned by the police. She nodded her agreement.

Going back into the ante-room the nurse looked at the policewoman and said rather officiously, 'You can see her now. Only for a few minutes mind. She's in a lot of pain and needs to sleep.'

It was difficult to understand much of what Amanda was saying, her lips were so swollen, but the policewoman managed to get the gist of what had taken place.

The curtains were suddenly pulled back and Amanda's father, accompanied by the nurse, walked in. This gave the policewoman her cue to leave and she dutifully said goodbye to Amanda and her parents. She left without even acknowledging the nurse.

Mr Saunders was visibly shocked by the appearance of his daughter.

'My God!' he exclaimed. 'What's happened to you?'

His wife related what had happened, until a pretty young nurse with short blonde hair interrupted. 'I'm sorry. I have to ask you to leave now. I'm going to take your daughter up to the ward. She needs some rest.'

After handing them a card detailing visiting times, she pulled back the curtains and ushered them out.

During the train journey back to London, Jennifer felt smug and pleased with herself. She had not planned to be so rough with Amanda, but was glad that she had been. One thing was certain. It would be a long time before Amanda dared go near Trevor again.

Her head was beginning to ache. She was hungry, having only had four glasses of wine all day. Jennifer felt sure Trevor would be at home when she arrived. She planned to take him out for a romantic dinner and not mention anything about Amanda. A complete new start was the way forward, she told herself.

It took longer than usual to get a taxi at Kings Cross as the rush hour was beginning. This irritated her but, when she arrived at the top of the mews and saw the Jaguar outside, she felt relieved.

Turning the key in the lock she went in and was curious as to what the candlestick was doing standing on the floor of the hall. Picking it up she found it was wet and sticky. She placed it on the bottom stair while she hung her jacket on the clothes stand. She called out to Trevor, but there was no answer.

After checking the kitchen and lounge, she ventured upstairs. The shock of what she saw turned her legs to jelly and she fainted. As she passed into oblivion, the doorbell rang.

Jennifer did not hear the bell ringing continuously; neither did she hear the thumping on the door. Finally, two policemen forced their way in while another two stayed outside examining the Jaguar. Just as they reached the top of the stairs, Jennifer regained consciousness.

The sight of what was left of Trevor's face caused one policeman to turn away as he fought off the need to be sick.

'Help him,' Jennifer screamed.

'I think it's too late for that, my dear,' the policeman said as he helped her to her feet.

The sound of sirens from police cars and ambulances speeding down the mews bought home to Jennifer the horror of the situation and she began to cry. She was helped downstairs to the kitchen where a policewoman made her a cup of strong tea.

Upstairs in the bedroom Detective Inspector Russell and Detective Sergeant Crossman watched as photographs of the body were taken from various angles.

The mews had been cordoned off and the press had been kept at bay.

Crossman carefully picked up the heavy candlestick and placed it in a large polythene bag. The bloodstained pillow was next. Both items were sent off for forensic tests.

'Over here, Inspector!' a man in white overalls called out. With a pencil he lifted some strands of hair from Trevor's hands.

After whispering to each other the two detectives left the room. 'Be back in a minute, Jack,' Russell called out to the Police pathologist who was still examining the body.

Once outside the door he spoke to his colleague. 'Let's take a good look around. You take upstairs and I'll do the down.'

As he approached the kitchen he heard Jennifer refuse to go in the ambulance. 'I'm alright. I don't need to go to hospital.'

'Is there anyone I can contact for you?' the policewoman asked.

At that point Detective Inspector Russell entered the kitchen. 'Get her out of here,' he said quietly out of the corner of his mouth.

Two ambulance men arrived and, despite Jennifer's protests, began helping her out to the ambulance.

As they reached the front door, Russell called out, 'Just a minute.' Carrying the bloodstained raincoat, he walked slowly towards Jennifer. 'Is this your coat?'

She looked at it and replied, 'I think so … I'm not sure.'

'What was it doing in the washing machine?'

'How should I know? Jennifer replied.

Turning to the policewoman, Russell said, 'Okay, you can take her off to hospital now.' Lowering his voice, he continued, 'I want you to stay with her. Don't let her out of your sight until you hear from me, and no visitors.'

'Sir,' she replied, following Jennifer to the ambulance.

Back upstairs, Russell asked, 'What do you think, Jack?'

'Difficult to say at this stage. I don't think he's been dead for more than thirty, maybe forty-five minutes. He doesn't appear to have put up much of a struggle. Made an attempt to grab at the attacker's hair. Can't say for sure yet whether the candlestick was the weapon or not, but it looks pretty obvious.' He grinned. 'Nasty one for you, Inspector.'

'Thanks a million,' Russell replied.

Chapter Thirty-Seven

That same evening Anne was drawing the living room curtains. With a heavy heart she gazed at the 'For Sale' sign outside her house. There had been no news from Ralph and she now accepted that that part of her life was over. Feeling extremely tired after house-hunting, she planned on having a nice fragrant bath followed by an early night with a book.

She had not entirely given up on trying to confirm whether Jennifer's mother was indeed her dear friend, but it was proving difficult without talking to Trevor or Jennifer, and this she was trying to avoid.

Anne was about to go upstairs when the doorbell rang. Looking at her watch she frowned. It was almost 9.30.

Since Trevor had gone, she had installed a chain on the door. Checking it was secure, she opened the door as far as it would go.

Detective Sergeant Crossman stood in the porch accompanied by a policewoman. After producing an identification card he said, 'Sorry to trouble you, ma'am, but are you Anne Stacey?'

'Yes, I am,' she replied letting the chain off in order to open the door wider.

'May we come inside for a moment?'

'Of course. Whatever's the matter?' she asked quizzically.

Guessing this would be something that Trevor had been up to, she motioned them to sit down.

'I'm afraid we have some bad news for you, Miss Stacey,' Crossman began.

'What's my brother been up to now?' she interrupted.

'Is your brother a Trevor Stacey?' the policewoman asked nervously.

'That's right,' Anne replied.

'I'm sorry, Miss Stacey. We have to inform you that your brother is dead.' Crossman looked at the floor as he delivered the tragic news.

Anne went white. 'What! How?'

'At this stage we're treating it as a murder investigation.' Crossman still did not look up. He was experienced at delivering this sort of news, but never found it easy.

'There must be some … mm … mm … there must be some mistake,' Anne stammered. She could tell by the sympathetic look on the policewoman's face that this was no mistake.

'Can Margaret here make you a cup of tea?' Crossman asked.

'No, thank you. I mean, yes … Oh! I don't know.' Anne buried her face in her hands. She felt sick. Trevor, the dear little boy she had loved and cared for, dead. She shook her head.

'This can't be true,' she said removing her hands from her face.

'Miss Stacey, do you mind if I ask you some questions?' asked Crossman. Realising Anne was still in trauma, he quickly added, 'After you've had a strong cup of tea.'

She stared at him. 'How do you know it's Trevor?' she asked, her voice trembling.

'We found his girlfriend, Jennifer Freeman, with him. She confirmed that it was Trevor Stacey,' he replied.

'Jennifer was with him? Where? How did it happen?'

At this point the policewoman came into the room with a steaming hot cup of tea and placed it on the table in front of

Anne. Contrary to what he had said, Crossman began his questioning before she had even taken her first sip.

'When did you last see your brother? What do you know about Jennifer Freeman?'

Anne answered as best she could, but she could see the detective becoming confused as she began relaying the story of how she thought Jennifer was the daughter of her childhood friend.

'Do you see her mother often?' he asked.

'No, I haven't seen her for twenty years,' Anne replied.

'Miss Stacy. I'm afraid I have to ask you this. Where were you between the hours of two thirty and five o'clock today?'

Anne was stunned. 'What! You surely don't think that I had anything to do with this.'

'I'm afraid everyone is a suspect at the moment,' he replied curtly.

The policewoman winced, thinking that Crossman was being rough on Anne.

'I've been house-hunting in London most of the day. I got back about four, I think.' She leaned forward to sip her tea. 'Detective Crossman. Where was my brother found?'

He looked her full in the face as he replied, 'At Jennifer Freeman's house in London.'

'Where's Jennifer now?'

'She's been taken to hospital suffering from shock,' the policewoman interjected. 'Don't worry, she's got an officer with her. Now, is there anyone you would like me to call? You don't want to be on your own tonight.'

Not for the first time in her life, Anne realised there was no one. Not wanting to admit this she replied, 'No, don't worry. I'll be alright.'

Crossman brought them back to the real reason they were there. 'Miss Stacey. Did you go house-hunting with the help of an estate agent?'

'Yes. Of course I did,' she replied.

212

'Then you won't mind giving me their name and address?'

'No, I don't mind at all,' she said nervously.

'Were you alone at any point during the times I mentioned?'

'Yes, of course. I was alone when I travelled to London and back.' Her voice had changed from sounding nervous to being indignant. 'I think I've answered enough of your questions for now Detective Sergeant. I must get ready to go and see Jennifer.'

'I'm afraid that won't be possible,' he said as he stood up. 'We have to interview Miss Freeman before she can see anyone.'

'Oh my God! That poor girl. Don't tell me you suspect her.'

'Like I said, Miss Stacey. Everyone's a suspect at the moment.'

'Are you sure you're going to be alright by yourself?' the policewoman asked kindly.

'Perfectly,' Anne replied. 'I really do need to be alone now, if you don't mind.'

As they were leaving, Crossman said, 'I see you're selling up. Don't leave the area without letting us know, Miss Stacey.'

Chapter Thirty-Eight

The following morning Mary woke early after having had a good night's sleep, helped by the black shadows that had engulfed her the previous evening. She had no difficulty putting her actions of the day before completely out of her mind.

Taking care to make herself look nice, she put on a cream cotton dress that she had never worn before. Looking at her reflection in the mirror, she decided to cover her hair with a straw hat.

Twice she attempted to phone for a taxi, but got nervous and hung up. The third time she succeeded. Feeling proud of herself and with a smile on her face, she set off to collect Dorothy.

'Please wait,' she told the taxi driver as they arrived at the hospital.

'How long will you be, love?' the driver asked.

Mary did not answer. She quickly got out of the cab and went up the steps to the hospital. The fact that she had not paid him left the driver with no option but to wait.

Dorothy was sitting by her bed, fully dressed, with an anxious look on her face. As soon as she spotted Mary walking towards her through the ward, her face lit up.

'Hello my dear,' she said with a big smile. 'Am I glad to see you.'

'How are you?' Mary asked.

'I'm fine,' replied Dorothy. 'I told you I would be, didn't I?' At that point, Sister arrived.

'Well, you can take her home now. You must let us know if she gets any headaches or dizziness,' she said kindly.

Mary nodded.

Back home, Dorothy thought she noticed a change in Mary. There was a look of contentment and a smile on her face for most of the morning.

'Have you had any breakfast?' Dorothy asked.

'No,' Mary replied. 'I'm going to make us boiled eggs with toast while you go and get into bed.'

Dorothy laughed. 'I'll do no such thing. There's nothing wrong with me. I feel fine.' Popping some bread in the toaster she went on, 'I had my breakfast at six this morning but I'll make you some.'

There was a loud knock on the door. Dorothy looked at her watch. It was a quarter past nine. Looking up she said, 'Who on earth can that be at this time in the morning?'

Mary shrugged her shoulders.

WPC Margaret Holmes, who stood on the doorstep beside Detective Inspector Russell, was hoping he would do a better job than Crossman had done the previous night with Anne Stacey. Dorothy opened the door and Detective Inspector Russell made the introductions as they both produced their identification cards.

Dorothy was terrified. Had Jennifer carried out her threat? Were the police here to take Mary away?

'Are you Dorothy Maitland?' Russell asked.

Dorothy nodded.

'May we come in and talk to you for a minute?' WPC Holmes asked gently.

Without saying a word, Dorothy stood back to let them enter. After ushering them into the lounge, she closed the door.

'I understand you're the live-in housekeeper, cum carer of Mary Freeman,' Russell said as he sat down on the chester-field.

'That's right.'

'I also understand that she is of a very nervous disposition.'

'Yes, that's true. But she's getting better all the time. If you take her away and put her in a home, it will break her heart and mine. I don't know why her daughter's doing this. I'm quite capable of looking after her and it was her father's dying wish that I should stay and take care of her.'

'Hold on there, Dorothy. We haven't come here to put Mrs Freeman into a home.'

'I'm afraid we have some bad news regarding Jennifer Freeman's boyfriend. He was found dead last night and we have reason to believe he was murdered.'

Dorothy gasped, 'Murdered!'

Russell continued. 'Now I understand you've lived with the Freemans for many years?'

Ignoring the question, Dorothy asked, 'Does Jennifer know?'

'Yes, she does. But you don't need to worry about her. She's being taken care of. At some stage I'll need to interview her mother. Do you think she's up to it?'

'Oh dear me,' Dorothy moaned. 'When will that poor woman's troubles end? You know, Inspector, I can probably tell you more about Jennifer than Mary can.'

He smiled at Dorothy. 'That'll be very helpful, but I'm afraid I will still need to talk to Mrs Freeman at some stage. It might help if you sat with her while we ask her a few questions.'

Dorothy nodded.

For the next 30 minutes she answered all their questions and told them everything she knew about Jennifer, without holding anything back.

'You've been very helpful, Dorothy. Just one more question before you fetch Mary. Is she prone to any violent outbursts? You know, does she ever lose her temper?'

Dorothy gave a quiet nervous laugh before replying,

'Never. There were times when I wished she would, then perhaps she wouldn't have been treated so cruelly by her daughter.'

The door suddenly opened and Mary came in. Dorothy wondered whether she had been listening outside. Standing very still she looked from the policewoman to Detective Inspector Russell. She had taken off her hat and the bald patches were still visible.

After Dorothy had made the introductions, Russell asked Mary to come and sit next to him. She walked straight past and went and sat on the chair near the window.

'Do you know Trevor Stacey?' Russell asked.

Mary shook her head.

Dorothy was about to remind Mary who he was, when Russell put his hand up to silence her.

'Have you ever seen him, Mary?' he asked.

Mary nodded. 'I've seen him, but I don't know him.'

'Do you like him?' The inspector was being as gentle as he could.

'No,' Mary replied. 'His father raped me.'

'Mary!' Dorothy interrupted. 'That's not true.' Turning to the Inspector she said, 'Mary doesn't know Trevor's father. I told you he's in prison for rape, but Mary has never met him.'

Russell was uncomfortable taking the interview any further.

'One last question, Mary,' he said. 'Where did you go while Dorothy was in hospital yesterday?'

Mary thought for a minute. 'Came home in a taxi and went into the garden.'

Russell took a deep breath. 'After that, did you go out at all? You know, shopping or anything like that.'

Mary shook her head.

As they were leaving, the policewoman asked, 'What happened to your hair Mary?'

Touching her hair Mary replied, 'She did it.'

217

'Who is she?'

'Jennifer,' Mary replied.

Dorothy gasped. She had always thought that Mary had ruined her own hair.

Chapter Thirty-Nine

With the help of medication, Jennifer slept until six the next morning. A timid young nurse woke her, putting a cup of tea on her bedside locker. Having heard the news on the radio, she was aware that this woman was somehow connected with a dreadful murder. Jennifer opened her eyes and stared at the nurse who immediately, in accordance with her instructions, ran off to fetch Sister.

It took a little while for Jennifer to realise where she was. Sitting up she looked around the small room before the horror of the night before hit her. She fought back the tears that came into her eyes at the thought of life without Trevor.

The door opened and Sister walked in. 'Good morning, Jennifer,' she said cheerfully.

'Where are my clothes? I need a telephone,' Jennifer replied rudely.

Ignoring her request, Sister plumped up her pillows. 'I want you to drink your tea. A policewoman is waiting outside to talk to you.'

'I want my clothes. I'm getting out of here. You can tell her that I don't want to talk to anyone.'

At that moment the policewoman came in. 'Hello, Jennifer. I'm WPC Simmons.'

'I don't care who you are. You can get the fuck out of here. I'm going home,' Jennifer replied.

Looking shocked at this outburst the Sister said, 'Now there's no point in upsetting yourself. Why don't you settle down and answer a few questions for the lady and then you can go home.'

After much more protesting and bad language, Jennifer agreed.

'Did you visit your friend Amanda yesterday?' the policewoman began.

'No!' replied Jennifer.

'Did Trevor visit Amanda yesterday?'

'I don't know. Why should he?'

'Where did you go yesterday?' the policewoman continued.

'I was at home in the morning and went to the bank in the afternoon. When I came home I found Trevor lying there …' She began to cry and scream at the policewoman. 'Why aren't you out looking for his killer instead of asking me these stupid questions?'

At this point the door opened and Detective Sergeant Crossman walked in. The WPC gulped before introducing him. Sergeant Crossman had a reputation for being brutal with his questioning.

He went straight for the jugular. 'Miss Freeman. Did you ever purchase a black raincoat from Harrods?'

'I don't know. I've bought lots of clothes from Harrods.'

'Did you take the candlestick from the lounge up to the bedroom?'

'Yes, I did. It was on the floor downstairs.'

'Why didn't you open the door for the police yesterday?' he asked.

'Because I bloody fainted, that's why,' she shouted. 'Now can I have my bloody clothes?'

'You certainly can,' Crossman replied. 'Take your time getting dressed. We'll be waiting outside. I'd like you to accompany us to the station.'

Jennifer realised she was being treated as a suspect.

'What for?' she screamed. 'Do you think I killed Trevor?'

Before Crossman could answer, she continued, 'I'm not coming to your bloody police station with you or anyone else. You can piss off. Rest assured, you'll be hearing from my solicitor.'

Crossman shrugged his shoulders and said nonchalantly, 'You can do it either way. Come with us willingly to help us with our enquiries or I can arrest you and take you by force. The choice is yours.'

Jennifer was shocked. The seriousness of the situation was beginning to scare her.

Knowing that Crossman would carry out his threat without giving Jennifer time to think, the policewoman said, 'You do want us to find Trevor's killer, don't you? It would be much better if you came voluntarily.'

Crossman, who always got irritated when WPCs intervened, left the room saying, 'You're wasting time, Miss Freeman.' Glancing at the WPC, he said, 'I'll be in the car.'

'How long is this going to take?' Jennifer asked the policewoman angrily.

'I'm not sure,' she replied. 'The quicker we get you there the quicker it will be over. Come along now. Detective Crossman doesn't like to be kept waiting.'

Sister came in with some clothes and laid them on the bed.

'This had better not take long,' Jennifer mumbled. She hesitated as she went to pick up her clothes. 'These aren't mine,' she snapped.

'I know,' replied the WPC. 'They belong to the hospital. We can return them later.'

'Where are my own clothes?' Jennifer screamed.

'Detective Crossman sent them off to forensic for tests. There's nothing to worry about. This is just normal routine,' replied the WPC, trying to console her.

Jennifer got dressed in the cheap navy blue skirt and T-shirt. Drawing the line at wearing a pair of old-fashioned slippers, she walked out to the car in her bare feet.

221

Arriving at the police station, she was ushered into an interview room. WPC Simmons sat with her.

Upstairs in CID, Detective Inspector Russell sat with his feet up on his desk. 'OK, Crossman,' he said. 'What have we got?'

'Harrods confirmed the raincoat was purchased with her credit card. Albeit some months ago.'

'Confirmation that she had not fainted when Uniform arrived at the scene.'

'Confirmation from the bank that she was there that morning to close the joint bank account she had with Trevor Stacey. Not in the afternoon, as she claims.'

'Confirmation that no one else's footprints were found at the scene apart from Jennifer Freeman's and the victim's.'

'Confirmation from a cabbie that he took a girl matching Jennifer Freeman's description to Amanda Saunders's house.

'Confirmation that there was no break-in other than when Uniform bashed the door in.'

'I can also confirm that she is a real looker with long brown hair, big brown eyes and legs up to her armpits,' said Crossman finally, with a glint in his eye.

Ignoring what he thought a tasteless comment, Russell asked, 'Fingerprints?'

'Just a matter of time,' Crossman replied. 'We've only just brought her in. I don't think we'll get a match on the hair found in Stacey's hands until late this afternoon.'

'OK. Make the arrest and hold her. Check back with me when you get Forensics' results.' Russell removed his feet from the desk.

'Will do,' Crossman replied, and left the office.

Something was bothering Russell as he sat with his elbows on the desk, deep in thought. Trevor Stacey was the son of the rapist who was now behind bars. Could there be a connection here? He remembered that it had taken place in Denton and that his old mate, Detective Inspector John

222

Harris, had handled the case. If Jennifer had been a victim of that animal and not said anything, she could be seeking revenge through his son. He picked up the phone and asked his secretary to get him Denton Police Station.

'You just caught me, Russell. I was just going out. What can I do for you? I'm sure you haven't called to enquire after my health,' Harris said jokingly.

'No, you're right. I need a favour. If I drive down there now can you spare me an hour? I want to pick your brains about the Denton rape case.'

'Sure,' Harris replied. ' I was just going to the pub for lunch. You can buy me a beer. Be good to see you, mate. Get here as quickly as you can.'

Russell grabbed his jacket and left for Denton.

Chapter Forty

Anne sat reading the gory details of her brother's murder in the newspaper. She couldn't cry. She had shed so many tears, blaming herself for failing to do a proper job of bringing him up. She remembered how hateful he had been to dear Mrs Davidson. That should have been the signal that things were not right.

As she read on, it mentioned Jennifer, his girlfriend. Brought up by a nanny in Ramsden, it said. Anne stared at the print before her. Ramsden. That wasn't very far away.

She put the paper down and tried to think what to do. Should she go and see Jennifer? The poor girl must be distraught. She wondered whether she had gone home to her mother. Anne picked up the phone to see if she was at home in London.

A man's voice answered and told her that Jennifer was not there.

'Do you know where she is?' Anne questioned.

'Sorry, ma'am. I can't say,' he replied.

Anne went back to the newspaper and began reading more details of the murder.

Who could have done such a terrible thing? He must have been mixing with some real thugs, she thought to herself.

Finding it increasingly difficult doing nothing, Anne decided to visit the local police station believing they might be able to help with finding the address of Jennifer's mother.

She thought that even if she turned out not to be her old friend it was her duty to visit Jennifer anyway, assuming that was where she was.

She put on her jacket, glanced at herself in the mirror and made her way out to the car.

Detective Inspector Russell pulled up outside Denton Police Station at the same time as Anne. He sat in his car and watched her walk into the station. He couldn't help but notice that this girl had the same long, thick brown hair as Jennifer Freeman.

Once inside, he heard Anne ask the desk sergeant if he could help her find the address of a Mrs Freeman who lived in Ramsden. 'I think her name's Mary, and she has a daughter, Jennifer.'

Russell's ears pricked up. Instead of going upstairs to John Harris's office, he hung around the Reception.

The desk sergeant disappeared. 'Someone will be out to see you shortly,' he said on his return.

Russell ran up the stairs two at a time and barged into John Harris's office. 'There's a girl in your reception trying to find the address of the Freemans. Do you have a problem with me handling it?'

Harris looked surprised and replied, 'I don't, but Uniform might.'

'Fix it for me, John. I'll explain afterwards,' Russell said breathlessly.

'OK,' Harris replied, picking up the telephone. 'And hurry up if you're going to buy me that beer.'

Russell ran down the first two flights, took a deep breath and walked slowly down the remaining stairs. He walked across to Anne. 'I understand you're looking for the address of a Mrs Freeman.'

'That's right,' replied Anne.

'Do you mind if I ask why?'

At that moment John Harris walked downstairs and

whispered, 'My office is free if you need it. See you at the White Horse.'

Russell turned back to Anne, 'Sorry about that. Come this way.'

She followed him up the stairs to Harris's office. Deliberately not sitting behind the desk, Russell sat down and motioned Anne to sit opposite.

'Where were we? Now, you want to find the address of a Mrs Freeman.'

'Is there a problem?' she asked.

'No, not really,' he replied. ' But I need to have your name and address first.'

'Of course. I'm Anne Stacey and I live at number seven, School Road, Denton. Mrs Freeman's daughter, Jennifer, is … I mean was, my brother's girlfriend. Due to circumstances that you probably already know about, I'm quite anxious to find her.'

'I see,' he replied, his eyes widening. 'You're Trevor Stacey's sister.'

'Yes. Well, half-sister,' she replied. 'You see, I happen to think that Jennifer's mother is a childhood friend of mine who I haven't seen for nearly twenty years.'

'Why haven't you seen her?'

'I explained all this to a Detective Sergeant Crossman yesterday,' she replied.

'Would you mind explaining it again to me?'

Anne relayed the story in detail of how Mary had disappeared after her marriage to David Freeman.

Russell cleared his throat. 'Anne, do you mind if I ask you a very personal question?'

She shook her head.

'Is Jennifer Freeman your daughter?'

'Of course not. Whatever makes you think that?' She was obviously shocked at the suggestion.

'Oh, I just thought she looked remarkably like you,' he said smiling.

'Detective Inspector. For your information, I have never had a child and I'm not likely to. My looks, especially my hair, were unfortunately inherited from my father, John Stacey the rapist, who is now in prison.'

What Russell had wanted to ask, but chose not to, was whether Jennifer was the result of Anne being raped by her father.

He got up from his chair. 'I've got to meet someone Anne. I'll be about an hour then I'd be happy to pick you up and take you to the Freeman's house.

'That's very kind of you, but you don't have to do that. If you could just give me the address I'm sure I can find it.

'I'd like to,' he replied. ' I need to ask the housekeeper some questions anyway.'

Dorothy and Mary were having lunch when Detective Inspector Russell, accompanied by Anne, knocked loudly on the door. Hoping it was not the police again, Dorothy pushed her chair back from the table. Mary had been in surprising good humour all morning and she didn't want her upset.

After she had opened the door, the Inspector made the introductions and she ushered them into the lounge and returned to the kitchen.

'I've got some visitors, Mary. I won't be long. Perhaps you could carry on weeding the patch behind the tree when you have finished your lunch,' Dorothy said with a smile.

Mary nodded.

Returning to the lounge, Dorothy said, 'Miss Stacey. Please accept my sincere condolences. What happened to your brother is just too awful for words.'

Anne pushed her hair back from her face and thanked her. Dorothy could not help noticing the similarities between Jennifer and Trevor's sister.

'Now, how can I help, Inspector?'

Playing a hunch, Russell began by asking, 'Do you think you could find Jennifer's birth certificate for me?'

Dorothy looked puzzled. 'I wouldn't know where to look. I've never even seen it.'

'That's a pity. You see, it's very odd, Somerset House claim to have no record of a Jennifer Freeman.'

'Well, you know she was born and presumably you've seen her,' Dorothy replied jokingly. 'Why do you need her birth certificate?'

'Just routine,' he replied.

'I suppose I could look in Mr Freeman's old room. If it's anywhere that's where it will be,' Dorothy suggested.

'Thank you. That would be most helpful.'

Russell shifted in his chair. 'I've read Detective Sergeant Crossman's report and I'm under the impression that neither you or her mother got on too well with Jennifer.'

Dorothy looked embarrassed. 'She was a very difficult girl who inflicted a lot of misery on everyone. Her mother is not a well woman. I told Detective Crossman that she suffers from a very nervous disposition and, quite often, goes into a trance and doesn't speak to anyone. I have to say that a lot of her problems, not all, were brought about by Jennifer's behaviour.'

'Was Mary Freeman ill when you arrived to take care of Jennifer?' he asked.

'Yes. She was worse then. According to Mr Freeman it all started after she gave birth. He was a kind man. Did everything he could for her. It was my job to look after both of them,' Dorothy replied.

Russell frowned. He seemed to remember hearing that David Freeman was a pervert who had probably caused his own death.

'Were they happily married?'

'When I arrived, Mary had suffered several nervous breakdowns, so I don't think you could call it a happy marriage,' she replied sadly.

'Thank you. You've been a great help Dorothy. Now for

some good news. Anne thinks that there's a possibility Mary may well be the close friend she hasn't seen for almost twenty years.'

Dorothy looked puzzled but then remembered Mary saying, 'That's my friend,' when she saw Anne's picture in the paper.

'Can I see her?' Anne asked excitedly.

'Well, of course, but you must be very careful not to upset her,' Dorothy replied.

'Does she get violent when she's upset?' Russell asked, suddenly thinking this might be another lead.

'Goodness me, no! She just goes into a trance.' Dorothy sounded indignant. 'She's in the garden, Anne. I'll go and explain why you want to see her.'

'Would it be better if I looked through the window? There's no point in upsetting her if I've made a mistake,' Anne said quietly.

'Perhaps you're right,' Dorothy said thoughtfully. 'Inspector, I think it better you wait here.'

Russell nodded.

With heart pounding, Anne followed Dorothy into the kitchen. What she saw through the window made her gasp. Mary, who had finished weeding, was sitting in a deck chair reading.

'What's happened to her hair?' Anne asked, tears forming in her eyes.

Surely this couldn't be Mary. But, as Anne walked towards her, there was no mistaking those large pale blue eyes.

'Hello, Mary. Do you remember me?' Anne asked in a trembling voice as she squatted down by the side of the deckchair.

Mary dropped her magazine and stared at her. The fear in her eyes upset Anne so much that she couldn't hold back her tears.

'Anne,' Mary whispered. 'Why didn't you come before?'

'Oh Mary. What's happened to you? Anne asked between sniffles.

Trying to remember what had happened caused the black shadows to engulf Mary. She closed her eyes and then opened them wide. Staring at Anne she said, 'My father's a vicar you know.'

Dorothy came back into the lounge, after taking Mary to her room, and apologised for not offering them tea. 'I'll put the kettle on right away,' she said.

The Inspector looked at his watch. It was nearly four o'clock. They should have had the results from Forensics by now. He thanked Dorothy, but explained he was running late and had to get back to London.

Anne looked disappointed. 'Could I stay for a bit, Dorothy? I can easily get a taxi home.'

'Of course,' Dorothy replied. 'I'd like the opportunity to have a chat with you.'

Detective Inspector Russell left, and Anne followed Dorothy into the kitchen. She had been visibly shaken by Mary's behaviour and welcomed the strong cup of tea. They chatted for almost two hours.

'From the day she left after the wedding, no one saw or spoke to her,' Anne said. 'I kept trying to ring her during the day when I knew David would be at work, but the phone just rang and rang. No one ever answered it.'

Dorothy explained that, for a long time, there was only one phone in the house and that was in Mr Freeman's room, which he kept locked.

'Why?' asked Anne.

'Well. Mr Freeman gave me to understand that the ringing of the telephone upset her,' replied Dorothy.

'But she'd have heard the phone ringing in his room. Being unable to answer it would have made her even more upset, I would have thought.' Anne's dislike of David Freeman was beginning to show, so she changed the subject.

230

'I wonder what the Inspector wants Jennifer's birth certificate for? Do you know, Dorothy, he asked me if Jennifer was my daughter. What on earth would make him think that?'

'Probably because you look alike,' Dorothy replied. 'It's funny. I thought your poor brother looked somewhat like Jennifer too.'

Anne began to think the unthinkable. She knew that both she and Trevor looked like her father, but Jennifer? Mary was as blonde as could be, while David Freeman had thinning light mousy-coloured hair. So where did Jennifer get her looks from?

Dorothy brought Anne back down to earth. 'I think we ought to think about getting you a taxi, my dear. It's getting late and I have to see to Mary's dinner.'

Anne was disappointed. She was hoping to be invited to stay. 'Can I just have a peep at Mary before I leave?' she asked.

'You go and see her while I ring for a taxi. It's the last room along the landing. Don't wake her up, though,' Dorothy said firmly.

Kneeling by her long-lost friend she whispered, 'I'm so sorry I wasn't there for you Mary. 'I'll make it up to you, I promise.' She tiptoed out of the room.

As they were saying their goodbyes on the doorstep Anne asked, 'Is Mary getting any proper psychiatric help?'

'No,' replied Dorothy. 'That was something Mr Freeman never wanted to happen. But don't worry, she's improving all the time.'

'I bet he didn't want it to happen,' Anne thought as she climbed into the taxi.

On the way home she felt relieved that she did not have to drive. Her head was spinning. She had to get Mary some proper treatment and find out, for certain, who Jennifer's father was. Thinking of Jennifer made her realise that she had not asked how she was, or indeed where she was.

Chapter Forty-One

Striding back into the police station, Detective Inspector Russell went straight to his office and summoned Detective Sergeant Crossman. He arrived with a smug look on his face and sat on the windowsill.

'What have you got from Forensics?' Russell asked curtly, hoping his manner would show his annoyance at his Sergeant sitting perched on the sill.

'OK. Here we go,' Crossman began cheerfully, ignoring the curtness in Russell's tone.

'Fingerprints on candlestick. Dead match to suspect.'

'Hair samples. Dead match to suspect.'

'Blood on raincoat. Dead match to victim's.'

'Motive? He was spending too much of her money and was having it off with her best friend.'

'Learnt anything else?' Russell asked.

'Yeah. Odd this. No hospital in London has a record of Jennifer Freeman's birth.'

'Regarding her mother's mental state. No nut-house has any record of treating her.'

Russell flinched at Crossman's terminology.

'And since we can't find any trace at Somerset House, how do we know her name is Jennifer Freeman? That's it, Gov.' He closed the file and put it under his arm.

'Did you talk to anyone at the college she attended near Cambridge?' Russell asked.

'Constable Holmes is out there now,' replied Crossman looking pleased with himself.

Inspector Russell was not so pleased. He had expected Crossman to be doing it, not a young policewoman, and quietly told him so.

'Sorry, Gov. I had a lot on. In any case, we've got more than enough here to charge her with.'

'Don't be in such a hurry,' Russell snapped. 'How long have we got?'

'We can hold her until twelve o'clock tomorrow. Her lawyer's on his way to see her. Quite a big shot, so I'm told.'

Before he left the office Crossman looked quizzically at Russell. 'Any reason why you want to wait, Guv?'

'I'm just not sure yet. Shut the door behind you, please.'

Crossman shrugged his shoulders and left.

An hour later Russell sat at his desk looking at photographs. Displayed before him were pictures of John Stacey the rapist, Trevor Stacey the son, Anne Stacey the daughter, and the supposedly completely unrelated Jennifer Freeman.

He frowned. Something very odd about all this, he thought to himself. The likeness of all four had to be more than a coincidence.

Reluctantly, he called Crossman in again. 'Look at these,' he said getting up from behind the desk in order for his sergeant to take a closer look.

'Jesus Christ!' Crossman exclaimed. 'They're all the same family.'

'It certainly looks that way,' replied Russell.

The sergeant scratched his head. 'So maybe her name isn't Freeman?'

'I don't know. Maybe she was adopted.' Russell began pacing the floor.

'Well, we can't ask her father, he's dead and ... Well, you've seen her batty mother,' Crossman said callously.

Russell thought for a minute. 'We know Anne and Trevor Stacey's father is that rapist from Denton – which just happens to be where Mary Freeman was born.'

Crossman sat down. 'You're right, Gov. Phew, what a mix-up.'

Russell sat back behind his desk. 'What bearing does any of this have on Jennifer Freeman, or whatever her name is, killing Trevor Stacey?'

'Did she know he was her brother? And if she did, why would that make her want to kill him?' Crossman was talking to himself.

'It's late,' Russell said. 'I'm off home. First thing in the morning I'll go and see if I can get any more out of Anne Stacey. You make the necessary calls and see if we can interview old man Stacey. I'm not sure which prison he's in, but you can soon find that out.'

'Don't forget, we've only got until twelve o'clock, then we have to charge Jennifer or let her go,' Crossman reminded him.

Russell picked up his car keys from the desk. 'Well, the earlier you get started the better.'

Chapter Forty-Two

Charles Witherton, a renowned lawyer, was being chauffer-driven across London to the police station where Jennifer was being held. He had been briefed by old Cornell.

'Spoilt little rich girl,' he had said, but, in his opinion, not capable of committing murder.

'Well, we shall see,' he thought as he entered the police station. He was a very tall man in his fifties, immaculately dressed and full of self-importance. The desk sergeant treated him with the utmost respect and immediately accompanied him to the cell where Jennifer was being held.

'About fucking time,' Jennifer yelled at him. She was sitting on the bed crouched up in a corner. Still wearing the hospital's clothes, she didn't look anything like as attractive as he had been led to believe.

'Good afternoon, Miss Stacey,' he said in a cultured voice. He remained standing but put his briefcase on the floor.

Fighting to hold back the tears, Jennifer said, 'They think I killed my boyfriend.'

'I'm going to try and prove that you didn't,' he replied.

'I have to get out of here. I can't stay another night. I'll double your fee if you get me out of here today,' Jennifer ranted.

Charles Witherton smiled and informed Jennifer that it didn't quite work like that. 'The police are quite within their rights to hold you here until tomorrow lunchtime. That is, of course, if they have any real evidence. This I will find out in due course. In the meantime I have to ask you some questions.'

'I'm not answering any questions until you get me out of here,' Jennifer shouted.

'That behaviour will not help. I can't get you out of here if you won't answer my questions,' he said patronisingly.

'First of all, do you have an alibi?'

'What!' she screamed.

'Where were you when this murder took place? Think hard. This is important.'

'If you must know, I was on a train coming back from Ramsden,' she replied.

'Can anyone verify that?'

'It was very crowded, so hundreds of people would have seen me, but I don't know any of them,' she snapped.

He spent half an hour trying to make her see sense and, before leaving, instructed her to refuse to answer questions unless he was present.

Jennifer hurled abuse at him as he left. 'You were supposed to get me out of here, you bastard.'

Chapter Forty-Three

Detective Inspector Russell sat in his car outside the police station. He was trying to figure out whether there could be a connection between Jennifer murdering her brother and possibly being the daughter of a rapist.

Turning the key in the ignition he decided not to wait until tomorrow, but go out to Denton tonight to see Anne Stacey. He called her from the car and she sounded almost delighted that he was coming to see her.

'I feel so useless sitting here on my own. I know it sounds daft, but I feel as if I should be doing something,' she said.

She was shocked to read in the paper that a 20-year-old woman had been arrested and was helping the police with their enquiries. She had assumed it would have been some thug Trevor had double-crossed who had murdered him.

The loud knock on the door sent her rushing to open it. 'Come in, Inspector,' she said as she stood aside for him to enter. 'Would you like some tea, or perhaps something a little stronger?'

'Something stronger would be great, but unfortunately I'm on duty, so tea would be fine,' he replied as he settled himself into a chair, clutching a folder.

Anne brought in the tea.

'I want you to look at something,' said Russell as he opened the folder and spread three photographs out onto the coffee table.

Anne was stunned as the photographs of her father,

brother and Jennifer stared up at her. Guessing what his suspicions must be, she remained silent. She had thought of nothing else during her taxi ride home from Ramsden.

'Do you think there's a possibility that your friend Mary was raped by your father and went off to get married to hide the fact that she was pregnant?' he asked, trying not to sound too blunt.

Anne leaned back in her chair and closed her eyes. 'Inspector it doesn't bear thinking about. I thought once he was locked up I could forget all about him and begin a new life but, once again, his wrongdoings have come back to haunt me.

'So you do think it's possible?' he said.

'I don't know the exact date that Mary became pregnant, and I don't know when Jennifer was born, but I must confess I was amazed she had chosen to marry David Freeman. On her wedding day she behaved as if she was in a dream. I put that down to nerves. Inspector, could the fact that she was raped have caused her illness?'

'It's very possible,' he replied. 'It would certainly explain why Mary had no time for her daughter.'

'I meant to ask you earlier on. How is Jennifer? Have you seen her? I feel guilty not having been to see her.'

The inspector ducked the question by asking, 'Have you read the papers today?'

'Yes, I have and I was going to ask you whether you really think that a woman could have done this terrible thing?'

'At this point in time the answer is yes,' he replied.

'I don't suppose you can tell me who this woman is?'

He thought for a minute. 'Well, I'm not supposed to, but since you'll probably read about it in the paper tomorrow it might be better you hear it from me.' Anne gave him a puzzled look. 'All the evidence we have, which is quite substantial, points to one person. I'm afraid it's Jennifer.'

The colour drained from Anne's face. 'Jennifer! You must have got it wrong.'

'I don't think so. I was hoping to find some connection between her mother being raped and Jennifer murdering her boyfriend, but I think I'm barking up the wrong tree.' He quickly changed the subject. 'You live here alone, don't you?'

She nodded.

I feel such a heel having given you a shock like this and leaving you alone,' he said.

'Oh, please, don't worry. I've had worse things to deal with in my life,' she replied, shaking her head.

As he was leaving, she asked, 'Do Dorothy or Mary know about this?'

'No,' he replied. 'I'd be grateful if you kept it to yourself until tomorrow.'

He shook Anne's hand. 'Thank you for your time, Miss Stacey. Call me any time if you think of anything that I should know about.'

The following morning Detective Inspector Russell arrived at the police station to find Crossman had already left to interview Stacey in Pentonville prison.

WPC Holmes was waiting for him. 'Can I have a word, sir?' she asked, as he was opening his office door.

'Of course. 'Have you got something for me?'

'Sergeant Crossman asked me to let you know that Jennifer Freeman was wearing a black raincoat when she visited Amanda's house,' she said, following him into his office.

'Has he been to see her?'

'No sir. He spoke to her on the telephone.'

'Hmm!' Russell pursed his lips. 'Anything interesting from the college?'

'Not really, sir. It seems she broke every rule in the book. Very popular with the male students, not so popular with the females. As I understand it, she was never short of money.

One thing I did discover; Trevor Stacey was Amanda's boyfriend to begin with. She apparently caught them necking at a party and there was a lot of drink thrown about. That's about it sir.'

At eleven o'clock Crossman, without knocking, came barging into Russell's office.

'Bingo, Gov,' he said cheerfully. 'For two packets of fags he admitted raping the vicar's girl, as he called her. Not officially, mind. He wouldn't sign a statement, but told me on the QT.' Crossman took a deep breath. 'Where do we go from here Gov?'

'I think we go ahead and charge Jennifer Freeman and stop wasting any more time worrying about whose daughter she is. Sorry you've had a wasted journey, Crossman. I have to admit I was barking up the wrong tree. I'm sure that what you found out is true, but it has no bearing on the case.' Russell stood up. 'Get an interview room set up and get her lawyer down here.'

'Her lawyer's already with her. Practically the whole station can hear her screaming at him,' Crossman replied.

Detective Inspector Russell put on his jacket and said, 'Let's go.'

Jennifer Freeman was charged with the murder of Trevor Stacey at exactly twelve o'clock that day.

Once the formalities were over, Russell drove to Ramsden to break the news to Jennifer's mother and Dorothy. This was a job for one of the WPCs, but for some reason he decided to do it himself. He wanted to see Mary Freeman's reaction when she heard the news. There was something about this case that was still bugging him.

He was halfway up the hill when, to his surprise, he saw Mary, clutching a magazine, walking up to the Lodge alone. Dorothy was standing at the gate waiting for her. He got out of his car and, before Mary was within earshot, asked Dorothy, 'Does Mary often go out on her own?'

'Not often. You're getting to be quite a regular visitor. Do go in. I'll just wait for Mary.'

Mary sat in her chair by the window and Dorothy went bustling into the kitchen to make some tea. 'I won't be a moment,' she called out.

'Hello, Mary,' Russell said with a smile.

She stared at him but made no reply.

He smiled at her again and asked, 'Did you have a nice walk, Mary?'

She nodded her head.

There were a few seconds of uncomfortable silence before Mary suddenly asked, 'Did you bring my friend Anne to see me yesterday?'

'I certainly did,' he replied. ' Don't you remember?'

'I thought it may have been one of my dreams,' she said quietly.

'Is she coming to see you again?'

'Yes. This afternoon,' she answered with a faint smile.

'Mary,' he said gently. 'Why did Jennifer cut your hair off?'

She looked down at the floor. 'Because I had been to the hairdressers. She tried to strangle me, too.'

Russell raised his eyebrows. 'Why did she try and strangle you?'

'Because I was ill,' she replied.

'You said … was ill. Are you better now?

Mary lowered her head.

At this point Dorothy came in and placed the tray on the coffee table. 'Have you got more questions to ask us, Inspector?'

'No, not today. I'm afraid I have some rather shocking news for you.'

Dorothy handed them each a cup of tea. 'Oh, I'm getting quite used to shocking news. What is it now?'

Russell cleared his throat. 'This morning we've charged

Jennifer Freeman with the murder of Trevor Stacey. I wanted you to know before you read it in the newspapers.'

Dorothy's hand shook and her cup went crashing to the floor.

Mary continued drinking her tea quite unperturbed. Russell watched as she put her cup back on the table. Returning his glance, Mary gave a faint smile.

By this time, Dorothy had picked up her cup and saucer from the floor. Clasping her hands together, she said, 'There has to be a mistake, Inspector. Jennifer isn't a very nice girl, but murder? No! Whatever makes you think it was her?'

'I'm afraid we have some pretty conclusive evidence,' he replied.

'She wouldn't kill anyone.'

He placed his cup back on the table. 'I understand she tried to strangle Mary on more than one occasion.'

'She wasn't trying to kill her, though,' Dorothy said, exasperated.

'Yes she was!' Mary interrupted.

'Mary, please!' Dorothy said in an unusually loud voice.

Mary got up and left the room.

Dorothy was relieved to hear a car arrive. 'You'll have to excuse me now, Inspector. Anne Stacey has come to see Mary.'

'Thank you for your time,' Russell said.

'And thank you for sparing us the horror of reading about this in the newspapers.' As Dorothy saw him to the door she said, 'I must say, Inspector, I think you're making a big mistake.'

She watched as Anne got out of her car and went across to Detective Russell. They stood talking for a while and she wondered whether he was telling her about Jennifer. Finally, Anne shook his hand, turned and walked towards the house.

'This is a terrible business,' Dorothy said, as she ushered

Anne into the house. 'I suppose you've heard about Jennifer?'

'Yes, I have, and I have to say I find it very difficult to believe. How's Mary? Does she know they've charged Jennifer?'

'Yes. We were together when the Inspector told us. Strangely enough, it doesn't seem to have bothered her at all. I don't know. I really don't.' Dorothy shook her head.

'She didn't get upset when she heard?'

'No, she seems fine,' Dorothy replied. 'She's up in her room. You can go up if you like.'

Anne quietly opened Mary's door and found her sitting on the bed twiddling her fingers. 'Hello Mary,' she said nervously.

Mary jumped up and ran into Anne's arms. They hugged each other for several minutes, each one's tears dropping on the other's face.

'Try not to cry,' Anne said. 'I'm here now and nothing bad is ever going to happen to you again.'

For several more minutes Mary just clung to Anne, sobbing.

After bringing Mary a glass of water, Anne sat beside her on the bed. They had been chatting for about an hour when Anne said, 'Mary. I'm not going to ask you what happened any more because I know. I don't want you to go off in a trance when you think about it. I want you to share it with me. I know why you went off and married David Freeman. You were carrying my father's child.'

Mary began to close her eyes. Anne gripped her hand. 'No, Mary. Please don't go to sleep. Stay with me. I know what my father did to you. I understand why you wanted to hide it from me and your father.'

Mary opened her eyes. 'Anne. Oh Anne. Is it really you?'

'Yes. It's really me, and once you're better we'll go and sit on our log and catch up on all the time we've missed.' She put her arm around her friend's shoulders. 'Do you want to lie down, or would you like to come down for some tea?' Anne asked.

Mary looked up at Anne, closed her eyes and said, 'My father's a vicar, you know.' She then smiled and lay back on the bed staring up at the ceiling.

Anne panicked and began to shake her. 'Mary. It's Anne. Please sit up and talk to me,' she pleaded. Mary continued to stare at the ceiling with a vacant look in her eyes.

Anne ran to the top of the stairs and called Dorothy.

'Oh dear, what did you say to her? Whatever it was, it must have been something she doesn't want to face,' Dorothy said as she removed Mary's shoes. 'Leave her alone for a while. She'll soon be alright.'

Downstairs, Dorothy explained that this was what happened when you talked about something she didn't like or was scared of. 'I think it's a sort of barrier she puts up to hide behind. This is only what I think, mind. I'm not a psychiatrist, but I think I know what's best for her.'

'I know you don't want Mary to go away for treatment. Neither do I. But do you think she would benefit from having psychiatric treatment at home? I would be quite willing to pay for it if necessary,' said Anne.

'Oh, my dear, there would be no need for that. Mary has plenty of money. In fact I don't know whether she realises how rich she is,' Dorothy replied.

'Would you mind if I made some enquiries about getting her some help?' Anne asked.

'My only fear is that if a psychiatrist saw her in the state she is in now, for instance, they would send her away. I promised Mr Freeman I would never let that happen.' Dorothy looked out of the window at the garden. 'She loves her gardening, you know.'

Anne wanted to say, 'Damn David Freeman. He kept her in captivity for long enough,' but restrained herself and said, 'That won't happen, I promise you.'

244

Mary suddenly appeared at the door. Her eyes still had a vacant expression as she walked slowly in and sat down at the kitchen table.

'I suppose you're ready for your dinner,' Dorothy said as she stroked Mary's head.

Mary just nodded.

Anne stood up. 'I really must be going now.'

Mary smiled at her and said goodbye as if she was a complete stranger.

Back home, Anne began thinking about where she could get help for Mary. Once more it brought home to her how friendless she was. Her thoughts strayed to Ralph. He would know what to do. Her stomach churned at the thought of what might have been. She knew deep down that she was still very much in love.

The following morning she telephoned for an appointment with Dr Wright. Anne decided to walk to his surgery, as she needed some fresh air. On the way, she began to have misgivings about seeing him. He had been so supportive during her mother's illness but she couldn't help wondering what sort of response she would receive now that he knew her father was a rapist.

Her worries were unfounded. He greeted her in his usual cordial way. Without going into detail, Anne explained that she had met up with Mary again and that she was suffering from a nervous breakdown.

'I'm so sorry to hear that,' he said sympathetically.

'I want Mary to have the best possible help that money can buy. I wondered whether you knew of anyone who would treat her at home. She lives in a place called Ramsden and, as I understand, is not even registered with a local doctor.'

'Well, aggrieved as I am at having to admit it, I have to tell you that the best psychiatrists are based in London,' he said leaning back in his chair.

'Do you think any of them would come out to Ramsden?'

Dr Wright smiled. 'They would probably go to the moon if the price was right. We could be talking about a substantial amount of money, Anne.'

'Believe me, Dr Wright, that is not a problem. Mary has inherited a great deal of money from her late husband.'

He got up from his chair. 'You go home, Anne, and after surgery I'll make some enquiries and give you a ring.' He rested his hand on her shoulder. 'My dear, I know what you've been through and I can only imagine how difficult things must be for you. I want you to know that if I can ever be of any help, you only have to call.'

Anne felt tears beginning to well up in her eyes. 'Dr Wright, thank you very much indeed. I'll wait to hear from you.'

She walked home feeling somewhat comforted by the doctor's words.

Five days later Mary began her treatment with a Dr Mayer attending her at home. Anne visited every day.

It was six months later, two days before Jennifer's trial was to begin, that Dr Mayer was able to establish that Mary had not only been raped but also systematically abused by her husband.

'She's a very frightened, lost soul,' he told Dorothy and Anne one morning after a consultation. 'As you can see for yourselves, she is progressing very well, but I have to warn you, whether Mary will ever be her old self again is doubtful. The medication will prevent her escaping from the real world. That's what she's doing when she shuts out everything.'

'Doctor, could this all have been caused by the fact that she was raped?' Anne asked.

'Initially, yes. Of course it was compounded by the years of sexual abuse she suffered at the mercy of her husband.'

'Years of sexual abuse!' Dorothy repeated.

'Yes. You see it's rather like an open wound that doesn't get the chance to heal, and another wound opens up in another

246

part of the body. Not knowing which one to face, and not wanting to face up to either of them, she hides away from the real world.'

Dorothy, who was sitting with her mouth open, suddenly said, 'What are you talking about? Mary may well have been raped but she certainly did not suffer abuse from her husband. Not any that I've seen anyway. I've never heard such nonsense.'

'Miss Maitland, it is very rare that anyone notices when a woman is being abused. You see, in almost every case, it is done in secret. Unfortunately the victim is too scared to say anything. In Mary's case this all started very early on, after she had been raped, resulting in her becoming mentally ill. But don't feel too gloomy about it. You can see for yourselves how much better she is, and I can assure you that she will improve even more as time goes on.

'I must be getting along now. I'll be back in three days at about the same time.' He picked up his briefcase and made ready to leave.

As she walked to the door with him, Anne asked, 'Dr Mayer. Is it in order for me to talk to her about any of this?'

'I gather from Mary that you've already spoken to her about the rape. I think it would be unwise, at the moment, for you to venture into the torment she suffered from her husband. I don't want her to lose confidence in me at this crucial stage. One other thing. She's been through quite a session today and she'll be very tired and washed out. Give her a chance to have a rest before you go up to see her.'

Anne nodded, 'Of course. Thank you, Dr Mayer.'

She returned to the kitchen to find a very indignant Dorothy. 'How dare he suggest such a thing,' she said angrily.

'Dorothy, he wasn't suggesting anything. He was stating a fact,' Anne said firmly.

'That man was so good to her. I know he was a bit strange, but abuse Mary? Never.'

247

That night, Dorothy found it impossible to get off to sleep. She began thinking about the day that Mary had bruises on her cheek. The times she could not sit still at breakfast, almost as if in pain. The dreadful weals that she had caught a glimpse of when Mary was changing her clothes. Her standard answer was always, 'I fell.'

So many things began to click into place. The occasions when she had seen him going to Mary's room late at night. What a fool she had been. She realised now that she had let Mary down badly.

Chapter Forty-Four

Jennifer stood in the dock looking ashen but defiant. The first witness for the prosecution was Amanda. Photographs of the injuries caused by Jennifer's attack were distributed to the jury. For 30 minutes the prosecution questioned Amanda, who answered truthfully up until the last question.

'What was Miss Stacey wearing when she arrived at your house?'

Amanda cleared her throat and, looking straight at Jennifer said, 'A fawn suit with a black sweater underneath.'

Crossman closed his eyes and said to himself, 'Shit!'

Amanda then continued. 'She had a long black raincoat around her shoulders.'

Crossman breathed a sigh of relief.

Jennifer screamed from the dock 'She's a liar.' Horrified, her counsel watched as, in her naivety, she batted her eyelashes at the Judge and said, in a babyish voice, 'Your Honour. She hates me. I wouldn't kill Trevor. I loved him.'

The Judge, seemingly irritated, adjourned the court for two hours.

The trial lasted for three weeks and Jennifer's behaviour showed no sign of improving. Charles Witherton tried his hardest to make her see sense, and suggested that she change her plea to guilty. He explained that they could go for a crime of passion, suggesting that Jennifer was so upset by Trevor's behaviour she was not responsible for her actions.

'Jennifer, if you do this, I can almost guarantee you a shorter sentence,' he said.

She became hysterical and screamed, 'How many times do I have to tell you. I did not kill Trevor. I did not wear a black raincoat when I went to Amanda's. She's lying. I'm not going to plead guilty to something I didn't do.' Composing herself, she went on, 'In any case, this is England. They don't put innocent people in prison.'

The counsel for the prosecution began his summing up. Walking slowly up and down in front of the jury, he described Jennifer as a spoilt rich girl with no thought for anyone but herself. 'We have learned that she even terrified her own sick mother. Ladies and gentlemen, these are the facts.

'The black raincoat that belonged to Jennifer Stacey was covered in bloodstains and hidden in her washing machine ready to destroy the evidence.

'Her fingerprints were found on the solid brass candlestick that was used to bludgeon Trevor Stacey to death.

'She was found at the scene of the crime with the candlestick at her feet.

'Traces of her hair were found in the victim's hands.

'She claims her reason for not letting the police in was that she fainted, but when the first officer arrived at the top of the stairs, she was fully conscious.'

Prosecuting counsel went on and on incriminating Jennifer, and finished by saying, 'Ladies and gentlemen. These are the facts and I recommend that you find the defendant, Jennifer Freeman … Guilty.'

Chapter Forty-Five

Anne was getting ready for her visit to Mary. It was only nine o'clock in the morning but she liked to get there early on the days that Dr Mayer was visiting. It gave her a chance to chat before he arrived. She pulled her hair back and clipped it on top of her head. She had decided she was now too old to let it hang down over her shoulders. As she did so she thought she might suggest that she took Mary to the hairdressers. She felt sad when she recalled her friend's long blonde hair. It was such a mess now.

The telephone rang interrupting her thoughts. It was the estate agent. Anne had taken her house off the market after Trevor was killed and she had found Mary.

'I know you decided not to sell,' a woman's voice said. ' But I have someone with me who could be very interested in your property. I wondered if you had thought any more about selling your house.'

Anne thought for a minute. It would be nice to leave Denton and make a fresh start. Perhaps buy something closer to Mary.

'Yes,' she replied. 'I could be interested.'

The agent arranged for a Mr and Mrs Patterson to view the property that evening.

Replacing the receiver, Anne noticed that the newspaper had arrived. Picking it up the headlines jumped out at her. '20-Year-Old Jennifer Freeman Sentenced to Twenty Years'.

With legs that had turned to jelly, Anne walked into the

lounge and slumped into a chair. Reading on, she couldn't help wondering how the girl could have committed such a horrible crime. Her father, who she loathed, was behind bars paying the price for his sins. Jennifer was about to pay the same price. Poor Trevor had paid the ultimate price. She felt a degree of guilt about the way she had always put her career first. Maybe, if she had spent more time with her brother, things could have turned out differently. But knowing that if she had, she would never have met Ralph, she remembered something her mother used to say: 'Better to have loved and lost than not to have loved at all.'

Snapping out of her melancholic mood, Anne looked at her watch and realised she was going to be late getting to Mary's. Deciding it would make sense to have a cup of coffee and calm down before she drove, she telephoned Dorothy.

'I'm going to be a little late this morning,' she said.

'Don't worry, Anne. I thought you might.'

'You've read the paper, then?' Anne asked.

'No, my dear. I heard it on the radio.'

'How is Mary? Does she know?'

'No, not yet. I thought I would wait until Dr Mayer arrives.' There was tiredness in Dorothy's voice as she went on, 'Anne, don't worry if you don't feel up to coming today. I'm sure you must feel very upset about your brother.'

'Yes, I am feeling a little gloomy, but I promised Mary I would come every day. I'll never let her down again, Dorothy.'

When she eventually arrived at the lodge, Dr. Mayer was already in consultation with Mary.

To Anne's surprise, Dorothy gave her a hug and kissed her on the cheek when she opened the door. 'You're a good girl, Anne,' she said emotionally.

Settled in their usual place at the kitchen table, Anne asked, 'What did Dr Mayer say?'

'He said that he would tell Mary the news this morning

252

and come again tomorrow to make sure it's had no adverse effect. Oh, Anne. Will this nightmare never end?'

Noticing that Dorothy looked and sounded very tired, Anne asked, 'Are you alright?'

'Just tired,' she replied. 'I haven't slept much thinking about what that poor girl went through. I was fooled by David Freeman and I feel partly responsible.'

Anne was consoling Dorothy when Dr Mayer tapped on the door.

'Well, the deed is done,' he said as he pulled out a kitchen chair and sat down. He felt quite at home now coming into the kitchen for a cup of tea.

'How did she take it?' Anne asked.

'Strangely enough, she looked almost relieved. But I suppose it's not too surprising considering their relationship. In fact I don't think there's any need for me to visit tomorrow. She seems in remarkably good shape. If you're worried at all, just call and I'll be here as soon as I can.' He finished his tea and said cheerfully, 'See you in three days.'

Minutes after he left, Mary came downstairs and asked, 'Anne, are you alright? I missed you this morning.'

Anne got up and gave Mary a kiss on the cheek. 'I'm fine.'

'Can you stay for lunch?' Mary asked Anne chirpily.

'Well, I think Dorothy's got enough to do without entertaining me. She's tired. Perhaps another time,' Anne replied.

To Dorothy and Anne's surprise Mary said, 'Dorothy, you go and put your feet up. Anne and I will get the lunch ready.'

'Don't be silly. You two go in the other room and chat. I'll see to it.'

They were both delighted when Mary repeated, 'Anne and I will get the lunch!'

While preparing cold meats and salad, Anne told Mary she was thinking of selling up and coming to live nearer.

'That would be wonderful,' said Mary excitedly.

Anne was pleased to see that Mary was behaving almost normally apart from the occasional vacant stare.

During lunch Anne told Dorothy of her plans. She was equally delighted.

'Now you two have the job of keeping your eyes open for any property that comes on the market. Not too expensive, mind.'

'Don't worry about how much it costs,' said Mary. 'We've got plenty of money, haven't we Dorothy? We could probably buy a house for you.'

Anne laughed and replied, 'I don't think that will be necessary.'

After lunch Dorothy went upstairs to take a nap while Mary and Anne sat in the garden and chatted about all manner of things.

'This is just like old times,' Anne said

Mary smiled. 'Anne, I can never put into words how happy I am that you're here at last. I'm terrified that I'm going to wake up and find that it's all been a dream.'

'Do you feel like telling me what happened?' Anne asked.

'No,' Mary said. 'Not today. Another time, perhaps. I'd like to hear what you've been up to all these years.'

Deliberately not mentioning the deaths of Mrs Davidson and Mary's father, Anne told her all about Ralph and her job as area manager working for the supermarket chain.

'What a clever girl you turned out to be,' said Mary.

'I like to think that it was because of my hard work, and nothing to do with the fact that Ralph, who was a director there, fell in love with me.'

'Why did you leave?' Mary asked.

'I'm not sure you want to know. It might upset you.'

'Why will it upset me?'

'Because it concerns my father. The pig that raped you. I'm sure you're not ready to talk about him yet,' Anne replied.

Mary stared at her. 'Oh, Anne. Did he rape you too?'

'No. Nothing like that. Thanks to Trevor, they found out that my father was the Denton rapist and sacked me. Mind you, they paid me off handsomely.'

Mary looked puzzled. 'I thought you said the boss was in love with you.'

'I thought he was. I was very much in love with him. Unfortunately, the chairman made him choose between his career and me. He chose his career and sacked me. I was heartbroken for a long time. I'm over it now. Well, sort of over it. But, to be honest, I'm still in love with him.' Realising she was upsetting herself, Anne changed the subject. 'I've got some people coming this evening to view my house, so I had better start looking right away otherwise I shall be homeless.'

'Anne, you can always come and live here until you find something,' Mary said excitedly.

'That's very kind of you, but I'm sure it won't be necessary,' Anne replied.

Mary's face suddenly lit up. 'Why don't you come and live here anyway? We've got plenty of room. You could have …' Mary stumbled over her next words, '… his room.'

'Mary, I don't know whether you've noticed, but Dorothy is looking very tired. She's not getting any younger and I think it would be too much for her, don't you?'

'But I'm getting stronger every day. We could look after her, for a change. She's been so good to me. I can't bear to think what would have happened if it hadn't been for Dorothy. Anne, will you just think about it?'

It was five o'clock and a chill breeze made them decide to go indoors.

Dorothy was looking refreshed after her nap and had already put the kettle on. Taking a sponge cake from a colourful biscuit tin, she said, 'You two must have smelled the tea leaves.' They all laughed.

To Dorothy's surprise, Mary immediately got the cups and saucers down from the dresser and put them on the table.

Once they had finished their tea, Anne said, 'I really must be going. Those people are coming to see the house at seven.'

'Would you mind just helping me wash up before you go?' Mary said as she began clearing the table.

'Mary!' Dorothy said indignantly. 'You don't ask guests to help wash up. What are you thinking of. Now go and see Anne to the door. This is my job.'

Mary giggled. 'Not any more it's not.'

Dorothy had never seen Mary giggle before. It was like a breath of fresh air.

Two weeks later Anne received an offer for her house. It was far more than she could ever have imagined. The estate agent informed her that the buyer would pay cash providing the house would become vacant in 10 days. Instead of the excitement she thought she should be feeling, she felt sad and somewhat scared.

Looking at the gateleg table in the corner of the lounge, Anne remembered the reason she had bought it. She had been ashamed to entertain Ralph in the kitchen.

It was going to take a great deal of courage to pack all her belongings and leave this house. There were so many reminders of her mother. As she looked around, it occurred to her that Mary might like to come and help with the packing. Feeling somewhat relieved that she would not have to attempt the daunting task alone, she went upstairs to tidy her bedroom before leaving for Mary's.

Looking a lot better, Dorothy opened the door and said, 'We're in the kitchen in deep discussion. Come and join us.'

A newspaper lay opened on the table at the 'Houses for Sale' page.

Anne sat down. 'Goodness me. You're both looking serious.'

256

They looked mischievously at each other.

'You ask her.' Mary grinned at Dorothy.

'We've got some people coming tomorrow to clear out Mr Freeman's room and we were wondering what use we could make of it.' Dorothy cleared her throat. 'We've been looking out for a house for you, but those that are for sale are either unsuitable or outrageously expensive. I thought about it, then suggested to Mary that you might like to consider coming to live with us.'

Anne frowned and looked at Mary who quickly said, 'I did not say a word. This is all Dorothy's idea.'

Looking embarrassed, Dorothy continued, 'It's just that you spend most of your time here anyway. It seems such a waste for you to spend all that money on a house just to sleep in.'

Anne found it impossible to hide the excitement and comfort she felt at the thought of moving in with Mary and Dorothy. She blushed. 'I don't know what to say.'

'Oh, please say yes,' Mary pleaded.

'Now, Mary. Please don't pressurise Anne. She has her own life to lead. After all, she may want to pick up on her career and that could result in her having to move out of the area,' Dorothy said seriously. 'I think the best idea is for Anne to think about it for a few days and let us know.'

'I think that's the perfect solution,' Anne said. 'I know I'm not going to find a place in the next ten days and that's when I have to be out of my house. So, if you're both sure, I would be more than grateful to stay for a while.'

Mary beamed.

'There's one condition,' Anne said. 'You Mary, will have to come and help me pack.'

'Of course I will. I'd be delighted to help.'

Three days later, Anne drove over to collect Mary at nine o'clock in the morning as they planned to spend the whole day packing.

As they drove into Denton, Anne noticed Mary's face change. In order to avoid going past the Vicarage, she took the long route through the high street. Throughout the journey Mary stared straight ahead so as to avoid looking at any of the old familiar surroundings.

Once inside the house, Anne asked, 'Was that very painful for you?'

Mary nodded.

They immediately set to work filling large cardboard boxes that Anne had organised.

They laughed and giggled as they reminisced at some of the pranks they had got up to when they were young.

Once the living room and kitchen had been cleared of everything but the furniture, Anne sank down on the armchair and said, 'Now the hard part.'

'What do you mean?' Mary asked.

Anne looked up at the ceiling, 'Mrs Davidson got rid of all my mum's things after she died, but the bottom drawer of her dressing table contained a lot of personal things like letters and photographs. I've never been able to bring myself to go through them. Maybe it's time to throw them away.'

'Why do you have to get rid of those things?' Mary asked.

'I have to start a new life Mary. I must stop living in the past.'

'Why don't you let me clear that drawer? I'll put everything in a suitcase and you can bring it with you. That way you won't get upset and we can sort it out later,' suggested Mary.

Anne smiled as she remembered how, in the past, she had dumped her problems on Mary who had always come up with a solution. How supportive she had been when her father had left. How she wished she could have been around when Mary needed her.

'I can't tell you how good it is to have you around again,' Anne said as she got up from the chair.

A few minutes later, Mary was upstairs with an old brown suitcase. She pulled at the bottom drawer with all the strength she could muster before realising it was locked.

She called down the stairs to Anne. 'Have you got a key to the drawer? I think it's locked.'

Anne put the tape down she was using to seal up the last of the tea chests and went upstairs.

'It's probably got a bit stiff,' she said as she went into the bedroom.

After a few minutes, with them both pulling, Anne had to admit that it was locked.

How strange, she thought to herself. She had opened it several times before trying to pluck up courage to go through it. The last time was just before her father had moved in. She shuddered as she wondered if he had tampered with it.

'Let's leave it for now,' Anne said with a troubled look on her face.

Mary had noticed how upset she looked and was determined to get this unpleasant job done for her friend. While Anne began packing in the other bedroom, Mary struggled with a knife and the key from the bedroom door, trying to shift the catch on the drawer.

'Done it!' she called out.

'Well done,' Anne shouted back.

The drawer was stuffed full of old brown envelopes, photograph albums, loose photographs and letters that had gone brown around the edges with age. Without paying any attention to them, Mary began packing them into the suitcase. The last one was a beige folder and, as she picked it up, several photographs fell out onto the floor.

The first one she picked up caused her to go as white as a sheet. It was a picture of a girl, naked apart from her shoes. It looked as if she was crying. She was lying on what looked like a dirty old mattress. With a trembling hand Mary picked up another, and recognised herself lying half-naked on the old mattress, only this time she could see it was in the back of a van.

Mary began to tremble. She could feel her head being pushed back and the smell of alcohol. The excruciating pain as he bit her nipples went through her body. With the key in her hand she quietly went and locked the bedroom door. Her eyes glazed over as she said quietly, 'You can't get me now.'

She crawled under the bed and, lying on her side, pulled her knees up to her chest. They were all in the room after her now. David Freeman with his cane and Anne's father with his stinking breath. Her mind was in turmoil as she realised what Anne had done. She must have known they'd be here. She tried in vain to hide behind her black shadows but they would not come.

Thinking Mary had gone quiet, Anne called out, 'How are you getting on?' Getting no answer she called again, 'Are you alright?'

Mary pulled her knees tighter to her chest and remained silent.

Hearing Anne trying to open the door, she began whimpering. 'Leave me alone. Please leave me alone.'

Anne was now twisting the doorknob, shouting, 'Mary! Open the door. What are you doing?'

In her mind Mary was determined that they were not going to get her this time. She crawled from under the bed, picked up a vase from the dressing table and hurled it at the door. It smashed into pieces and the noise was deafening.

'Mary,' Anne screamed. 'What are you doing? Let me in.'

What followed was the sound of the matching vase being hurled at the door.

'Please, Mary. Let me in,' Anne begged.

'Leave me alone,' Mary screamed as she hurled the clock at the door before crawling back under the bed.

Terrified by Mary's behaviour, Anne ran down the stairs and telephoned Dorothy. Without going into detail she asked for the telephone number of Dr Mayer. 'Mary's gone into a trance and I think Dr Mayer should see her,' she said breathlessly. 'I'll call you back as soon as I can.'

Heart pounding, she dialled the doctor's number and explained to him what was happening.

'Don't try and talk to her,' he said. 'Leave her alone until I get there.'

'But she might hurt herself,' Anne protested.

'She is more likely to do that if she thinks you're going to open the door. Now stay calm. Fortunately I'm only twenty minutes away. I'll be there as soon as I can.' Doctor Mayer hung up.

Anne sat on the bottom of the stairs for what seemed like hours. No sound came from the bedroom. She could only hope that Mary was alright. She wanted to ring Dorothy and explain properly what had happened but was terrified in case Mary heard her.

A car pulling up outside made Anne jump to her feet and open the door.

'Thank goodness you're here,' Anne said in a panic-stricken voice as Dr Mayer walked calmly up the path.

'You wait here,' he said with a reassuring smile. Anne was somewhat irritated by his calmness as he walked slowly up the stairs.

He talked to Mary in a very quiet voice for about ten minutes. Suddenly Anne heard a window smash and, through the living room window, watched as a bedside lamp came hurtling down, landing in the front garden.

Soon after, Dr Mayer came downstairs and informed Anne that Mary had to go to hospital. 'Don't worry,' he said. ' I'll go with her.'

'Can't I come?' Anne asked.

'I don't think that's a very good idea,' he replied. 'Why

don't you drive over and keep Dorothy company and I will call you later this evening.'

Anne nodded, trying hard to keep back the tears.

She sat in the kitchen listening as the two men who had arrived in white coats broke down the bedroom door. For a few minutes she heard Mary screaming, 'Leave me alone! Leave me alone!' Then silence. Dr Mayer told her they had given Mary an injection that had put her to sleep.

Anne watched as they carried her friend out to the ambulance strapped to a stretcher.

The Priory was a private nursing home for the mentally ill. It stood on one level in 10 acres of beautiful grounds. Mary spent almost a year there. Not one day went by without either Anne or Dorothy visiting her.

She got worse before she started to get better. As a result of the medication, her skin paled and her face shrunk, which made her eyes seem larger than ever.

The terrible guilt Anne felt for what had happened was beginning to take its toll. Not only had she not been there to prevent the prolonged nightmare she had endured at the hands of David Freeman, she had now been the cause of Mary's acute nervous breakdown.

Moving in with Dorothy had been a great help. She had been so supportive and kept trying to convince Anne that it was not her fault.

'If only I had not let her open the drawer where my sick demented father had kept the photographs of his victims, she would not be in hospital today,' Anne had said to herself and Dorothy so many times.

They sat at the breakfast table one Friday morning, in silence. This was the day they were going to bring Mary home for a weekend to see how she got on. They were both anxious as to how things were going to work out, but tried not to show it.

'I know one of the things she'll say,' said Dorothy breaking

262

the silence. 'She'll take one look at that overgrown garden and ask us why we hadn't looked after it.'

'I know,' Anne replied. 'But Dr Mayer said it will be good therapy for her once she's feeling a bit stronger.'

Mary was waiting in Reception for them when they arrived. Anne had bought her some new clothes to come home in but they hung on her like a scarecrow. She had lost so much weight.

During the drive home Anne said, 'Those clothes I got you are all too big. I think we will have to go shopping tomorrow.'

'Can I come with you?' Mary asked.

'Of course,' replied Anne. ' It'll be fun.'

Dorothy patted Mary's knee. 'It's good to have you home, my dear.'

After lunch both Dorothy and Mary went for an afternoon nap. Anne sat in the lounge, drinking a cup of coffee. She had vowed to herself she would spend the rest of her life looking after her friend. It was a daunting task but she was determined to do it.

Resting her head back in the chair she began to think how things might have been. She still thought about Ralph and wondered whether, if he came back, she would still devote her life to looking after Mary. She swallowed hard and faced the fact that he was never coming back any way, and so she would never have to make that choice.

The weekend went extremely well. Anne took Mary shopping and they had fun trying on clothes. On the Sunday, the day Mary was due to return to the nursing home, Dorothy cooked the most delicious roast beef lunch with all the trimmings.

Mary had little appetite, but appreciated that Dorothy had cooked her favourite meal.

'We are going to have to fatten you up, young lady,' she said. They all laughed.

Anne worried that Mary would not want to go back to the

nursing home and was dreading bringing the subject up. To her surprise and relief it was Mary who looked at the clock and said, 'I hate to go, but I think you ought to be getting me back now.'

Dorothy stayed to clear up and Anne took Mary back to the nursing home.

As they were saying their good -byes Mary said, 'Funny isn't it?

Anne smiled at her friend and asked, 'What's funny?'

Mary's eyes glazed over and she replied, 'I got rid of Trevor because he was going to have me locked up, but it didn't work. I still got locked up. My father's a vicar, you know.'

Anne was shocked. 'Don't be silly, Mary, you didn't get rid of Trevor.'

Mary's eyes became focused again and she smiled.

Anne hugged her and whispered, 'Soon you'll be home for good and I'll be there waiting for you. I'm going to look after you, Mary, and help you get well.'

Pulling herself away Mary, said, 'And when I'm better, will you leave?'

Sensing the anxiety in her friend, Anne replied, 'Of course not. I'm going to be with you forever.'

Driving home, Anne worried about the enormity of the commitment she was making but, since she had nothing else in her life, she convinced herself that it was the right thing to do.

Chapter Forty-Six

Ralph Stevens stood back and surveyed his office. He felt very depressed. It seemed that he had given up the love of his life for these large, expensively furnished, surroundings. It had taken him all this time to realise that there was nothing for him in life without Anne.

He had cut out and kept the picture from the newspaper of Anne sitting on the log. His heart still skipped a beat when he looked at it, but now it also caused an ache in the pit of his stomach.

Picking up the telephone he asked his secretary to make an appointment for him to see Chandler. 'Tell him it's urgent and must be today,' he said curtly.

While he waited, he toyed with the idea of getting in touch with Anne first. Maybe she wouldn't want him after all this time. He knew he had behaved very badly.

His secretary popped her head round the door and said, 'He has a lunch appointment today, but if you're there at eleven o'clock he can see you for ten minutes.'

'That's fine,' Ralph replied. The door closed and he muttered, 'What I have to say won't take long.'

He arrived at five minutes to eleven and was shown straight into the chairman's office.

'This had better be important. I've got a very busy schedule today,' Chandler bellowed in his usual arrogant way.

'Well it might not be for you, but it certainly is for me,'

Ralph said enjoying the moment. He threw an envelope onto Chandler's desk. 'That's my official resignation.'

Chandler stood up. 'What are you talking about? Are you mad?'

'Only inasmuch as I should have done this a year ago. I can't bear the thought of working for you any longer.'

'Now look, Ralph. I know we've not seen eye to eye since that ridiculous situation over that girl, but I thought you were over all that.'

'That girl, as you so rudely call her, is the woman I love. I only hope that I haven't left it too late. I've been a fool. I don't ever want to end up like you, stuck at business dinners with no one to go home to.'

The veins stood out in Chandler's forehead as he said angrily, 'You don't have to be so bloody rude.'

Ralph grinned. 'I'm surprised you know the difference between good manners and being rude, since I've never heard or seen you display anything but the latter.'

Chandler, ignoring what Ralph had said, walked around the desk and stood opposite him. 'Now come on, Ralph. Is it money? We can come to some arrangement.'

'I don't think so. You see, every time I see you I'm reminded of what I've lost because of your inhumane attitude. Now, if you'll excuse me, I'm going to try and put my life back in order.'

After packing all his personal belongings into two briefcases he said goodbye to his secretary and left.

Back in his flat he poured himself a large vodka and tonic and thought about how best to approach Anne. It was two o'clock in the afternoon. He spent the next hour tormenting himself with thoughts of Anne having fallen in love with someone else but then realised she was not the sort to go headlong into another relationship. Having no idea where she was working and, not wanting to telephone, he made up his mind to drive out to Denton and wait for her to arrive home from work.

It had been such a long time but he could still remember what it felt like to hold her in his arms. Looking out of the window over Hyde Park he recalled how they had spent the day there and how he had pointed out his apartment to her.

Strolling aimlessly into the bathroom he pictured her stepping out of the shower and coming into his arms soaking wet. He had lifted her up and carried her into the bedroom and made love so tenderly.

With tears in his eyes he looked at his reflection in the mirror and said, 'What a fool you've been, Ralph Stevens. A love like this only comes by once in a lifetime. When she needed you most, you broke her heart.'

Taking out his wallet, he took out the newspaper cutting and stared at Anne's picture. 'I will make it up to you, my darling. You will never have a problem again that you can't share with me. I love you so much it hurts.'

He cringed as he thought that she must have been so alone. He had read about the murder of her brother and still had not made contact, and found it hard to believe that he had behaved in such a callous way.

By four o'clock he had showered, changed, and set off to drive to Denton. On his way, he stopped and picked up an enormous bunch of red roses. The sight of the bouquet lying on the seat beside him lifted his spirits. He sang along with every love song that was played on the radio.

As he turned into her street his stomach churned at the thought of her soon being in his arms. Not wanting her to see his car, he parked at the end of the street where a tree partly shielded him from view, but he could clearly see the outside of her house. Checking his watch he saw it was 5.30. He could be in for a long wait but he had already made up his mind. He would wait till midnight if he had to.

After just 20 minutes he saw a car pull up outside Anne's house. He didn't recognise it as her car, and a pang of guilt went through him as he thought she had had to downgrade her car when she lost her job.

His heart sank as he saw a couple he did not recognise get out of the car. He watched as they walked up Anne's path and put their key in the door. He waited for ten minutes, resting his head on the steering wheel.

A lump came in his throat as he walked up the familiar path to the front door.

The pregnant lady greeted him with a bright smile. 'Hello,' she said.

'I'm looking for Anne Stacey. She used to live here,' he said. 'I wonder if she left you a forwarding address.'

'Yes, she did, but where I've put it I really can't think. Would you like to come in for a minute and I'll see if I can find it.'

Ralph declined, as he could not bear the thought of going into the house without her being there. It held too many memories for him.

A few minutes later he was sitting in his car studying the address he had been given.

Chapter Forty-Seven

Dorothy had gone down to the bottom of the garden to find some mint. Anne was soaking in a nice hot bath. Mary was in her room putting some clothes away having just been brought home for the weekend. The view from the window was not nearly as picturesque as at The Priory, but this was home and she stood and watched the trees swaying in the breeze.

She was about to turn away when she saw a car stop at the top of the drive. A tall man got out and looked up at the Lodge. Mary shuddered. She knew at once who he was. The unruly blonde hair and expensive car were just as Anne had described.

She immediately went downstairs and quietly opened the front door. Walking up the drive towards him she asked, 'Are you lost? Can I help you?'

He looked at the thin, fragile woman and replied, 'My name is Ralph Stevens. I'm looking for Anne Stacey. I was told she lived here.'

'You're a year too late,' Mary replied. 'She did live here but got married and went to live in America. I'm afraid she never left a forwarding address.'

The devastation on his face prompted Mary to add, 'She was very happy when she left.'

She watched as his car disappeared down the hill.

'What are you doing out there?' Dorothy called out.

'Nothing. Just looking at the trees,' Mary replied with a satisfied smile that no one could see.

Contented, she walked around the house to the back patio and sat in her old wicker chair.

Three weeks later, Dorothy and Anne were preparing for Mary's homecoming. Dorothy had spent the morning cooking and Anne had cleaned and polished her room. Putting a small vase of flowers on the windowsill, Anne stared out over the garden. She had not been altogether happy with her last few visits to Mary.

Her friend seemed quieter than usual and, when she did speak, Anne detected a note of aggression.

She had mentioned this to Dorothy who said she had not noticed anything untoward. 'If you're worried about it, have a word with the doctor before you bring her home,' she had suggested.

Making up her mind to take Dorothy's advice, she stood back and admired her flower arrangement.

Having first phoned the doctor, Anne arrived half an hour early and was shown into his office.

Doctor Braithwaite was a small, thin man who spoke very quietly. Anne had seen him several times in the past for an update on Mary's progress. 'What is it you're worried about?' he asked.

Anne explained how she had noticed a change in Mary during her last few visits. 'She doesn't say very much, and when she does, it is always in an aggressive way. She also seems constantly irritated.'

'Well, I'm surprised to hear that. I spent an hour with her yesterday and she seemed fine,' he said disarmingly.

'I was just wondering if she's being discharged too soon.'

Dr Braithwaite shifted in his chair. 'I don't think so, my dear.'

'Are you sure you haven't noticed any change in her?' Anne asked.

'None whatsoever. In fact, we're all very pleased with Mary's progress.'

Anne fidgeted with the buttons on her jacket. 'Could you not keep her here for another week and keep a close eye on her? You know, under observation?'

Dr Braithwaite got up from his chair. 'I don't think that would be a very good idea. She is set on coming home today and you know she is not actually being discharged. We intend seeing her once a month. It's quite normal for us to keep an eye on patients anyway, just to ensure things are going well. What I would like you to do is take her home and, if you have any problems, call me or Doctor Mayer.'

Anne nodded. 'Thank you Dr Braithwaite. I'll go and find Mary.'

As she went to leave, she saw the door was ajar. But what she did not see was Mary, who had been listening outside, scoot down the corridor.

On their way home, Mary asked Anne if she could stop at the Vicarage and sit on the old log for a while.

'I don't think that's a very good idea. Dorothy will be worried about us. In any case, we've got all the time in the world to visit our log and chat,' Anne replied as gently as she could.

For the rest of the journey Mary appeared to be sulking.

'Are you alright?' Anne asked.

Ignoring her question Mary replied, 'You've got lovely hair you know.' She leaned across and stroked it.

'Stop it. I'm trying to drive,' Anne said laughing.

Mary giggled.

Arriving back at the lodge, Mary seemed to be her old self again. She hugged Dorothy and followed her inside. She turned suddenly and, out of earshot of Dorothy, said to Anne in a commandeering voice, 'Take my luggage up to my room.'

Anne was shocked at her tone but laughed and got Mary's case out of the car.

The next morning, at breakfast, Anne noticed Mary staring at her hair. 'What's this fascination with my hair?'

'It's nothing,' Mary replied. 'I just wondered why you

sometimes pile it on top of your head with a clip and sometimes have it hanging loose.'

'Well, there are times when I think I'm far too old to wear it loose.'

'Nonsense!' Dorothy interrupted. 'With lovely hair like that, you should show it off.'

Neither noticed the strange look on Mary's face as she felt for her own hair.

'I'm off to tidy my room. I can't sit here all day talking about hair,' Dorothy joked as she left the kitchen.

Anne turned to Mary. 'Well, when shall we start getting your garden sorted out? Let me know and I'll help you.'

'Why didn't you look after it for me?' Mary snapped.

Stunned again by Mary's tone, Anne replied, 'What with visiting you everyday, we really didn't have the time. Anyway, Dr Mayer told us it would be good therapy for you when you got home.'

'What does he know?' Mary asked curtly.

'Mary, what on earth is wrong? Why are you in such a bad mood?'

Mary gave an artificial smile. 'I'm sorry Anne. Maybe I wasn't ready to come home. I think I'll go and lie down.'

That evening, Mary took special care dressing for dinner. She wore a pair of black corduroy trousers and a pale yellow silk shirt.

Anne was in the kitchen, laying the table. They had stopped eating in the dining room soon after David Freeman had died.

'Wow! Look at you,' Anne teased as Mary entered.

Ignoring her remark, Mary asked why they were eating in the kitchen. 'I'm home now and I want things done properly. Put all that away and lay the table in the dining room.'

Anne stood with her mouth open. Before she could reply, Mary left the room and met Dorothy coming down the stairs.

'Dorothy. Do you mind if we eat in the dining room

tonight? A sort of celebration. You know, my first night home for good.'

'Of course, my dear. What a good idea,' Anne heard Dorothy reply.

During dinner, Mary was back to her normal polite self. 'Anne is going to help me get started on the garden. We'll soon have it looking nice again, won't we Anne?'

Deciding to forget Mary's rudeness, Anne smiled and replied, 'Of course we will.'

'I'll help as much as I can,' Dorothy chimed in. 'But my old legs aren't what they used to be.'

'You'll do no such thing,' said Mary. 'Anne and I can manage, can't we, Anne?'

During the following week, Anne noticed that whenever Dorothy was around, Mary would be her normal polite self. But when the two of them were alone, she would, quite often, bite Anne's head off and become distant. She did not want to worry Dorothy and so decided to talk to Mary about her behaviour.

They were working together in the garden when Dorothy brought out cups of coffee.

'Let's take a break,' Anne said. They walked over to the patio and Mary sat in her wicker chair. Anne pulled up a garden chair and sat opposite.

Once Dorothy had gone back into the kitchen, Anne said, 'Now Mary. Do you want to tell me why you're so nasty to me when Dorothy's not around?'

To Anne's horror she saw Mary's eyes glaze over as she said, 'My father's a vicar, you know.'

'Mary, don't. Please don't hide. Let's talk,' Anne said anxiously.

Mary opened her eyes suddenly and staring at Anne said, 'Yes, my father was a vicar. But your father was a rapist. You know he raped me, don't you Anne?'

Anne hung her head. 'Yes, I know Mary, and I cannot tell

273

you how sorry I am. I thought we'd put all this behind us and were starting a new life.'

Mary continued staring at Anne but, in her mind, was seeing Jennifer. 'You wicked girl,' she hissed. Jumping up she ran inside and called Dorothy.

'Are you going to the shops today Dorothy?'

'Yes,' the old woman replied. ' Why?'

'I would like to come with you. I want to buy Anne a present. She's been so good to me.'

'What a kind thought. I shan't be going until this afternoon, though.'

'That's fine,' said Mary.

In order to safeguard Mary's surprise, Dorothy asked Anne to stay behind and prepare the vegetables for dinner. Anne readily agreed.

During dinner that evening, Mary gave Anne a beautifully wrapped gift of her favourite perfume.

'This is a little thank-you for all you've done for me,' she said sweetly.

'Oh, Mary, you shouldn't have.'

'You've been so kind to me. I know I haven't always been appreciative.'

Tears began to well in Anne's eyes. 'Oh, Mary, I'll do anything for you.'

'Anything?' Mary joked.

'Yes. Anything.'

'In that case, will you tidy up my hair for me and trim all these jagged ends off?'

'I'll do better than that. I'll take you to the hairdressers.'

'No!' Mary shouted.

Dorothy interrupted. 'She doesn't like hairdressers.'

Anne suddenly remembered the scene that Dorothy had told her about. 'Right. I'll have a go at your hair. Remember, now, I'm no hairdresser, but I'm sure I can tidy it up.'

Mary smiled sweetly and said, 'Thank you Anne.'

Chapter Forty-Eight

Ralph Stevens had spent the past couple of weeks feeling absolutely wretched, and had made no attempt to look for a new position.

The news of his departure from the company soon spread around the industry. Those who knew him were of the opinion that he was a key figure in the success of the Anderson's supermarket chain. His answering machine was full of messages from competitors asking him to call them, each one indicating there was a job on offer. In addition to this were three calls from Chandler. Ralph hardly recognised his voice, it sounded so conciliatory. He did not respond to any of them.

He had been drinking quite heavily over the past few days and decided he had to call a halt and pull himself together. Making up his mind to try again to put Anne out of his thoughts once and for all, he got up and went to make breakfast.

But cutting up some grapefruit his thoughts, as always, returned to Anne. Why didn't she leave a forwarding address in case he tried to contact her? Who was that woman she was living with in Ramsden? Why hadn't he asked around at the local shops? She must have made some friends there. Had she taken the first offer of marriage that came along in order to forget him?

'Ouch!' he exclaimed, as he realised he had cut his finger. 'Damn!' he said out loud. 'I just can't concentrate.'

Throwing the knife down, he gave up and went and sat in the lounge.

He wanted to follow up and find out more about what had happened. Although he knew he had lost Anne, he needed to know more. Part of him wanted to see what he could find out. The other part was telling him to give in and get on with his life.

The following morning he drove to Ramsden. Parking the car in a side street he began walking along the parade of shops. His first visit was to the chemist. The shop was empty except for the young girl standing behind the counter. He purchased some aspirin. As she handed him his change he asked, 'I wonder if you can help me? I'm looking for a lady by the name of Anne Stacey. She used to live up the hill in a house called Grange Lodge. Do you have any idea where she moved to?'

The girl looked a little embarrassed. 'I'm sorry,' she said. 'I'm only looking after the shop for my uncle. He's gone to the wholesalers. I don't live in the village. I'm just here with my mother, visiting for a few days.'

Realising he was making the girl nervous, he thanked her and left. Continuing down the street, full of gloom and despair, he stopped outside the paper shop. 'One more try,' he thought as he opened the shop door. The cheerful, plump lady behind the counter smiled. 'Good morning, I haven't seen you around here before.'

He picked up a newspaper from the counter and handed it to her. 'No, I don't live in the village. I'm here trying to find the whereabouts of an old friend of mine. You may have known her, a young lady by the name of Anne Stacey.'

The smile left the plump woman's face. 'Are you a newspaper reporter?'

'No, nothing like that,' he replied. 'She's very attractive with long brown hair and eyes to match. She used to live up the hill at Grange Lodge but left and went to America. I'm

276

trying to find out whether she left a forwarding address with anyone.'

'I don't know anyone who has left Ramsden to go to America. That's not what people do around here. The only Anne I know who fits that description, and I'm not sure of her surname, is the one who still lives at the Lodge along with Mary Freeman.'

Ralph felt his stomach turn over. He thanked her, paid for his paper and left.

Back in his car his head was spinning. So that was who the strange lady was, Anne's best friend. She had found her. The story of her going to America must have been Anne's idea. She did not want to see him. 'And who could blame her!' he said out loud. His spirits were lifted by the fact that she had not gone and probably not married. He decided to wait outside the Lodge until she came out.

It was two o'clock in the afternoon when he saw the strange woman, accompanied by an elderly lady, leave the house and walk down the hill. Waiting until they were out of sight he crossed the road and, with heart pounding, walked up the drive and rang the doorbell.

Anne was just about to go upstairs. Thinking Dorothy had forgotten something, she hastened to the door.

Totally unprepared, she stood rooted to the spot. Her hair hung loose and her large eyes stared at him as if he were a ghost.

'Anne. Can I come in for a minute please?' His voice wavered.

Dressed in a pair of jeans and soft white silk shirt, she continued staring at him.

'Please, Anne,' he begged, thinking how beautiful she looked.

Anne had still said nothing. She just stood and moistened her lips.

'Anne, if I can't come in, will you meet me somewhere?

277

Just to talk?' The anguish in his voice unnerved her.

She nodded.

'There's a café down in the High Street. Can we meet there?' he asked. 'Today, tomorrow, any time that suits you.' Stepping towards her he moaned, 'Oh Anne.'

She backed away, whispering, 'Tomorrow, at four o'clock.'

Watching him walk back down the drive, her legs turned to jelly. She closed the door just in time to prevent him seeing the tears in her eyes.

As if in a dream she went up to her room, lay on the bed and let the tears pour down the side of her face.

By the time Dorothy and Mary returned she had splashed her face with cold water and tried to behave as normally as she could. Deciding not to mention her visitor she pleaded a headache after dinner and went to bed. Twice she woke in the night and thought it had all been a dream.

At breakfast the next morning, Mary asked Anne when she was going to cut her hair. 'Could you do it this morning?' she asked sweetly.

Thinking it would keep her busy until the afternoon, Anne readily agreed.

'Don't forget I have to go to hospital for my check-up today,' Dorothy reminded them.

'I know,' Mary replied. 'We can take you to the hospital and come back here so Anne can cut my hair. Then we'll come back to pick you up.'

Dorothy laughed. 'You've got it all worked out, haven't you young lady?'

Anne sat quietly. She had forgotten about Dorothy's hospital appointment. Thinking things through, she said, 'That's fine. We'll still be back by three the latest.'

'Why, what's happening at three?' Mary asked.

'Never you mind, just wait and see,' Anne teased. 'I may have a surprise for you both.'

Returning after dropping Dorothy off at the hospital,

Anne asked, 'Mary, do you want a cup of coffee before we start?'

'No thanks,' Mary replied. 'Shall we do it in your bedroom? There's a better mirror in there.'

'If you like,' said Anne. 'You go and put a towel or something round you and I'll get the scissors.'

'I've already got the scissors,' Mary called over her shoulder as she went upstairs.

Anne looked at the clock. She had four hours to wait. She knew she had to handle the meeting with Ralph sensibly, but her emotions were running high.

'Are you ready?' she called out as she went up the stairs.

'Ready and waiting,' Mary called back. Anne smiled to herself.

Opening the bedroom door she found Mary sitting with a towel draped over her at the dressing table looking at herself in the mirror. After combing her hair through, Anne asked, 'Where are the scissors?'

Suddenly, Mary leapt from the chair sending Anne sprawling across the bedroom.

'Here they are!' she screamed, waving the scissors in the air.

Anne made a move to get up. 'Mary, what are you doing?'

With her foot, Mary sent Anne crashing to the floor again. Standing over her with an evil look on her face, she yelled, 'I'll tell you what I'm doing. I'm going to cut your hair the same as you cut mine.' In her sick mind she was looking down at Jennifer.

'Mary please,' Anne begged. 'Stop this.'

Before Anne could get to her feet Mary grabbed a candlestick from the dressing table and brought it crashing down on her head.

Seeing the blood pour from the wound, Mary smiled. She was no longer seeing Jennifer but Anne, her so-called friend who had tried to prevent her from coming home. 'You wanted to keep me locked up,' she snarled. 'Just like Trevor.

279

He wanted to get me locked up, and look what happened to him.'

Sitting astride Anne's unconscious body, Mary began hacking at her hair. When she was unable to get the scissors close enough she tugged chunks out.

Anne began to murmur. Mary slapped her hard across the face and shouted, 'Shut up!'

Satisfied there was very little hair left to cut, Mary went downstairs and got the first aid box. Putting a plaster over the gash in Anne's head she left, locking the door behind her.

Downstairs she sat and watched the clock, knowing it would soon be time to collect Dorothy. Ordering a taxi to pick her up at 1.30 she sat in the kitchen, humming.

Dorothy had undergone her check-up and been informed that her blood pressure was high. Knowing that Mary and Anne would be arriving any minute to collect her, she began to get agitated at having to wait for a prescription. At the very moment her name was called to collect the medication, Mary came rushing towards her.

'Hurry, Dorothy,' she called out.

On the way out, the old lady had a job keeping up with Mary. 'Whatever is the rush dear?' she panted. 'Is something wrong?'

'I'll tell you in the taxi. Now hurry.'

Dorothy stood still. She was very out of breath. 'What do you mean, taxi? Didn't Anne bring the car?'

'No, she's hurt. Now please hurry.'

Dorothy began walking again as fast as she could and Mary practically pushed her into the taxi.

As the driver pulled away, Mary said anxiously, 'She's fallen and cut her head. I've put a plaster on it but I couldn't wake her up. I was going to call for an ambulance but I thought it better to come and get you first.'

'Oh, my dear,' the old lady gasped, still out of breath from rushing. 'How did she fall and where is she now?'

'Lying on her bedroom floor. She came in to cut my hair, tripped, and the next thing I knew, she was on the floor with blood pouring out of her head. Oh, Dorothy, I didn't know what to do.' Mary hid her face in her hands.

Arriving back at the Lodge Dorothy opened the front door and hastened up the stairs.

'The door's locked,' she called down to Mary.

'I know. I locked it in case she fell down the stairs,' Mary said as she arrived at the bedroom door, key in hand. She opened the door and stood back to let Dorothy go in first.

Dorothy's scream stuck in her throat as she looked down at Anne. The piece of sticking plaster covering the main wound on Anne's head was soaked in blood which was trickling down either side of her neck. Her cheek was bruised and tears seeped from beneath her closed eyes.

With difficulty, Dorothy got down on her knees beside Anne. 'Oh my dear girl. What has happened to you?' Very gently she patted the cheek that was free of bruising. 'Anne, wake up, dear. Whatever's happened to your hair?'

Anne still lay motionless.

Dorothy looked up at Mary who was standing at the door staring. 'What's happened to her hair?' she asked, her voice trembling.

'It wasn't like that when I left her. Whatever has she done? Is she still alive?'

'Yes. Now go and call an ambulance at once. Tell them it's an emergency,' said Dorothy struggling to draw breath.

'You do it. I'll stay here with Anne,' Mary replied.

Shaking her head from side to side, Dorothy said quietly, 'Mary, please go and do what I ask. I'm having difficulty breathing.'

Irritated, Mary left the room. This was not what she had planned.

Dorothy looked at the little clock on Anne's windowsill. It

was almost 4.30. How long had the poor girl been like this, she wondered.

The ambulance men finally arrived and were visibly shocked at what they encountered. A pair of scissors and a towel lay on the floor beside an ashen-faced woman crumpled unconscious on the floor.

As one man quickly put an oxygen mask on Anne's face, the other turned to Mary. 'What happened?'

'She fell,' Mary replied calmly.

'What happened to her hair?'

'We don't know,' Mary replied. 'We think she did it herself.'

The paramedic who was still bending over Anne looked up and said, 'You'd better call the police.'

His colleague left the room to make the call.

Dorothy, who had been sitting on Anne's bed asked, 'Is she going to be alright?'

'Hard to tell at this stage,' the paramedic replied.

Dorothy's hands were shaking as she continued, 'I'll come with her in the ambulance.'

With panic in her voice Mary interrupted. 'No. I'll go with her. If she's going to die I want to be with her.'

'Mary, don't talk like that,' Dorothy snapped. 'You stay here. You'll be perfectly alright. I will call you as soon as I have some news.'

'No,' Mary repeated firmly. 'You stay here. I want to go with her to the hospital.'

'Mary, please be a good girl and wait here,' Dorothy pleaded.

'Don't argue. You can both come,' the paramedic said as he began strapping Anne onto the stretcher.

'No,' Mary snapped again. 'I want to come on my own.'

At this point the doorbell rang and one of the ambulance men ran downstairs and returned with a young policewoman accompanied by a detective.

On hearing that the policewoman would be going in the ambulance, Mary turned to Dorothy and said, 'Perhaps you should go with her.'

Dorothy patted Mary's back. 'There's a good girl. I'll call you as soon as I can.'

As the policewoman followed them out to the ambulance, the detective turned to Mary. 'I know you've had a bit of a shock, but it's important I ask you some questions.'

Mary nodded.

Chapter Forty-Nine

Ralph stood at the doorway of the café looking up and down the High Street. It was almost five o'clock. He had drunk three cups of tea and felt miserable. Just as he was about to go back inside and order yet another, an ambulance came racing by with its siren wailing.

He had forced half of the tea down before deciding to drive up to the Lodge. As he came close to the house he had to stop. His stomach lurched as he saw the ambulance backing out of the drive.

He waited until it had sped away before parking in the drive and ringing the doorbell.

The strange woman opened the door. 'I'm sorry to bother you again, but Anne was supposed to meet me in the café at four o'clock this afternoon and ...' He was cut short by her outburst.

'I don't know what you're talking about. Anne Stacey left here and went to America a year ago. Now will you please leave.'

'But I know she didn't. You see, I saw her yesterday and we arranged to meet.' Ralph was trying his best to remain patient with her.

'You couldn't have seen her. I've told you, she's in America.'

A voice from behind Mary said, 'Can I help?'

The detective had walked down the hall.

'Goodbye,' Mary said, and slammed the door.

'Why are you telling him that Anne is in America?' The detective looked puzzled.

'It's none of your business,' Mary snapped.

Ralph rang the doorbell again, and this time the detective opened the door.

'My name is Stevens and I'm looking for an Anne Stacey,' said Ralph.

The detective remained silent but motioned him to come inside. Mary had been answering questions in the kitchen but now she was nowhere to be seen. After looking in every room he found a bedroom door that was locked.

'Are you in there Mary?' he called out.

'Yes. But I'm not coming out to answer any more of your questions until you get rid of that man.'

Walking back down the stairs he phoned the station to ask for another policewoman to be sent immediately.

Back in the kitchen, he asked Ralph to explain his relationship with Anne. When he had finished, the Inspector said, 'I'm afraid I've got some bad news for you,' and went on to explain the events of the past hour.

Ralph held his head in his hands. 'And you think she did this to herself?'

'Can't answer that yet,' the Inspector replied.

'What hospital have they taken her to? Can I go and see her?'

'No reason at this stage why you shouldn't. I don't know whether they'll let you. She's in a pretty bad way.' The suspicious look on the detective's face unnerved Ralph.

The doorbell rang and the detective let the policewoman in. They stood in the hall as he gave a quick briefing of the situation. She nodded and went straight upstairs

'Do you need me for anything else?' Ralph asked.

'Not for the moment,' the Inspector replied. ' She's been taken to Ramsden General.'

Ralph handed him his business card. 'That's where you

can reach me. I don't work for that company any more but I've ringed my private number.'

The Inspector studied the card and nodded.

Arriving at the hospital he spotted the old lady he had seen walking down the hill with Anne's strange friend. She was sitting in the waiting room, a small, hunched-up figure, looking lost and upset. Her eyes were red from crying.

He approached slowly and said gently, 'Excuse me, are you with Anne Stacey?'

Dorothy looked up. 'Yes. Is there any news?'

Ralph sat down beside her and apologetically explained that he was not a doctor. 'My name is Ralph Stevens. You've probably never heard of me.'

The old lady began to cry.

Ralph gave her his handkerchief. After drying her eyes she said, 'Oh, I've heard of you alright. You're the man who broke her heart!'

It was as if she had put a knife in him. He swallowed hard. 'I'm here to try and put things right, if she'll let me.'

'Let's hope you're not too late,' Dorothy said shaking her head from side to side.

'What have the doctors said?' Ralph asked.

'Nothing yet. They told me to wait here and they'd come and see me as soon as they had some news.'

Ralph put his arm around her shoulders. 'Would you like me to get you a cup of tea?'

She nodded.

He soon realised that this was no London clinic when the nurse he asked to fetch the tea looked at him as if he had just come down from Mars and pointed him in the direction of a vending machine.

Sitting back down next to Dorothy he looked around at what he thought had to be one of the most depressing places he had ever been in. The walls were painted cream but were in need of a good wash down. Grey linoleum covered the floor and, here and there, cigarette ends lay under the grey plastic-covered chairs. It was the Casualty department and nurses were flying around everywhere, doing their best to pacify some of the disillusioned and bad-tempered people who were still waiting to be seen.

He watched Dorothy's hand shake as she tried to drink the tea from a paper cup. Leaning forward with his head in his hands, he thought, Anne, I've just got to get you out of here.

After what seemed an eternity, a nurse came across to Dorothy. 'Dr Barnard will see you now, Miss Maitland.' She looked questioningly at Ralph, who to Dorothy's amazement said, 'I'm Ralph Stevens, Anne Stacey's fiancé.'

They were shown into a small room with a sign on the door saying 'Consulting Room 3'.

Dr Barnard sat on the edge of a somewhat dilapidated desk and motioned them both to sit down on two equally dilapidated chairs. Ralph once again introduced himself as Anne's fiancé. Dorothy remained silent.

'Well, Mr Stevens. Your fiancée has had a very narrow escape. If the main wound to her head had been a fraction deeper I would have been worried about brain damage. The bruising to her face is mostly superficial.

'Will she be alright?' Ralph asked anxiously.

'Yes. She should make a full recovery.'

Dorothy began to cry. Ralph immediately went across and put his arm around her shoulders. 'Come on, now,' he said, holding back the tears in his own eyes, 'She's going to be alright.'

Composing himself he asked, 'Do we have any idea as to why she did this to herself?'

The doctor looked puzzled. 'Didn't you know? She was attacked. The police had five minutes with her before we put her under sedation and she was able to tell them something about what had happened. They're on their way to see you anyway, and can answer any further questions you may have.'

Dorothy gasped, 'Tell me this isn't true.'

'Can we see her?' Ralph asked

'You can for a few minutes, but remember, she's heavily sedated.'

They had put Anne in a small room on her own. Her head was completely swathed in bandages and her long brown eyelashes sparkled with tears. A policewoman sat in the corner reading a book.

Ralph moved to the side of the bed and took her hand in his. 'My darling, my beautiful darling. I love you so much.' His teardrops fell onto the mustard-coloured counterpane.

Dorothy slumped onto a small chair. The policewoman looked up and whispered, 'You look tired.'

'Yes, I'm very tired, but relieved that she's going to be alright.'

After kissing Anne on her forehead, Ralph went across to Dorothy. 'There's no way you're staying around to talk to policemen tonight. I'm going to drive you straight home. Wait here while I go and sort this out.'

The sympathetic detective told him he could take Dorothy home, but warned there would probably still be police at the house.

Before they left, a nurse came to ask for some particulars for hospital records. The question of who was Anne's next of kin made him cringe. This poor girl had none, and so without hesitation he gave his name and telephone number.

'We need to leave the number of your house too, Dorothy,' he said. The poor old lady had trouble remembering, but after sitting quietly for a minute, was able to tell them.

It took almost an hour for WPC Janet Phillips to coax Mary out of her room. When she finally opened the door, Mary smiled at her and said, 'My father's a vicar, you know.'

'Yes, and my father's Jesus Christ,' she replied sarcastically. 'Now let's get you downstairs.'

'Would you like a cup of tea?' Mary asked the detective as she entered the kitchen, her eyes ablaze with excitement.

'No thank you,' he replied. Janet will make you one if you like. I want you to sit down and answer some questions.'

Mary sat down opposite him at the table. 'I don't know whether you know this, but Anne Stacey raped my father.' Her mind was in such turmoil that she didn't know who had raped whom.

Ignoring her remark, he asked, 'Did you hit Anne and cut off her hair?'

Mary's eyes glazed over and she rocked backwards and forwards laughing hysterically. She suddenly stopped, looked at the constable, and said, 'It was only a game. I didn't mean to hurt her. She's my best friend.'

'But you did hurt her,' the constable said.

Mary began to cry. 'I want my father here to help me.'

The constable looked at the detective questioningly. 'Her father's dead,' he mumbled.

Suddenly becoming calm, Mary asked him, 'Did you kill my father?'

Shaking his head he looked at the WPC. 'You had better get some help.'

She immediately left the room.

'I can help you,' Mary said excitedly. 'What is it you want done?' Quick as a flash she jumped up from the table and took a carving knife out of the drawer. 'Do you want me to kill Ralph Stevens? He's evil, you know.'

Trying to stay calm, the detective smiled. 'No, that's alright Mary. Put the knife down.'

She walked towards him, pointing the knife at his throat. 'I killed Trevor Stacey. They never found out, you know. He wanted to have me locked up.'

The detective backed away.

'That's why I killed Anne. She wanted to keep me locked up. But I didn't kill my husband, he just died.'

'You didn't kill Anne. She's in hospital.'

Mary's face changed. 'In hospital? With my father? I must go there at once. She'll kill him, I know she will.' Putting the knife down on the table she made a move to get her coat.

The WPC returned. Having heard what Mary had said, she put an arm around her shoulder. 'It's alright Mary. Someone is coming to take us to the hospital.'

Ralph and Dorothy arrived at the Lodge just as Mary, strapped to a stretcher, was being put into the ambulance.

Jumping out of the car, Ralph ran over to the police-woman. 'What's happened? Who are you taking in the ambulance?'

After he explained who he was, she told him briefly what had occurred. By the time Dorothy joined them, all she heard was, 'She's gone completely mad. It seems Mary was responsible for attacking Anne.'

This was more than the old lady could take and she fell in a crumpled heap to the ground.

Chapter Fifty

Ralph looked exhausted. He had been up all night, sitting at Anne's bedside. She was conscious, but very weak. He held her hand and intermittently kissed it.

'Did you wait long at the café?' she whispered.

'I would have waited forever, Anne. I want to ask you one question and then you must sleep.'

'What is it?' she murmured.

He knelt down by the side of the bed. 'Anne. I know I let you down badly but believe me, I suffered for it. I love you more than life itself. Will you marry me?'

Tears ran down her face as she mouthed, 'Yes.'

Ralph left the hospital a very happy man. On the doctor's advice he had not told Anne that poor Dorothy had died of a heart attack and that Mary was now locked in a secure wing of a mental hospital.

One year later, having just visited Mary who had been pronounced mentally unfit to stand trial for the murder of Trevor Stacey, Anne and Ralph walked hand in hand through the grounds of Darlington Mental Hospital.

'Thank you for coming with me, Ralph,' she said squeezing his hand.

He stood still and took her in his arms. 'Darling, we will come and see her as often as you like. You will never have to face anything alone again.'